# DEAD TO RIGHTS
## MOUNTAIN SHADOW MYSTERIES BOOK TWO

TARAH BENNER

ALSO BY TARAH BENNER

*Better Off Dead*

*Witches of Mountain Shadow (Books 1-6)*

*Christmas in Mountain Shadow*

*The Witch's Fortune*

*Blood Ties*

*The Elven Blade*

*The Elderon Chronicles (Books 1-5)*

*The Lawless Saga (Books 1-4)*

*Bound in Blood*

*The Fringe (Books 1-5)*

*The Defectors Trilogy (Books 1-3)*

Copyright © 2023 by Tarah Benner

All rights reserved.

This book is a work of fiction, and any similarities to any person, living or dead, are coincidental and not intentional.

No part of this book may be reproduced in any form or by any electronic or mechanical means, including information storage and retrieval systems, without written permission from the author, except for the use of brief quotations in a book review.

ISBN: 979-8852061591

www.tarahbenner.com

*To Arlen.*

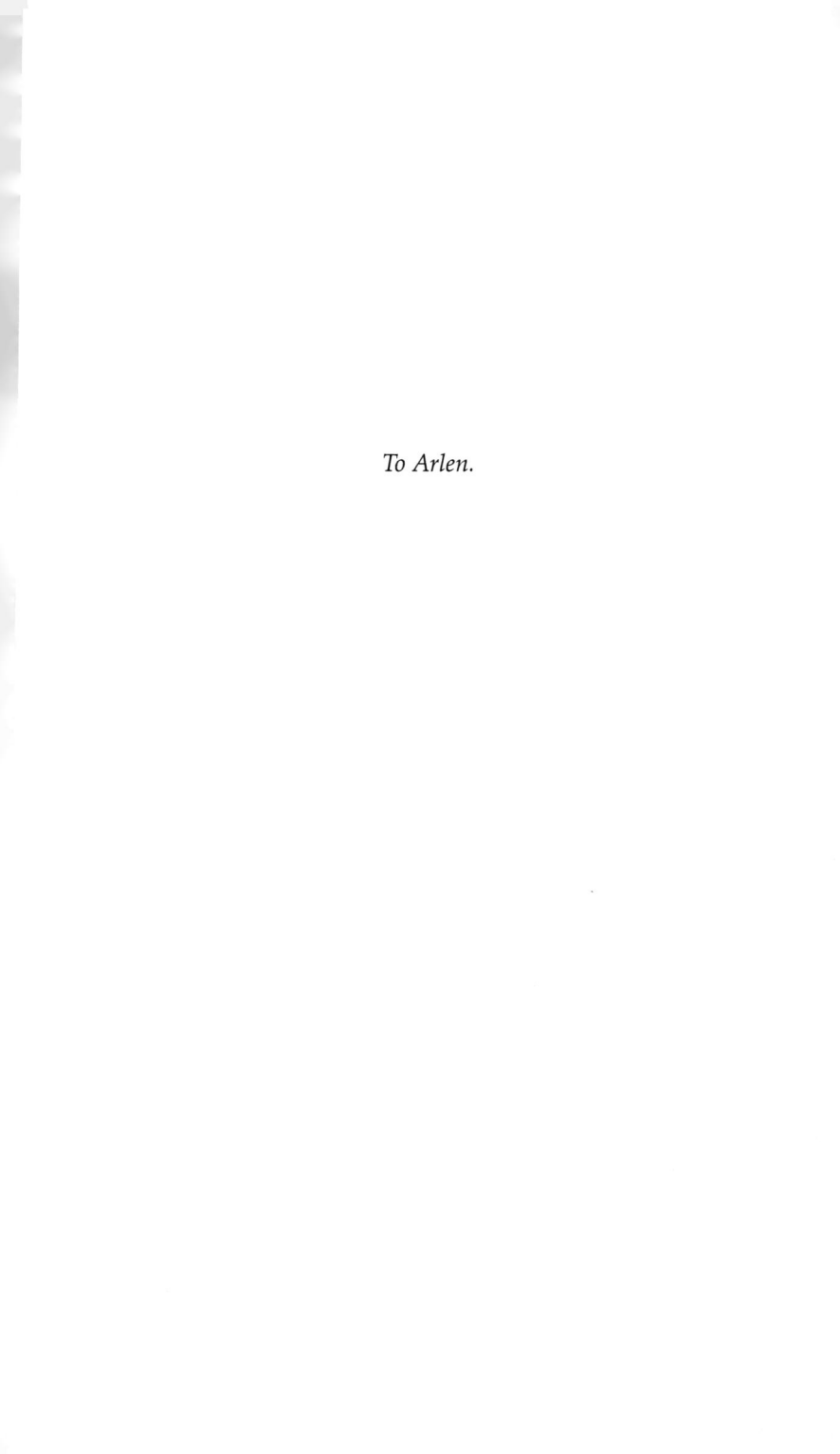

CHAPTER ONE

I n the bright light of day, The Mountain Shadow Grand didn't *look* haunted. The towering red-brick building on Phantom Canyon Boulevard looked almost as grand as it had in its heyday — or at least it *would* have, if it weren't for the boarded-up windows, the cracked marquee, and the overgrown thicket of weeds that grew along the foundation.

From the outside, one couldn't see the dilapidated furniture, the rotted floorboards, the crumbling ceiling, or the moldy carpet. Inside, The Grand looked like the perfect home for the ghosts who still roamed the building.

I had a list as long as my arm of things around the hotel that needed fixing, but I still wasn't sure what to do about *them*. Still, I got a fresh burst of giddy pride as I stared up at the hotel — *my* hotel, which I'd inherited from my aunt Lucille when she'd died.

"Welcome home, Des," I said, parking the rental van along the curb just past the front entrance for easy unloading.

Desmond stretched lazily in the passenger seat and blinked up at me with those eerie yellow eyes. He'd slept nearly the entire ride from Chicago, and I grimaced when I saw the layer of fine black hairs he'd left all over the upholstery. Cats weren't specifically prohibited in the rental agreement I'd signed, but traveling cross-country with a furry companion in the front seat was probably frowned upon.

Figuring I'd have to work my magic with the lint roller before returning the van, I got out to stretch my legs, sip my latte, and drink in the glorious mountain views. Naturally, I'd already paid a visit to Déjà Brew, my favorite coffee shop, to fortify myself with caffeine. Three shots of espresso drenched in chocolatey goodness had already begun to take effect, and I found myself moving with much more vigor than I usually had for hard physical labor.

Slipping in my earbuds, I hit play on my podcast and started schlepping boxes up to the front steps.

*Mindset is everything,* intoned the cheesy voice in my ears as I dragged a particularly heavy box to the very edge of the cargo area. *Whether you think you can, or you think you can't — you're right.*

I rolled my eyes but filed that little tidbit away nonetheless.

Ever since I'd been fired from my job in marketing, I'd been riding a rollercoaster of crippling self-doubt mixed with screw-you-I-can-do-whatever-I-set-my-mind-to energy. I'd been consuming a steady diet of motivational self-help books and entrepreneurship podcasts as I thrust myself into figuring out how to renovate The Grand.

It wasn't easy to keep a positive attitude when I had no

money and a bid for six million dollars sitting in my inbox, but I was trying my best.

After hauling the first eight boxes up to the door, I paused to reward myself with a few sips from my latte. As I savored the rich bite of espresso, I got a familiar tingle on the back of my neck. It felt as though I was being watched.

I turned around, but there was no one there. Phantom Canyon Boulevard was empty.

Pivoting back around to face the hotel, I caught a glimpse of myself in the van window and shuddered. During my time in Colorado, I'd felt like a flaxen-haired goddess for the first time in my life. But after four days back in the Midwest humidity, my blond curls had returned to their usual frizzy mess.

"Moving in?" came a voice from the side of the van, startling me so much that I jumped. Coffee sloshed all down my front, and my heart galloped into overdrive.

Turning toward the sound of the voice, I was surprised to see Gideon — the yummy tattooed bartender who worked at the dive across the street. He was tall and muscular, with thick dark hair and a perpetual five o'clock shadow.

"Oh . . . sorry," he said, glancing down at the chocolatey espresso dribble that now marred the front of my white T-shirt. "I didn't mean to scare you."

"Y-you didn't," I said, cheeks heating as I tugged my earbuds out and searched the pockets of my shorts for a napkin. "I, uh . . . just wasn't paying attention." I smiled and jerked my head toward the van. "Long drive."

Gideon nodded in understanding, and I followed his gaze from my grubby moving attire to the stack of boxes piled in front of the door. "Boy, when you make up your mind to go for something, you *really* commit."

I chuckled. "Yeah, I guess." I decided not to mention that the move from Chicago to Mountain Shadow was more of a force play than some calculated life choice.

When I'd learned that my fiancé was a con artist who'd swindled me out of my life savings, I knew I couldn't return to the apartment where the two of us had lived. After the ordeal with Todd, I'd also had a *teensy* little breakdown at work, which may have contributed to me losing my job.

"I'm not actually moving in here," I said, gesturing up at the graffitied plywood covering the first-story windows. "I'm just storing some of my stuff here while I figure out my next move."

Officially, I was living with my ninety-two-year-old grandmother until I could come up with the money for the hotel's renovations, but that didn't seem like a sexy thing to say.

"I heard you were the one who inherited this place."

I nodded. "My great-aunt left it to me in her will. It was her dying wish to see it restored, so I'm gonna give it my best shot."

Gideon raised his eyebrows. Either he was impressed by my gumption, or he thought I was totally nuts. He cracked a grin. "Well, I'm glad you decided to stay."

My stomach did a little flip, and I suddenly wished I'd bothered to put on some deodorant and fix my sweaty ponytail after sixteen hours in a van.

"Let me help you."

"Oh, no. You don't have to —" I started. But Gideon

was already climbing into the van and hefting two of the larger boxes into his thick, muscular arms.

I decided not to complain. I could definitely use the help, and I would have been lying if I said it was a drag to watch Gideon lift heavy objects.

I scurried to open the front door of the hotel, and Desmond hopped out of the passenger-side door, which I'd left cracked for air flow.

"Some cat you've got there," Gideon muttered as Des slinked past him into the lobby.

"Sure is," I agreed, bending to grab the top box off the stack I'd left by the front door. In addition to the hotel, Lucille had left me her ornery black cat, and he had the funny habit of following me everywhere I went.

"Where do you want them?" Gideon called over his shoulder.

"Uh . . . here in the lobby is fine."

Gideon pivoted on the spot and raised one bushy dark eyebrow. "Caroline, where do you *want* them?"

"No, really." I swallowed. "I was going to store them up on the fourth floor for the time being, but the elevator's hau—"

I clamped my mouth shut. I'd been about to say the elevator was haunted by the hotel's former handyman but stopped myself just in time. "It's . . . out of order," I finished lamely.

Gideon grunted in understanding and started up the sweeping wooden staircase, which creaked loudly under his weight.

"Wow," he muttered as he rounded the second-story landing and gazed out over the banister. "I've never been in here. This place is incredible. You're really going to renovate it?"

"Yeah," I huffed, simultaneously annoyed and impressed that Gideon didn't sound remotely out of breath. I decided not to mention the fact that, since I was freshly unemployed, I really had nothing better to do.

"You secure funds for the remodel?" he asked, turning down the hallway and continuing up the next flight of stairs.

"Not yet," I said, hoping my voice didn't convey the full extent of my desperation.

In reality, I had no idea how I was going to swing the remodel, but since my gran had fronted me the money to pay back the taxes Aunt Lucille had owed, I was committed to making it happen one way or another.

"It's a big job," said Gideon, pausing as we reached the third floor and gazing up and down the gloomy hallway.

I made a note of assent in my throat as I pulled out the long brass key that opened the door to the fourth-floor stairwell, hoping he couldn't hear how winded I was. Since when was Gideon so chatty?

He led the way up the last flight of stairs and nudged the door at the top open.

"Just inside that first room is fine," I said as he turned down the fourth-floor hallway. The entire top floor of the hotel had been closed off since the late forties, and it would probably be the last to be renovated.

Gideon drifted into the first room he came to and set his box down, pausing as his eye caught the little black-and-white sticker I'd made with my trusty label maker.

He turned to look at me, eyes twinkling with mirth. *"Jammies/good underwear?"* He chuckled. "I'm not sure which I'm more curious about — the jammies or the underwear."

My face immediately caught fire, and I pivoted — utterly horrified — and fled down the stairs. I could hear Gideon's smug laughter following me all the way back down, and a sting of irritation mixed with my embarrassment.

That was the *last* time I let anybody help me move.

Cheeks still flaming, I flung open the front door and came face to face with Officer Will of the Mountain Shadow PD.

Will Hamby — Officer Handsome, as I'd dubbed him in my head — looked just as surprised to see me as I was to see him, which was weird, considering he'd been about to knock on the front door of my hotel. His cruiser was parked behind the van, and Will was in full uniform.

His blue eyes widened as he took a half step back, opening and closing his mouth. His speechlessness was kind of adorable, and I smiled as he ran a hand through his neat blond hair. "Caroline."

"Officer Hamby."

Will's eyes moved swiftly over my bare legs before snapping back to my face in a businesslike fashion. "I, uh . . ." He cleared his throat. "I was just out on patrol and thought I'd check in on the property. I saw the van parked outside and —" He broke off, mouth pulling into a frown as his gaze drifted over my shoulder.

I *sensed* rather than felt Gideon's presence behind me, though I couldn't bring myself to look at him.

"Problem, officer?" the bartender rumbled.

Will's eyes narrowed ever so slightly, and his mouth hardened into a thin line. "Nope. I was just telling Caroline that this property has been sort of a stopover for vagrants in the past. When I saw the van parked outside, I stopped to make sure everything was all right."

"Everything's fine," said Gideon in a measured tone that nonetheless betrayed the faint hint of a challenge.

"I rented the van to bring my stuff back from Chicago," I told Will. "Gideon saw me unloading from across the street and came over to help."

I wasn't sure why I felt the need to give such a detailed explanation for Gideon's presence. Will *had* accused my gran of murder. It wasn't any of his business who helped me move.

Something like relief flashed across his face, but his gaze darkened as it settled back on Gideon. "What's the expression? Four hands are better than two; six hands are better than four?"

He turned on his heel and started for the street. It wasn't until he'd climbed into the van that I understood his meaning.

"Oh, no . . . Will, you don't have to do that!"

But Will was already climbing out of the van with a plastic bin full of my five-, eight-, and ten-pound dumbbells. He grunted as he stepped down and adjusted his grip on the bin. "Where do you want 'em?"

"Fourth floor," said Gideon before I could answer. "You'll have to take the stairs. Elevator's out."

"Copy that."

I was pretty sure I could *smell* the testosterone in the air as I retrieved two of the smaller boxes and followed Will up the main staircase. At least I was making short work of the move.

Desmond came streaking down the stairs as we were going up, letting out an excited *ree-arr*!

Let the record reflect that I was trying very, *very* hard not to stare at Will's butt as I climbed the steps behind him. But in those tight uniform pants —

*Nope*, I told myself firmly as I followed him up the stairs. I was not in any shape to even think about dating anyone — not when the ordeal with Todd was still so fresh.

I could hear Gideon coming up behind me, though he still didn't sound even remotely out of breath. When did the bartender even have time to work out? I wondered. He always seemed to be working at Chumley's.

Will made his way up to the fourth floor with the confidence of someone who'd been there before — probably chasing off "vagrants." He set the bin of dumbbells neatly against the wall and made a wild movement with his shoulders to avoid running into Gideon.

The two men were silent as we headed back down, but the tension in the air was palpable. It seemed too intense to be the result of simple male jealousy, and it occurred to me that there might be more between Gideon and Will than I realized.

We'd nearly reached the foot of the stairs when the door leading to the third floor slammed shut with a bang. My heart gave a jolt as the stairwell went dark. Nobody moved a muscle.

"Well, that was . . . weird," said Will after a beat.

"Yeah," I agreed, my voice coming out at least half an octave higher than normal. "This place gets some weird drafts." Not to mention my hotel was haunted.

Will reached out to open the door, but the knob

wouldn't budge. "It's stuck," he said, rattling the doorknob and bracing his weight against it.

"Let me try," Gideon muttered, nudging Will aside.

I rolled my eyes as Gideon tried the knob himself, but then a feeling like cold water trickling down my back made my spine go stiff. My insides clenched as I fought a shiver, and I wheeled around just as the door at the top of the stairs slammed shut.

A resounding silence filled the stairwell, and that icy feeling seemed to spread from the base of my spine all the way around to my chest.

"Another draft?" Will asked as I stumbled up the stairs.

Wordlessly I tried the handle, but it wouldn't move.

My chest seized with sudden claustrophobia, and I got a whiff of a familiar woodsy scent as Will squeezed past me on the stairs. There was a thud and a rattle as Will rammed his shoulder against the door, but the thing wouldn't budge.

Then I heard something just on the other side of the door — a low, pained-sounding moan followed by some indistinct grumbling.

"What was that?" Gideon asked sharply.

"Hello?" called Will, pounding on the door with his fist. "Is someone there?"

"It's probably just my contractor checking on the . . . er, pipes," I finished lamely, grimacing as the indistinct muttering grew louder. I still couldn't make out any words, but I had a feeling the voice didn't belong to a person.

"Why doesn't he let us out, then?" asked Will in exasperation, continuing to pound on the door. "Hey! Hello? Could you unlock the door?"

The disembodied voice on the other side continued to grumble, and another loud thud shook the stairwell as Will tried once again to break down the door. Slivers of light shuddered all around the door frame. He rammed into it with his shoulder once again, and this time the door swung free.

A dim light filled the stairwell as Will careened through the opening. He landed in a heap on the musty carpet, looking adorably confused and disheveled.

A second later, I heard a creak from the stairwell and saw Gideon at the bottom, peering onto the third-floor landing.

Will looked up and down the hallway in bewilderment. There was no one else there.

"Well, that was weird," Gideon called, moving toward the next set of stairs.

Will muttered his agreement, following Gideon back down to the first floor. He didn't speak again until we'd reached the sidewalk. "You said it was your contractor up there?" he asked, glancing up at the fourth-floor windows.

"Uh . . . probably," I lied, unable to keep the nervous squeak out of my voice.

Will's gaze swiveled to the curb, where only his police cruiser and the van were parked. "There's no one else here."

"You know contractors," I said, attempting a blasé shrug. "It's hard to pin them down."

"Uh-huh."

Gideon and Will made quick work of the rest of my belongings, though I noticed that neither of them lingered in the fourth-floor stairwell. They said their goodbyes and left in a hurry — Will climbing into his cruiser and Gideon shuffling back across the street to the bar.

Once they were gone, I slammed the door of the hotel behind me and closed my eyes with a sigh of relief.

"Caroline! You're back!"

My eyes flew open at the sound of Aunt Lucille's voice as my heart gave a startled jolt. I found myself staring at a black-and-white apparition who looked as though she'd been ripped from a glamorous old Hollywood film.

She appeared, as always, in her thirtysomething form, wearing a pair of high-waisted pinup girl shorts with a short-sleeved cashmere turtleneck. Her dark curls were piled on top of her head, and despite her more casual attire, her long false lashes were firmly in place.

"You *scared* me," I huffed, clasping my chest. "Don't just . . . pop up like that!"

"I'm sorry if I gave you a fright, dear. But you've only just arrived, and I have so many questions! How was the drive? Was poor Desmond traumatized? Is Chicago still windy? Did you manage to sublet your apartment? Did you sell your couch? How do you feel? And, most importantly, who were those *gorgeous* men?"

I let out an exasperated sigh. "The trip was fine, Aunt Lucille. Desmond did great. The Windy City's name doesn't have much to do with the wind in Chicago . . . I found a subletter . . . sold the couch. And I'm okay with it. It doesn't make sense to be paying rent on an apartment in another city — especially since I don't have a job." I hitched a thumb toward the door. "That was Officer Hamby of the Mountain Shadow Police Department and Gideon Brewer — the bartender who works across the street."

Aunt Lucille propped her hands on her hips and fixed me with a reproachful look. "Caroline McCrithers! Are you juggling both of those young men at once?" A devilish gleam appeared in her eyes, ruining the effect. "You are a girl after my own heart!"

"I'm not *juggling* them," I grumbled, circling slowly on the spot as I searched for my handbag, which I'd discarded just inside the hotel entrance. "I'm not even *seeing* them."

"Well, why not?"

"Need I remind you that I was recently *engaged*? And that the man I was supposed to marry turned out to be a total fraud?"

"Oh!" Aunt Lucille scoffed, waving her hand as if this was unimportant. "I was engaged just about every summer from the time I turned twenty-one. None of them stuck. And as for catching a dud here and there, that's just par for the course."

"I'm not ready to date anyone," I said, rummaging in my bag for my trusty magenta day planner and opening the snap closure. "Besides . . . I have bigger problems right now."

I glanced around at the dilapidated lobby. The parquet floor was missing boards in places, and the entire surface was covered in debris. The plaster ceiling was cracked, the wallpaper was peeling, and most of the windows were either broken or missing. The place needed a *lot* of work, but I couldn't exactly bring in a contractor until I dealt with the unfriendly ghost who'd trapped us in the stairwell.

Finally, I located the stained and battered business card I'd gotten from my elevator repairman. I could hardly read the name etched across the bottom — only the first name,

Jinx. The card bore the gold emblem of a hand with an all-seeing eye in the center of the palm, and the text under the name read "Medium."

Digging into my pocket for my phone, I dialed the number listed on the card and waited as it rang. A beat of silence greeted me on the other end of the line, followed by a recording of a smooth feminine voice.

*You've reached Jinx's Salon. If this is a psychospiritual emergency, please hang up and dial seven-one-nine, six-eight-five, zero-zero-one-one. For psychic readings, including tarot, palmistry, numerology, and astrology, please press one. For past-life regressions and energetic healing, press two. For dream interpretation, press three. For communing with spirits of the dead, press four. For all other calls, please remain on the line.*

Feeling slightly uneasy, I pressed four and waited as cerebral electronica music played over the phone. I shot Aunt Lucille a wide-eyed look and shrugged. This was by far the weirdest phone call I'd ever made.

Within just a few seconds, someone picked up. The trippy hold music went dead, and that same pleasant, chocolatey voice from the recording answered. "It's a vibrant day under the Aquarius full moon. This is Jinx. How may I help you?"

For a moment, I was speechless. I'd never dialed a psychic before, and to be honest, I felt a little silly.

"Uh . . . hi." I cleared my throat. "My name is Caroline McCrithers. I just inherited The Mountain Shadow Grand from my great-aunt's estate. I'm having a little issue with, um . . . a spirit."

CHAPTER TWO

I was jittery the following morning as I pulled up in front of the hotel. I wasn't sure why I was so nervous to meet Jinx. I didn't entirely believe in psychics, and I felt a little foolish for even calling the number.

But Jinx had come recommended by my curmudgeonly elevator repairman, Rusty. Rusty was the one who'd told me about the ghost of Roy Wilkerson, who'd been the hotel handyman way back in the thirties and now haunted the old birdcage elevator.

Jinx arrived at nine o'clock on the dot, though I didn't hear her pull up. As I busied myself sweeping up the broken shards of pottery and dead leaves that littered the hotel lobby, I felt a little tingle along the back of my neck just before I heard the knock at the door.

Desmond gave an excited *ree-arr!* and streaked across the parquet floor to reach the door before me. I flung it open to find a tall stately trans woman with light-brown skin and warm brown eyes standing on the steps.

Her tight gelled curls were shorn close to the scalp, and

she wore a colorful silk scarf tied around her head. Her eyes were done up with glittery orange eyeshadow, and her lips were stained a deep plum. Over her arm she carried an old-fashioned carpetbag, and several gauzy shawls completed the fortune-teller look.

"Hello. Are you Jinx?"

"I am," she said in that smooth voice of hers. "And you must be Caroline."

"That's me." I stepped aside to let her through, and Jinx seemed to float — rather than walk — into the lobby. "Th-thank you for coming over on such short notice."

"It's no trouble at all. I am already acquainted with several of the spirits who call this hotel home." She arched one perfectly manicured eyebrow. "It's not the first time I've been called out to . . . attend to their needs."

Swallowing down my skepticism, I forced myself to nod politely. It didn't matter that I'd recently gotten reacquainted with my dead aunt's ghost or that I *might* have brought down a teensy little brick wall with nothing but my mind. I still wasn't convinced that I hadn't suffered some kind of mental breakdown after the ordeal with Todd.

Oddly, I found that possibility more comforting than acknowledging the existence of things like ghosts and psychics.

"I'm sensing some resistance here," said Jinx, gesturing toward the center of my body as if something in my energetic field had given me away.

"Oh, well I . . ." I grimaced, not wanting to insult her.

"It's all right," she said, chuckling softly. "It's perfectly natural to doubt your own experiences. Most people do, at first. It can be difficult to accept that some part of us can remain in this realm long after we die."

"This *realm*?" I repeated as my right eye twitched. This was almost too much to swallow.

Jinx nodded. "Most people were brought up to think of the afterlife as some far-off place, but the veil between the earthen realm and the spirit realm isn't built like a brick wall. It's more or less a living thing that can become damaged or weakened where lots of spirits pass through."

"And that's why my hotel's . . . *haunted*?" I could hardly bring myself to say it while keeping a straight face.

Jinx smiled. "That's one way to put it. But I prefer to think of places such as your hotel as waypoints for troubled spirits."

I raised my eyebrows.

"Spirits that remain in the physical plane after death usually have unfinished business on earth," she explained. "This is why these spirits are so often agitated."

"Oh, he's agitated all right," I muttered. "Apparently, the ghost of Roy Wilkerson doesn't want me renovating the hotel."

A small smile tugged at Jinx's lips, though it didn't meet her eyes. "Mr. Wilkerson has been one of the more . . . *active* spirits here."

I let out a heavy breath. "You can say that again. He locked me and some friends in a stairwell yesterday."

Jinx nodded, and I realized that she looked sad. "That sounds like him."

"So . . . how do I get rid of him?" I asked, rocking back on my heels.

"Well, normally I would suggest that we invite the spirit to pass on. Sometimes the mere suggestion is enough to do the trick. However, seeing how Mr. Wilkerson has insisted on staying here all these years . . ." Jinx trailed off, and my heart sank.

"There's no getting rid of him?" I asked, dread seeping into my voice.

"Not necessarily." I noticed that Jinx seemed to be choosing her words carefully. "I could always perform a forceful banishment —"

"Yes!" I said before she could finish. "Let's do that."

Jinx chuckled softly. "I can see he has not made any new friends here."

"Nope."

She nodded. "Of course, the choice is yours. However, I must warn you that a forceful banishment is energetically heavy work. It is also permanent. Once I perform the banishment, the spirit will no longer be able to inhabit your hotel."

Despite Jinx's tone and the way she seemed to be warning me about something, I failed to see the drawbacks of banishing Roy Wilkerson. "Permanent" sounded nice.

"Although I try to be very specific when performing this kind of work, I must warn you that other spirits may be affected."

I frowned.

"Mr. Wilkerson is not the only spirit who calls The Mountain Shadow Grand home," said Jinx pointedly.

I squirmed under her gaze and swallowed. Was it possible that Jinx knew about Aunt Lucille's ghost?

"If I were to perform a forceful banishment, other spirits could be cast out, too — never able to return."

A shiver of unease swept through me at the finality of her words, and I chewed nervously on my bottom lip.

Aunt Lucille had told me once that her spirit seemed to be tied to the hotel. If she was cast out in Jinx's banishment, I may never see her again.

"Once spirits are banished, they sometimes return to the spirit realm," Jinx continued. "Other times, they are forced to wander between the realms for eternity — never finding peace."

At those words, my stomach clenched. The idea that I might never see Aunt Lucille again was bad enough. I couldn't risk sentencing her to an eternity as a ghostly drifter.

"I guess we'd better not do that," I said with a sigh. "Any other ideas?"

Jinx nodded as though she'd been expecting me to say that. "Since it seems that Mr. Wilkerson's spirit cannot be put to rest, it might be helpful to determine *why* he feels he must linger in this realm."

I squinted at her. This sounded a lot like therapy for ghosts, which for me was a bridge too far. Still, Jinx had taken the time to meet me at the hotel, so I felt I owed it to her to hear what she had to say. "How do we do that?"

"If I'm able to make contact with his spirit," said Jinx, "I might be able to learn what is keeping him tied to this realm."

"O-*kay* . . ."

Apparently, my reluctant consent was all Jinx needed. She immediately set down her carpetbag and began pulling out handfuls of crystals, sage, and giant white candles as if she was Mary Poppins — if Mary Poppins owned a metaphysical supplies store.

I got a whiff of something that smelled like the back of a hippie's van when Jinx jerked her head up and asked,

"Where has Mr. Wilkerson's spirit been the most persistent lately?"

"He made himself known about a week ago as I was getting off the elevator," I said. I didn't mention that the antique Otis elevator had the creepy habit of zooming up to the closed-off fourth floor whenever it felt like it — or that it had dropped me three stories. "Then yesterday, he trapped us in the stairwell."

"We'll start with the elevator," said Jinx. "I'm getting a lot of despondent energy from that general vicinity."

I pressed my lips together and nodded as Jinx gathered up all her witchy supplies and shuffled over to the far corner of the lobby.

I watched awkwardly from the sidelines as she placed lit candles all around the old birdcage elevator and began to smudge the cage, both inside and out. The smell of burning sage tickled my nostrils and made me sneeze, but the scent wasn't entirely unpleasant. Jinx moved fluidly around the elevator, placing a shiny black rock in each corner.

Finally, she sat down in the very center of the cage and readjusted her gossamer shawls. Her sparkly eyelids fluttered closed, and I watched her face in the dancing candlelight for any sign that she was getting a download from the spirit world.

After a while, Desmond appeared, sniffing Jinx's left knee and crawling delicately into her lap. Jinx didn't move as he settled in. She didn't even open her eyes.

I was just about to wander off to go do something else when I felt a faint prickle along the back of my neck. I shifted my weight from one foot to the other, and then a feeling like icy water being poured down my back made every hair on my body stand on end.

"Hello, Mr. Wilkerson," said Jinx softly, still not opening her eyes.

Well, *that* was creepy. The woman still appeared to be deep in meditation. Had she *sensed* him somehow?

Roy's ghost didn't answer her, but the tingling along the back of my neck seemed to intensify.

"He is here with us now," said Jinx, just in case I wasn't already dialed in to the very unpleasant ghostly sensations. Then, louder, she added, "Mr. Wilkerson, go in peace. Leave The Mountain Shadow Grand hotel. May your old wounds be forgotten, old loves laid to rest. Let the bonds that tether you to the earthen realm dissolve and the silvery veil call you home . . ."

At Jinx's words, a cold draft shot through the lobby, raising goosebumps all over my arms. The candles sputtered, and a few went out, filling the air with the scent of smoke.

Desmond gave an indignant *ree-ow!* and leapt out of Jinx's lap.

"Mr. Wilkerson does not wish to leave," Jinx said unnecessarily.

"Why not?" I asked, my gaze darting from corner to corner as if I expected the ghost of the hotel handyman to materialize in front of me.

"He will not tell me." Jinx's brow furrowed, and she shook her head. "I'm sensing deep sorrow — but also rage. Longing. His energy feels to me like unrequited love, but that's not entirely right."

I gaped at Jinx, who was still sitting with her eyes

closed. I didn't know how she could stand to keep her eyes shut with the foreboding presence of Roy around.

Then, suddenly, another icy draft stole my breath, and the rest of the candles went out. My skin prickled as I gasped for air and squinted through the gloom.

For a moment, I thought perhaps it was just a trick of the light — or maybe the smoke from the candles. But then I recognized the rail-thin form of the hotel's former handyman standing over Jinx.

My heart leapt. "B-behind you!" I spluttered, jumping back and pointing a shaky finger at Roy.

Desmond hissed, arching his back. His yellow eyes were fixed on the ghostly form of Roy Wilkerson, who was dressed in a pair of tatty overalls and a slouchy newsboy cap.

Jinx didn't look around at my warning. She didn't move a muscle. "He's still with us?" she asked.

I nodded mutely before remembering that she still had her eyes closed. "H-he's right behind you."

"On their own, the spirits of the dead cannot harm us," she said. "Though, if their foothold in this realm is very strong, they can sometimes manipulate objects on the physical plane."

At those words, I remembered when Gran had insulted Aunt Lucille and a pendant light had fallen from the ceiling. It also explained how Roy managed to control the elevator.

"He won't tell me what troubles him," Jinx murmured, sounding frustrated for the first time since she'd begun the ritual. "Mr. Wilkerson, can you *show* us?" she asked, speaking to the room.

Roy's ghost vanished almost as abruptly as it had

appeared, and I heard a light *thunk* that seemed to have come from the floor above our heads.

Frowning, I shuffled away from the elevator and stared up the grand staircase. The hairs along the back of my neck tingled.

Every bone in my body said it was a bad idea to go looking for the source of the noise. The upper stories felt like the ghosts' domain, which was ridiculous, since it was *my* hotel.

No. I needed to get to the bottom of things if I ever wanted to host guests at the hotel. I couldn't very well ask people to come and stay as long as I had light fixtures falling from the ceiling and an elevator with a mind of its own.

Swallowing down my fear, I started to climb — each step creaking under my weight. The squeaks and groans seemed much louder than usual, and my heart hammered against my ribcage.

For once, Desmond didn't come bolting up the steps behind me. He just watched from the landing, his yellow eyes glowing in the dark.

I didn't have to go far to see what had fallen. Directly across from the top of the staircase, a framed black-and-white photograph lay on the musty pink carpeting. The thin brass frame was badly tarnished from age, and the cracked glass was coated in a thick layer of dust.

Wiping away the grime with the pad of my thumb, I stared down at a portrait of a man and a woman. The man was clean-shaven and wore his hair slicked back. He was dressed in a boxy, expensive-looking suit and had the slightly smug air of wealth and good breeding. It *definitely* wasn't Roy.

The woman beside him wasn't smiling, though she had an attractive, youthful glow that told me she had to be at least twenty years younger than the man in the photo.

My eyes drifted down to the corner of the frame, where someone had handwritten the couple's name: *Ernest and Cecille Bellwether, 1933.*

The name Bellwether struck a chord. I knew the Bellwether brothers had opened The Grand, but that was Charles and Ulysses Bellwether. Besides that, the man in the photo only looked about fifty. He had to be one of their sons.

Still staring at the photograph, I came down the stairs to find Jinx packing away her things. She turned her head when she saw me, and her gaze drifted down to the photo in my hands. "Did you find something?"

"I'm . . . not sure," I said, frowning at the couple. Truth be told, I didn't have the slightest idea who these people were. The hotel's walls were full of creepy black-and-white photos, but this one must have meant something to Roy.

"I'm sorry I couldn't be of more help," said Jinx.

"You did help," I assured her. "This is more than I had to go on before."

She smiled. "Perhaps if you can learn what troubles Roy, you can help him pass on."

I let out a heavy breath. That sounded like a big project on top of the already big project of restoring the hotel. Good thing I was currently unemployed. "Can I ask you something?"

"Of course." A fine crease appeared between Jinx's brows, but her smile didn't falter.

"Do you think — I mean, is it *possible* . . ." I trailed off, not sure how to phrase my question. I sighed. "Someone told me recently that Mountain Shadow has its own magic — that it can trigger certain . . . abilities."

"Ah." Jinx lifted her brows in a knowing expression, and she nodded sagely. "I did wonder about you."

My stomach flipped over. "You *did*?"

Jinx nodded, studying me thoughtfully. "You could see him."

There was no point in denying it. It wasn't as though the town psychic was going to have me committed. I swallowed thickly. "Couldn't you?"

"No."

I stared at her, taken aback.

"I can usually *sense* spirits," Jinx continued. "Seeing them is . . . another matter entirely. Some people are born with extrasensory perception. They can see, feel, and know things that other people can't. Others have the innate ability to manipulate the world around them."

"Like . . . *telekinesis*?" I winced. I could feel my skepticism kicking in again.

"In some cases, yes. Anything outside the realm of what the average person is capable of can be explained by an enhanced connection to the elements — both seen and unseen. It's true that Mountain Shadow has a special energy that can unlock one's ability to tap into the elements." Jinx studied me for another moment. "Do you think you've experienced something like that?"

I shook my head quickly, wishing I hadn't said anything. I didn't want to think about the miniature earthquake that had brought down a solid brick wall or admit that I might have caused it.

The implication was terrifying.

Jinx's smile faded slightly as she searched my face for .

. . something. "Well, if you ever need to talk, Caroline, my door is always open. We have a community here for people like you — people who see things or experience the world differently than others do."

"A *community*?" I repeated dubiously. That sounded a lot like a cult.

"A coven," said Jinx, chuckling as if she'd somehow read my mind.

I gaped at her. *O-kay.* So I'd stumbled across the local coven. Cool.

"What do I owe you for today?" I asked, suddenly very tired.

Jinx just shook her head. "I don't charge for banishments that don't take. If you need further help, just call. I'm sure we'll be seeing each other again."

CHAPTER THREE

"I don't think emotional support animals count," I said to Gran as we pulled up in front of the Fireside Café. She sat beside me in the front seat of the Pinto, wrestling her white west highland terrier into a red reflective vest with "Emotional Support Animal" printed along the side.

Gran paused in her ministrations and gestured toward the restaurant. "All the patio seating's full, and it's too hot to leave him in the car."

This was why I'd left Desmond at home. "It says no dogs," I protested, pointing to a sign posted in the window.

"Service animals don't count."

"*Service* animals might not count, but the only service Snowball provides is barking at the mailman."

Gran waved away my protest and went back to buckling the vest as Snowball stared at me with a forlorn expression. "Snow comforts me and provides companionship."

"Still not a service dog," I muttered.

Gran scoffed. "Just be glad my emotional support animal isn't a miniature horse."

I sighed and climbed out of the Pinto, too drained and rattled from my meeting with Jinx to argue any further. The idea that Mountain Shadow had the power to unlock supernatural abilities was unnerving.

I didn't believe in magic, but then again, I hadn't believed in ghosts either until I'd inherited the hotel. And if ghosts were real, did that mean other supernatural beings existed?

Feeling rattled, I walked around and opened the door to help Gran out of the car. She was dressed in a white velour tracksuit with red-and-blue stripes along the sides. Her cloud of white hair stuck out the top of her American-flag printed visor, and she had her "going out" shoes on — a pair of pristine white Skechers with a sparkly silver "S" on each side.

As it was late July, the large stone hearth in the far corner of the restaurant was empty, but the unfinished red-brick walls and rustic pine furniture leant their own cozy warmth. People were packed into the café, chatting over eggs Benedict, gourmet pancakes, and mimosas. My mouth watered as I took in the sight of all the food, and we found ourselves a two-person table squished into the back corner by the kitchen.

From my seat, I could see a plump little redhead dressed in a lilac chef's outfit bustling around in the back. She flitted around the other line cooks, tasting things and swiping dishes off the line to place on the orders-up counter.

"Comp the mimosas at table twelve, will you? That eggs Benny took *way* too long to come out."

The server nodded and scuttled off to deliver the dish as the redhead came to take our order. As with Jinx, I felt a little tingle along the back of my neck and rubbed the spot absently. "Welcome to Fireside, ladies. Can I start you off with —"

The little chef broke off, her hazel eyes lighting up as they landed on the dog in Gran's lap. "*Snowball!*" Twin dimples appeared on either side of her mouth, and her voice jumped half an octave as she took on the tone reserved for dogs and babies. "Oh! Aren't you just the *sweetest widdle fing!*"

She bent to scratch Snow behind the ears, and Gran shot me a smug look.

"How are you, Ginger?" the chef asked Gran, returning to her normal speaking voice.

"Fine, Daphne. Thank you for asking. This is my granddaughter, Caroline."

"Nice to meet you," said Daphne the chef, still with that infectious grin. "I hope we'll be seeing Snowball at the show this weekend. I heard he was *this close* to a blue ribbon last year."

Gran nodded. "We wouldn't miss it."

I arched an eyebrow. "Show?"

"The Dog Days of Summer," Daphne supplied. "It's the annual dog show in town. It's no Westminster, but all proceeds go to charity. The restaurant is catering the event this year, and Doris Ashcroft has *not* made it easy."

"I'll bet not," Gran said with a chuckle.

Daphne rolled her eyes. "I'm supposed to be supplying four hundred gourmet peanut-butter-oat dog biscuits, four hundred pumpkin-spice puppy pies, and sixty pounds of jerky. Everything has to be soy-free, gluten-free, GMO-free

". . . and that's just for the contestants!" She said all of this in one breath, and her cheeks flushed a delicate shade of pink as she realized she was babbling.

"Sounds like you have your work cut out for you," Gran remarked.

"You can say that again." Daphne heaved a sigh. "Doris has been *extra* prickly since the historical society's committee for urban renewal opened applications for the big Main Street revitalization grant. The woman heads up *way* too many committees, if you ask me. But you didn't, so . . ." She gave a nervous chuckle. "What can I get you ladies to drink?"

"I'll have a coffee to start," said Gran. "Piping hot, if you don't mind. Caroline, would you like a coffee to drink, or should we ask Daphne if the server can administer your caffeine intravenously?"

I snorted at her deadpan tone and grinned at Daphne. "Coffee would be good, thanks."

"Coming right up." The little chef bustled away to get our drinks, good-naturedly barking orders at her line cooks as she went without even looking at the dishes.

"Snowball's competing in a dog show?" I asked in amusement. Then something else Daphne had said seemed to register in my brain. "Wait. What's the Main Street revitalization grant, and why haven't I heard about it?"

"The Mountain Shadow Historical Society awards it every three years," came a gravelly voice to my right.

I looked over to see a balding old man reading the paper at the table next to ours. He was dressed in a baggy T-shirt and a pair of worn Levis held up by suspenders.

He glanced up from his paper when I turned to look at him, but his gaze landed on Gran. "Mornin', Ginger."

"Drop dead, Herschel," came Gran's snappy reply a moment before a server appeared with two steaming mugs of coffee.

"What's put a kink in your oxygen tube?" The old man guffawed at his own joke and laughed even harder at Gran's scowl. He laughed *so* hard he began to cough and reached into his back pocket for a grimy bandana. This he used to mop under his bulbous nose, hacking and coughing all the while.

"It's rude to eavesdrop," Gran replied tartly.

"Tell me about the grant," I said, eager to learn whatever this old busybody knew.

Herschel's wiry gray eyebrows inched up, as if surprised to be consulted. "Well, it's a half-million-dollar grant that's supposed to go toward revitalizing historic downtown. Half of it comes from sales-tax revenue, and the state historic fund matches it. It's a pretty competitive process," Herschel added. "The last twelve years, the grant's gone to developers from out of state to rehab these old buildings."

"Don't listen to him," said Gran, staring determinedly at her coffee. "Herschel's mostly hot air."

"Hey," said Herschel with a wicked grin. "At least she called me hot."

Ignoring the weird dynamic between my gran and Herschel, I sat back and took a sip of my coffee as I turned this new information over in my mind.

A historic grant was just what I needed to jumpstart renovations at The Grand. Half a million dollars wasn't chump change — it was certainly more than the various grants I'd already noted in my research.

"How are projects selected?" I asked, ignoring Gran's irritation with Herschel.

"You just have to submit an application and make your case to the committee for urban renewal," said Herschel. "They're the ones who decide which projects to back. If you can impress those old biddies . . ." He let out a little *pfft* of air. "That's a half a million dollars in free money."

Free money — my favorite kind.

"We have to go for it," I whispered to Gran, wrapping my hands around my mug. Since Gran had leased the Blackthorne family farm to pay Lucille's back taxes on the property, I felt as though we were in this together. "This could be *exactly* what I need to get the building remodeled!"

"Half a million dollars isn't going to cut it," she reminded me.

Some of the air whizzed out of my balloon at those words, but I couldn't let that little detail get me down. "No, but it would give us enough to at least get started. I can't even secure a contractor without a deposit." I leaned forward. "Maybe if we got the grant, I could get a loan for the rest — use the building as collateral."

"Sounds like you have it all worked out."

Gran said this as if it settled the matter, and I watched out of the corner of my eye as Herschel folded his newspaper, set a crisp twenty-dollar bill on the table, and got up to leave.

"What's the deal with you and him?" I asked as Herschel ambled toward the door.

Gran looked affronted by my question. "Deal? There is no *deal*, Caroline."

I tilted my head to the side and shot her a disbelieving look.

"Herschel is just a nosy old goat with all the manners of a farmhand."

I lifted my shoulders. "It seemed like more than that to me."

Gran rolled her eyes and let out an indignant huff. "Well, if you *must* know . . . When you've been a widow for as long as I have, people start to think that you might be" — she lowered her voice — "on the market."

Whatever I'd been expecting Gran to say, it hadn't been *that*. I opened and closed my mouth several times and then clamped my lips shut to keep a laugh from escaping. "On the *market*?" I choked.

"Yes." Gran's brows knitted together. "What's so funny?"

"Nothing," I said, shaking my head and grinning in disbelief. "It's just . . . I thought the market closed once you hit ninety."

"Oh you did, did you?" Gran's tone was sharp.

I gave a helpless shrug. This was the type of conversation where it was impossible to say the right thing — and, to be honest, I wasn't all that jazzed to be discussing my ninety-two-year-old grandmother's love life.

"Well, it doesn't," she snapped, picking up her laminated menu and giving it a loud rustle. "People don't have expiration dates, Caroline. They just start to smell a little funny when they've been on the shelf too long."

CHAPTER FOUR

Three days later, I emerged from my frenzy of research and work with a crisp, quadruple-proof-read application for the Main Street revitalization grant.

I had five presentation booklets bound in faux-leather folders, which were full of snappy charts and graphs, as well as photos of the hotel I'd dug up from the archives down in Colorado Springs. My notes were typed up on a series of three-by-five cards, and I'd practiced my pitch for Gran and Desmond at least half a dozen times.

I may have bombed my last client pitch meeting at work, but I felt solid and prepared as I took the short flight of stairs up to the old city hall, which served as headquarters to the Mountain Shadow Historical Society.

In ad agency land, it was common to dress down for pitch meetings in an effort to look young and hip. But since I knew I'd be presenting to a panel of mostly older people, I figured it was better to dress like someone interviewing for a job as a White House staffer.

I'd donned a smart pencil skirt that hit just above the knee, a matching charcoal blazer, heels — and, as an afterthought, a pair of nude-colored pantyhose. I was already sweating bullets by the time I reached the top of the steps, but I was glad I'd gone the extra mile.

As I let myself in the front door, I was greeted by the scent of floor wax and a familiar musty old-building smell. I glanced around for some indication of where I was supposed to be going and saw a typed and laminated sign pointing me in the right direction.

I rounded the corner down a narrow hallway and heard a smatter of boisterous male laughter as two men in suits let themselves out of a room. One of them carried a large poster with a digital rendering of a building under his arm.

They passed me in the hallway without so much as a glance, and my stomach did a nervous flop. A familiar logo was printed along the bottom corner of the poster, and I recognized it as belonging to one of the top real-estate developers in Denver.

Were they *also* competing for the grant?

There were no chairs out in the hallway, so I cracked the door and stuck my head in. Three women and two men were seated at a table along the wall. I recognized the youngest committee member as Bellamy Broussard — owner of The Wind Chime Inn Bed and Breakfast. He wore his gelled black hair in a severe windswept style, and he was dressed in a pair of smart tweed slacks and a crisp lavender shirt.

None of the committee members so much as looked up when I walked in. They were all chatting amongst themselves, a few peering through bifocals at the glossy one-sheets left by the last applicants.

I straightened up and cleared my throat, and the older man at the table glanced up.

"Good morning," I said. "I'm Caroline McCrithers, representing The Mountain Shadow Grand."

"The Mountain Shadow Grand?" The old man frowned and shuffled the papers on the table in front of him before turning to his cohorts. "I don't remember seeing an application for The Grand. Do you?"

An older lady dressed inexplicably in a green Santa sweater shook her head, and I swallowed down my bubbling panic.

"I submitted it online yesterday," I said. "But I also have paper copies."

I preened a little at my own preparedness as I approached the committee, pleased I'd made a special trip to the office supply store to get the fancy résumé paper. The old man took my application, frowning as he examined it.

I hesitated. Was I supposed to give them a chance to read my application before I launched into my pitch? I decided to go ahead and hand out the folders so they could get acquainted with my proposal while I gathered my thoughts.

Retreating to the table opposite the committee, I opened my Filofax to retrieve my notes. I'd known exactly what I was going to say this morning, but the fact that they hadn't yet reviewed my application definitely threw a wrench in my plans.

"I thought Jay Mathers bought that building," said the

old man, whose tiny brass name badge told me his name was Nigel Williams.

"Nope," I said, deciding I'd take the time to field any questions before launching into my spiel. "Lucille Blackthorne was my aunt. I inherited The Grand when she passed away. It was her dying wish that I restore the hotel to its former glory."

Nigel made a harrumphing noise and went back to perusing my application, lifting the top page without reading it in its entirety. "What's your budget?"

I cleared my throat nervously. I'd been expecting this question, of course, though it didn't make it easier to skirt around the fact that I currently had two months' severance in my bank account and very little else.

"My contractor estimates that it will cost around five million dollars to complete the renovations. However, you'll see from my proposal that I plan to complete the project in stages, beginning with a remodel of the main floor to serve as an event venue. That phase includes an overhaul of the kitchen, dining room, and the grand ballroom. This way, the hotel could begin generating revenue as early as next year."

Nigel didn't glance up from my application, but his frown seemed to deepen.

"What are your other sources of funding?" asked Bellamy Broussard, leaning forward in his seat.

I took a deep breath. "I haven't pursued private investments at this juncture. However, I'm sure that securing such a prestigious grant will generate lots of interest in the project."

"Do you have any experience with commercial renovation?" asked a sweet-looking old woman with platinum-blond hair and a cleft chin seated at the end. I couldn't read her name badge from where I stood.

"No," I said, swallowing thickly.

"Any experience in hospitality?" asked the woman wearing the Santa sweater.

I shook my head. "I'm coming from the advertising industry. I've already begun a full rebrand of The Mountain Shadow Grand and a campaign to help generate grassroots support for the renovations."

"So what you're saying is that you have no budget, no investors, and no experience with this type of project *whatsoever*?"

This had come from a pinched-face old woman seated at the center of the table. Stiff gray curls protruded from her head in a style that reminded me of the bride of Frankenstein, and she wore what appeared to be a permanently sour expression.

I glanced at the name badge affixed to her polo shirt and saw that *this* was the infamous Doris that Daphne had been complaining about.

I opened my mouth to respond, but the old woman cut me off. "Why have you come here, Miss McCrithers? Is it your intention to waste this committee's time?"

"N-no," I stammered, heat rising in my cheeks as my chest fluttered with panic and humiliation.

"Because I cannot think of another reason why a young woman with no funding, no experience, and — frankly — no *clue* would be pursuing this grant."

I could feel a hard lump rising up in my throat, and I swallowed down the tears that threatened to burst forth.

Taking a slow, deep breath, I drew myself up and addressed the committee as a whole. "The Mountain

Shadow Grand is an icon," I began. "It meant a great deal to my aunt, but she never had the means to see it restored. It has stood vacant the past thirty years, becoming a target for vandals. This beautiful historic hotel, if revived, will create new jobs and generate tax revenue for Mountain Shadow. It will be a beacon that draws in tourists from all over the world."

"Miss McCrithers, it sounds like a very exciting project," said the kindly blond woman near the end of the panel.

"A very exciting project in *theory*," said Doris. "But I'm not one for theoretical projects."

"Of course not," I said. "But if you would just look at my projections for —"

"Miss McCrithers," Doris cut in. "I have no doubt that you are very skilled with a computer — skilled enough to make it look as though you know what you are doing. But when I look at you, I see someone who is inexperienced and fundamentally unqualified to take on this project."

I opened my mouth to answer her objections, but I had no words.

Doris rolled on. "Every time we open up applications for this grant, we get a flood of proposals from young fly-by-night developers who are just looking to turn a quick profit. This committee is not interested in these short-sighted endeavors. We are looking for someone who has a vested interest in the community — someone who cares about preserving the integrity and significance of our oldest structures while creating a positive economic impact through the revitalization of historic downtown."

Somehow, I managed to unstick my throat. "I assure

you, Mrs. Ashcroft. I have every intention of preserving the historical integrity of the hotel while —"

"That's what they all say, Miss McCrithers. But you landed in Mountain Shadow just a few weeks ago after having this property drop into your lap. You thought it might be fun to renovate an old hotel. You have no *idea* what that entails." She shook her head. "I do not believe for one second that you have what it takes to see this project through to completion."

For a moment, I just stood there — my whole body stinging from her assessment and my notecards hanging limp in my hand. A few committee members cleared their throats, but no one jumped to my defense.

What was I supposed to say? I *had* just come to Mountain Shadow, and I truly didn't have any experience in renovating old properties or running a hotel.

I was still trying to figure out how to respond when Nigel cleared his throat. "Yes, well . . . We'll review your application and be in touch."

My heart sank. That was a clear denial if I'd ever heard one.

Taking his words as the dismissal they were, I turned on the spot and hastily collected my things. I didn't look back at the committee as I fled the room. My face was still burning from the dressing-down I'd received, and I didn't think I'd be able to look Doris Ashcroft in the eye without bursting into tears.

It wasn't as though I'd expected this pitch to be easy. I'd known they would have questions — doubts about the project. I just hadn't expected to be the focus of their criticism.

Tears stung my eyes as I staggered into the hallway, but

someone caught the door behind me before it could swing closed.

"Miss McCrithers!"

I hurriedly scrubbed away my tears and turned to face the kindly old woman with platinum-blond hair who was hurrying to catch up to me.

"Yes?"

She searched my face, taking in my red-rimmed eyes, and her expression softened with sympathy. "I'm Selma Lewis, one of the committee members." The woman glanced over her shoulder and nervously adjusted the silver bracelet at her wrist. "I wondered if you had a moment to speak in private . . ."

"Uh, sure," I said, utterly bewildered but too traumatized from my presentation to ask what she wanted to talk to me about.

Selma skirted away from the door, ushering me down the long hallway so as not to be overheard.

"I'm sorry about what happened back there," she said once we were out of earshot. "Doris can be a bit . . . blunt sometimes."

Now *there* was an understatement.

"She means well, of course, but that doesn't always soften the blow. I'm sure that was hard to hear."

"It was," I admitted. "But I'd be lying if I said I hadn't expected some pushback."

Selma nodded and turned her head to face me, her lips curving in a warm smile. "I just thought you should know that the rest of us are *very* excited about your project."

I raised an eyebrow in disbelief. Had we been in the same meeting? If the other committee members were excited about me renovating The Grand, they sure had a poor way of showing it. "They were?"

"Oh, yes!" said Selma, so emphatically that I found myself believing that the woman was sincere. "You have no idea how long we've been waiting for someone to come along with the funds and the *gumption* to restore it. It's been downright painful to watch such a gorgeous old building go to wrack and ruin all these years."

I pulled a tight smile. "That's nice of you to say. To be honest, I wasn't sure how I was going to fund the renovations before I heard about the grant. My aunt didn't leave much in the way of cash."

Selma nodded. "I thought that might be the case. I also think Doris was wrong about you, and I don't mind saying so. I think you are the *perfect* person to head up this project. You're young, energetic, passionate, organized. And you seem to know how to get things done."

At those words, something like hope stirred in my chest, but it was quickly doused as I mentally replayed the highlights of my presentation.

"I appreciate you saying that, but Doris seemed pretty set in her decision."

"Well, I never did have a head for business," said Selma sheepishly. "I was a homemaker for most of my life, but nothing's decided yet. The way this works is we hear all the applicants' presentations. Then we take a few days to review the proposals before we come to a decision. If you could find another backer — someone with experience renovating commercial properties to partner with you — I think Doris could be swayed."

"Really? You think so?" I was honestly shocked to have

someone like Selma in my corner. I didn't think my presentation had been all that impressive.

Finding someone with experience to back the project sounded like a good idea, but bringing on investors at this stage felt like way more than I was ready for.

Selma nodded. "Think it over, will you? I believe I speak for the rest of the committee when I say that we would love to green-light this project."

CHAPTER FIVE

I felt thoroughly defeated by the time I stumbled into Déjà Brew, seeking the comfort of my usual oat-milk mocha with three shots of espresso.

Amber, my favorite barista, was working behind the counter. Her black hair was swept into an untidy bun at the top of her head, and her cut-off T-shirt gave a full view of her colorful sleeves of tattoos.

"Hey, girl!" she called, grinning at me over the espresso machine. Her hands moved with practiced efficiency as she made the drinks, and she was good enough at what she did to talk to me while she poured milk with one hand and knocked off the portafilter with the other.

"Hey . . ."

"Uh-oh."

My expression must have given me away, because Amber tilted her chin forward and gave me a look that said whoever had hurt me was about to have his tires slashed. "What *happened*?"

I sighed. This was what I loved about Amber. She was

always willing to listen to my problems — which was good, since I often used sugar and caffeine as a substitute for therapy.

I shook my head. "Nothing . . . I just gave the second-most humiliating presentation of my life. No biggie." I tried to shrug it off — both literally and figuratively — but I couldn't shake the sting of failure.

"Presentation?" Amber's pierced eyebrows rumpled. "Presentation for what?"

I told her all about the Main Street revitalization grant and how it had seemed like my very best shot at securing the funds to renovate the hotel. I gave her a play-by-play of my pitch — including Doris's very public assessment of all my shortcomings.

"Dude, that's *rough*," said Amber, her face crumpling in sympathy. "I know Doris, and she can be a real bi— Here's that biscotti!" she finished brightly, switching gears midsentence as she turned to hand a chocolate biscotti over the counter to another customer. Her plastered-on smile stayed firmly in place until the customer was out of earshot, and then she rolled her eyes. "She can be a real *biscotti*, if ya know what I'm sayin'."

"Well, she's not going to be president of *my* fan club anytime soon."

Something flickered in Amber's dark eyes. Then they narrowed in a devious expression. "Maybe that's your ticket then."

"What do you mean?"

Amber gnawed on her bottom lip. "Maybe you just need to . . . I don't know. Suck up to Doris a little."

I shook my head with a dark chuckle. "She seemed

pretty set on her decision. I don't think sucking up is going to get me very far."

"I'm not talking about helping little old ladies cross the street or anything. Seriously — do *not* offer to help Doris cross the street. I once made the mistake of holding the door open for her when she had her hands full of hot tea, and she spent the next ten minutes lecturing me on ageism."

"Yeah, that sounds like her," I sighed.

But that gleam of inspiration didn't leave Amber's eyes. "You know, Doris is heading up the big dog show this weekend. She's, like, *obsessed* with her whippet." Amber rolled her eyes. "That little greyhound-looking dog that's always shivering? Anyway, I guess Crumpet is a world champion or something. He's won best in show, like, three years in a row."

"Crumpet's a stupid name for a dog."

Amber snorted.

Come to think of it, I *had* seen Doris out walking a little dog before. Mountain Shadow was a small town, and I vaguely recalled a sad, skinny dog stuffed into a turtleneck sweater.

"Anyway, Doris is always in charge of Dog Days, and I heard they're short on volunteers this year. Doris was in here talking to Daphne Weaver last week. She's been scrambling to get everything together, which is probably why she seemed to have an extra large stick up her a—" Amber's eyes widened as another customer approached the counter, and she plastered that big, helpful smile back on. "And there's that cappuccino for you . . ."

The woman took her drink from Amber as I turned the idea over in my head. Doris *had* brought up the fact that they were looking for someone with a vested interest in the community — someone who wanted to stick around and really have a positive impact.

What better way to show that I was genuinely interested in improving Mountain Shadow than by volunteering for a good cause? I had no idea whom I might approach as an investor with experience in commercial renovation, but I could certainly give up a weekend to rip tickets and man the snack stand or whatever.

"You know, that's actually a good idea," I said after a moment's pause.

Amber waggled her eyebrows. "I'm always full of good ideas."

"I'll keep that in mind," I said as she poured the steamed milk into my cup and handed over my mocha. "I think I *will* sign up to volunteer. Who knows? It might be fun."

---

AT EIGHT O'CLOCK on Friday morning, I was standing in the town square, baking in the hot sun. I'd gotten up at the crack of dawn to get to my volunteer gig on time. With little rivulets of sweat dripping into my eyes and sliding down the backs of my legs, I was already beginning to regret that decision.

Doris Ashcroft was in charge of all the volunteers that morning. She'd looked surprised when I'd showed up, but I'd just plastered on my sweetest smile and joined the other volunteers in line.

She was dressed in a pair of pleated khaki shorts that hit below the knee and a royal-blue polo shirt bearing the

Dog Days of Summer emblem. With her top button fully fastened and her severe curls stuffed into one of those topless straw hats, Doris looked like an old-lady drill sergeant.

"Dog Days is one of the premier dog shows on the Front Range," she told the crowd of volunteers — mostly fit-looking retirees. "These contestants are canine royalty, and our standard is nothing short of excellence."

Doris began to pace before her troops, who shifted their weight nervously from one orthopedic sandaled foot to the other. "Our judges must be beyond reproach — irrefutable experts on the breeds which they are judging. Events must run *on time*. The town square must be kept free of litter and debris. Canine hydration and cooling stations must be kept full at all times. It's going to be a hot one this weekend." Doris gestured to the aforementioned "hydration and cooling stations" behind her — a collection of giant water bowls shaped like dog bones and five or six blue plastic kiddie pools.

I let out a long breath through my mouth. The shops on Main Street weren't even open yet, and it was already eighty-five degrees. The kiddie pools were looking pretty enticing.

"Check-in begins at nine a.m. sharp. Once I give you your assignment, please report to your station *immediately* to prepare —"

*"Adopt, don't shop! Adopt, don't shop! Dog shows drive demand that keep puppy mills alive!"*

A fervent chant broke through Doris's spiel, and we all turned toward the source of the noise. A hippie woman in a flowy green skirt was standing on the sidewalk in front of the square, brandishing a giant poster. Her long brown hair was ratty and unkempt, and on her shoulder she had a very detailed tattoo of a dog and a cat surrounded by a huge sun.

"Give a sweet dog like Sunshine a furever home. Or how about Biscuit, who was found in a dumpster at four weeks old? These fur babies don't need a blue ribbon. They only need your love!"

I assumed the poster she was brandishing had some sad-looking photos of dogs pasted on the front. She directed her plea at the steady line of cars that were already circling the block, trying to find parking for registration.

Most of the drivers simply ignored her, but a few people honked or made rude gestures. Still the woman kept up her tirade as she paced the sidewalk, her voice crackling over the low rumble of engines.

"One moment," said Doris, turning on her heel and marching straight over to the hippie woman. "Ma'am . . . ma'am!"

"I'd sure hate to be that poor woman," whispered the sixtysomething man beside me as Doris tapped the protestor on the shoulder.

"Ma'am? This is a private event."

"And this is public property! I have the right to peaceably protest."

Doris gestured at the sidewalk. "You're obstructing pedestrian traffic."

She wasn't wrong. Men and women with their dogs were stepping off the sidewalk and into the street to give the hippie woman a wider berth.

"You wouldn't have a problem with me being here if you weren't afraid that these people might learn the truth!

Many of these dogs have come from breeders who keep the mothers in abhorrent —"

"I'm going to ask nicely *once*," Doris cut in, her voice sharp and clipped. "Leave now, or I'll call the police and have you forcibly removed."

The hippie woman glared at Doris for a long moment before hitching up her skirt and stalking off — probably to take up her protest elsewhere.

I felt conflicted as I watched her cross the street. While I was sympathetic to the plight of Sunshine, Biscuit, and shelter dogs everywhere, I had to admit that Doris was impressively scary.

Shaking her head, Doris grabbed a cardboard box off the ground and went down the line, handing out blue volunteer shirts and assigning us to our stations.

"Size?" Doris barked when she reached me.

"Uh, medium, if you have it."

Doris dug around in her cardboard box and produced one tightly rolled blue shirt. "Piddle patrol," she said, slapping the rolled-up shirt into my hands.

I had a brief moment of panic when I realized that this wasn't one of the jobs she'd discussed during our brief orientation. "Excuse me?"

Doris gave me a deadpan look. "Or would you prefer 'poo platoon'?"

For a second, I just stared at her, and Doris rolled her eyes. "Contestants are not permitted to relieve themselves on the grass or in the right of way on Main Street." She turned toward the far end of the town square and pointed to an area on the other side of the gazebo. "Piddle patrol maintains the facilities."

Once she was finished handing out assignments, Doris

led me over to the area I'd be manning for the weekend. The "facilities" included half a dozen four-by-four platforms covered in fake grass — each with its own plastic fire hydrant.

My job was to stand by with a hose and spring-action pooper scooper to clean up after each contestant. It wasn't *exactly* what I'd had in mind when I'd volunteered to help out, but if Doris was trying to test my commitment, I would be the best poop scooper she'd ever seen.

Within the hour, the town square filled with every breed of show dog imaginable — poodles and Pomeranians, Dalmatians and Dobermans, beagles and basset hounds. Some of the contestants pranced alongside their owners on leashes, while others were wheeled into the square in rolling crates.

It hadn't occurred to me that there could be a rush to use the "facilities," but as owners and handlers piled out of cargo vans and RVs with their dogs, I realized that most of the contestants were in urgent need of a potty break.

I was just hosing down the fake grass after a very nervous Great Dane when I spotted Will in the middle of the road, directing a line of traffic. Despite the scorching heat, he was dressed in full uniform — the navy polyester sleeves clinging to his toned biceps.

As I stared, he reached up to wipe the sweat from his brow, and I was hit with an *extremely* inappropriate fantasy where Officer Handsome stripped off his shirt and I redirected my garden hose at that beautiful man-chest.

"Miss McCrithers? Miss McCrithers!" Doris practically barked my name, ripping me out of my heat-induced fantasy and sending me crashing back down to the AstroTurf.

I cleared my throat and gave my head a shake. "Hi. Yes! Sorry, what?"

Doris's brow was all scrunched up as she pointed at the nearest piddle pad. I squinted down at the turf and saw a teensy smear of poo residue stuck to the edge of the platform. "This isn't hygienic!" Doris snapped. "Would you care to relieve yourself on *soiled* turf?"

"Uh —" I stopped short of telling Doris that the last time *I'd* relieved myself on AstroTurf, I'd been two Long Island iced teas in at the Lake of the Ozarks and entrenched in a very intense round of mini golf. "No, ma'am."

I immediately turned on the hose and proceeded to spray down the piddle pad.

"I want these facilities spotless," Doris grumbled, jabbing her finger at the turf and glaring at me for another moment before making a tick mark on her clipboard, which I was sure meant that I'd just failed some sort of inspection.

"I'm *so* sorry. It won't happen again."

"Be sure that it doesn't," Doris snapped, stalking off to harass some other volunteer.

Just as I was rethinking all the life choices that had led me to that moment, I heard my name again — my first name this time.

My cheeks burned in humiliation at the sound of that voice, and I suddenly wished that I could shimmy under the pee-soaked turf and disappear from view. I looked up to find none other than Officer Will striding toward me with a cup of lemonade in hand. And *damn*, he looked good.

Even after sweating for hours in the sun, Will just

looked as though he should be running shirtless through the tide with a surfboard under his arm. It wasn't fair. My frizzy curls were plastered to the back of my neck, the sun was making my rosacea flare up, and my mascara was starting to run.

"Uh, good morning," I said, brushing back my hair and wincing when I felt a curl stick to my sweaty forehead. "It's a hot one today."

*Gah!* Was I talking about the *weather*? What was I, eighty years old?

"It's a scorcher," Will agreed, taking a sip from his lemonade.

"You want me to, uh . . . hose ya down?" I blurted, waggling my hose for emphasis.

Honestly, I wished that someone would swoop in right then and put an end to my misery.

A grin twitched at the corner of Will's mouth, and I was certain I wasn't imagining the way his blue eyes flickered down to my legs, which were bare to the hem of my white-denim shorts. "Maybe if I wasn't on duty," he mumbled, the tops of his cheeks turning pink.

At those words, I got a delicious flutter in my belly, and I almost forgot that I'd sentenced myself to an entire weekend of cleaning up dog doo.

"We . . . didn't get a chance to talk much the other day," said Will, who seemed to be choosing his words very carefully. "Since you moved all your stuff to The Grand, I suppose that means you're staying in town?"

His voice was casual, but when our eyes met, his face was etched with such hopeful expectation that I hardly even noticed the giant wrinkled bloodhound that was lifting his leg to the fire hydrant between me and Will.

"Uh, yeah," I said. "That's the plan. I just applied for a grant to renovate the hotel."

"Is that why Brewer was sniffing around?" Will asked, his tone laced with bitterness. "Or are you and he . . ." He trailed off, a deep crease marring his handsome face.

"Gideon?" I asked, simultaneously confused, annoyed, and a little flattered by Will's obvious jealousy. "Why would Gideon —"

"Miss McCrithers!"

At the sound of Doris's voice, my stomach curdled with dread.

"Miss McCrithers, will you *answer* me?"

I cringed and turned to find Doris standing over the very last pad of fake grass, clipboard in hand and a scowl on her face. "I'm here."

"Well, don't just *stand* there!" Doris spluttered. "We've got a number two and a number three over here! I need this cleaned up immediately."

"All right," I called, nodding so that she could see that I understood.

I would go and deal with the poop just as soon as I was done talking to Will. This conversation, while weird, felt too important to bail on, and it wasn't as though anyone was paying me to be there.

"*Now*, Miss McCrithers," Doris snarled, ramming her hands onto her hips.

I sucked in a breath, trying to remember why I'd rolled out of bed at six thirty to do unpaid work for a woman like Doris.

*You're here to make nice,* I told myself firmly. I needed Doris to like me so she'd green-light my project.

But in that moment, I was seeing red. Maybe it was the

heat or the awkwardness of the conversation with Will, but suddenly my hands felt . . . *weird*.

My skin was buzzing with electricity, though the sensation was concentrated in my palms. It was sort of like that pins-and-needles feeling I got when I slept on my arm wrong, but I could feel a strange sort of energy shooting toward my fingertips.

The sun beat down, scorching my arms, and blood pounded in my ears. What was Doris's problem, anyway? Why was she out to get me?

She really was a miserable old hag. She wasn't content to keep me from getting the grant I needed to restore the hotel. She *also* had to make it known that I was one of her poo platoon minions for the weekend.

Anger swirled in my gut, magnified by the heat of the sun. Sweat was gathering along my hairline, dripping slowly down my temples and down the front of my bra.

The itchy T-shirt suddenly felt much too tight — scratchy against my sensitive skin. In that moment, my anger and frustration reached such a fever pitch that I felt as though I might burst.

Then I heard a soft *pop*, and the hose gave a jolt in my hands. I looked down to where it trailed through the grass. The green rubber had sprung a leak.

*Pop . . . pop . . . pop!*

Three more little holes appeared in the hose, water gushing all over the grass. Then there was a loud *whoosh* as the rubber hose tore apart.

The length of hose in my hands instantly went limp, but the bit still connected to the spigot sprayed out in a wild flail. It doused me and Will with a torrent of cold water before falling limp on the ground.

I gasped at the unexpected cold shower, water dripping down my nose. "What the —"

What had just happened? Had *I* done that? My hands were still buzzing with that electric feeling, though the fury inside me had subsided. It was as if someone had released a pressure valve.

Will wiped his face, chuckling softly. I tore my gaze from the ruined hose, and my stomach gave a nervous little leap. Water droplets clung to his golden lashes, glistening in the sun. His front was completely soaked — the water making his navy uniform shirt cling to his strong chest.

Will shook his hair out, spraying me with water, and I let out a little shriek.

"Miss McCrithers, what are you *doing*?" Doris yelled.

"Sorry!" I called back, not sorry at all. "The hose just . . . sprung a leak and burst." Or I'd made it explode.

"Well, come with me to get a new one," she groused. "I need this place cleaned up!"

I sighed and squinted up at Will, my cheeks still flushed from embarrassment. This was going to be a *long* weekend.

"Sorry about that," I said.

"Eh, no biggie. The cold water felt nice, actually."

I grinned, highly aware of Doris standing fifteen feet away — glaring at me with her hands on her hips.

"Gotta go," I said with a helpless sigh. "Duty calls."

CHAPTER SIX

As it turned out, I didn't have time to replay the hose incident and come up with some plausible explanation for why it had burst. The square was soon packed with contestants and their handlers, and it was past eleven by the time registration slowed and I was finally allowed a break.

The breed competitions would begin after lunch, and all the handlers were milling around anxiously. I spotted Gran in the crowd with Snowball and hurried up to greet them.

Snowball was freshly groomed and sporting a jaunty American-flag-print bandana. Gran, to my astonishment, wasn't wearing one of her signature tracksuits, but a white collared shirt tucked into a pair of pleated red shorts. An American-flag scarf that matched Snowball's was tied around her neck, and she wore a straw visor in place of her usual rhinestone one.

"Hey," I said once I was within earshot, coming to a

stop outside an old-fashioned phone booth. "Snowball — looking *good*!"

"Caroline, what on earth are you doing?" Gran snapped by way of greeting.

I opened my mouth but closed it again, not having the faintest idea what she was talking about.

"Running around out here in the blazing sun without a hat!" She fixed me with a stern look. "The sun ages you, you know. And unless you've already found a man who's willing to marry you and give me several great-grandchildren, we need you looking your best."

I rolled my eyes, though the marriage comment stung. I'd been months away from walking down the aisle when I'd learned that my fiancé had been swindling me.

But all talk of husbands and great-grandchildren aside, I knew the sun was doing a number on my skin. I could already feel some tightness along my cheeks and forehead that told me I was getting sunburned.

But before Gran could say anything else, I heard a high-pitched squeal from behind me. I turned to see Daphne, the owner of the café, scurrying toward us from the refreshment table. Like Doris, she wore a royal-blue polo with the Dog Days logo on the chest, and her fiery red hair was covered in a wide-brimmed straw hat.

"Oh, Snowball. Don't you look handsome?"

Snowball whined and jumped up on Daphne, who giggled in delight. "Oh, you've got my number." She looked to Gran. "Can he have a T-R-E-A-T?"

"Why not?" said Gran. "We already did the swimsuit portion of the competition."

Daphne let out a full-belly laugh, shaking her head at Gran. "Oh, Ginger! You are a *card*!"

She reached into her fanny pack for what I suspected was a delicious homemade treat, but then her eyes snapped on to my face. "Ooh, honey. We need to get you a hat. You are burning up!"

"It's okay. I —"

But Daphne was already hustling away, fanny pack bouncing on her hips. She reappeared a few minutes later, clutching the most hideous piece of headwear I could have dreamed up.

It was a wide-brimmed straw hat like her own, but it had a stuffed Dalmatian head sewn onto the front and little stuffed limbs sticking out from the sides. The dog's head had clearly been cut off a cheap plush toy, and his eyes were sewn on a little crooked.

"It's all they have over there," said Daphne. "One of our vendors makes them. She said you could have it as free advertising."

I opened my mouth to politely refuse, but the little chef stuffed the hat over my head before I could get the words out.

"Looks very nice," said Gran approvingly, though the corner of her mouth twitched the way it always did when she was holding back something snarky.

I shot her a glare and sighed. Free advertising. I supposed that was just par for the course, since I already had a ridiculous job.

"Oh! I almost forgot," said Daphne. "It makes noise."

Of *course* it did. I gave a small shake of my head as Gran's eyes twinkled with mirth.

Standing on tiptoe, Daphne reached up and squeezed the Dalmatian's head. A tinny, mechanical bark erupted from my hat, and my face burned as several passersby turned to look in my direction.

"Oh, how *adorable*!" remarked an older woman, who was leading a whole pack of fluffy Pomeranians. "Where did you get that?"

"Fifth stall on your right as you head into the vendor's area," Daphne answered for me.

"Ooh! I wonder what other breeds they have!" the woman gushed, taking her husband by the arm and steering him toward the tents.

"What did I tell ya?" Daphne squealed, spreading her arms. "Free advertising!"

I sighed.

As Gran sauntered off for Snowball's first event, I wandered off in search of food. All I'd had for breakfast was a stale bagel with cream cheese, and the delectable scent of fair food was calling my name.

Main Street was closed off for the event, and food trucks from as far as Denver lined both sides of the street. There were vendors serving hot dogs, sliders, street tacos, pizza, turkey legs, gyros, funnel cake, fried mac and cheese on a stick, French toast on a stick, and Nutella crêpes.

All the lines were excruciatingly long. I couldn't afford to be MIA when Doris made her rounds again, so rather than loading up on a smorgasbord of refreshments, I narrowed it down to a hot dog, two carnitas tacos, and a jumbo-sized lemonade.

Sad puppy-dog eyes followed me and my hot dog all the way down Main Street. A few of their owners stared as I passed, too, but I was pretty sure that had more to do with the creepy dog sunhat than my delicious lunch.

When I reached the square, I saw handlers and their dogs lining up to enter the rings for the breed competitions. I cut through the "cooling station" area on the way to the pee pads but froze when I heard a deep-throated bark.

I looked up in time to see a huge German shepherd barreling toward me through the crowd. I took a step back, trying to decide if I should run, but the shepherd took a running leap over a blue plastic kiddie pool and launched himself right at me.

Long black claws dug into my arms, and the shepherd's mouth opened wide to reveal huge sharp teeth.

I screamed and stumbled backward, tripping over a yappy Maltese and nearly dropping my tacos in the process. I staggered, trying to right myself, and twisted my ankle in the uneven grass. I went down hard on my butt — landing with a splash in another kiddie pool.

Cold, sticky lemonade washed over me as the pressure from my grip forced the lid off my drink. My hot dog was long gone, having shot out of my hand like a bar of soap, and my shorts were completely soaked.

"Colonel! Down!" boomed a low male voice. "Oh my god. Are you all right?"

I looked up to see none other than Detective Pierce struggling to regain control of the rogue German shepherd. The dog continued to lunge for my head, whining with excitement.

"I'm so sorry," said the detective, reaching out a hand to help me up.

I took it and climbed awkwardly to my feet, wincing as a deluge of water gushed from the bottom of my shorts.

The German shepherd's whine turned into a growl,

and Detective Pierce gave his leash a hard yank. "Knock it off, Colonel! *Sit!*"

The detective glared daggers at his dog, who sat back on his haunches and wagged his tail as he looked up at his master. "I'm so sorry about him." The detective grimaced. "The Colonel has a *crazy* prey drive, and that hat —" He gestured at the stuffed Dalmatian, and my cheeks burned with humiliation. "I think he mistook it for a real animal."

"It's all right," I said, gingerly wringing out my shirt and trying to summon some dignity. It was difficult when my shorts were soaking wet and I was wearing such a stupid hat. I cast a wary glance at the Colonel. "Uh, is he a police dog?"

"Nah," said Detective Pierce, his mouth turning up in a grin. "He got kicked out of the police dog training academy for being too . . . aggressive."

"You don't say?" I muttered.

Okay, that was snotty, but the dog had just attacked me.

Detective Pierce nodded and then grimaced. "It's something we're working on."

"Uh-huh." I just hoped the detective's partner wasn't around. I didn't think I'd ever be able to look Will in the eye if he'd seen what just happened.

"Can I . . . buy you another lemonade?" Detective Pierce asked. To his credit, he directed his gaze to the half-empty cup in my hand, rather than the front of my shirt, which was soaked with the stuff.

"No, that's okay." I forced a smile. "I should be getting back." Doris would be wondering where I was, and if she thought I was slacking off, this whole day would be a waste of time.

Detective Pierce flashed an apologetic grin, and I ambled back to my station.

When I reached the piddle pads, Doris was nowhere in sight. I was just about to find a place to sit down and eat my tacos when a nearly frantic woman appeared, asking where the Yorkies were competing. I actually had no idea about the competition lineup, so I led her over to the booth where Daphne was handing out goodie bags.

"Excuse me . . . Daphne?"

"What's up, Sugar Pie?" Daphne beamed. "That hat looks great on you."

"Uh, thanks." After what had happened with the Colonel, I'd been tempted to ditch the hat. But since I could already feel the tops of my arms burning, I figured I'd better not risk it.

"Where are the Yorkies competing?"

"Um . . ." Daphne bent to consult a typed schedule affixed to a clipboard in front of her. "Ring four."

"Thank you," said the desperate Yorkie handler, scuttling off to take her place.

"The first rounds begin at one," Daphne said, more to herself than anyone else. "Someone should already have given the five-minute warning, but Doris *insists* on manning the loudspeaker herself." She rolled her eyes and turned to me. "You haven't seen her, have you?"

I shook my head. "Not since before lunch."

Daphne scoffed. "She's probably over at The Pampered Pooch giving Crumpet a bath before the show. Whippets are up next."

I nodded. The dog wash/pet store was one of the sponsors of Dog Days, and any owners or handlers participating in the show were given free washes for the entire weekend.

"Think you could go grab her?" Daphne asked as she handed a cellophane-wrapped bag of doggie treats to a woman with a nervous-looking pug. "I'm under strict orders not to leave my station except to use the restroom."

I nodded, though inside I was groaning. The *last* thing I wanted to do was go find Doris to tell her she was behind schedule, but as an event volunteer, I couldn't exactly avoid her.

I squared my shoulders and headed toward The Pampered Pooch, stopping at the volunteers' tent along the way to stuff the ridiculous hat into my tote bag. If I had to talk to Doris, I wasn't going to face her wearing a plush Dalmatian.

The Pampered Pooch was easy to find with its blue-and-white striped awning and the sign cut in the shape of a dog bone. The front windows were covered with posters for Dog Days, and a large metal water bowl sat outside.

There were two entrances to the shop — one for the dog wash and one for the pet supply store. I tried the door to the dog wash first and was surprised to find it locked. The little dog bone–shaped sign in the window said "Open," so I tried the door to the pet shop.

As I let myself inside, a scruffy little terrier the color of mop water waddled up to greet me. He wore a blue bandana that matched the awning, and I assumed he was the shop dog.

"Hey, buddy," I said in my sweetest dog voice, bending down to scratch him behind the ears.

The dog let out a savage bark, backing away fearfully. I straightened up. He wasn't a very friendly shop dog.

Maybe he smelled Desmond on me — or Detective Pierce's German shepherd.

"Doris?" I called, casting around.

No answer.

I could hear water running on the other side of the building — the side that served as the dog wash area.

Thinking Doris must not have heard me, I weaved around the islands of dog chews and squeaky toys until I reached the area with half a dozen industrial stainless-steel grooming tubs.

I spotted Doris at once. I would have recognized those Boy Scout–troop-leader khakis anywhere. She was bent over the side of a tub as if she were fishing something out of the bottom. Her tub appeared to be overflowing, and I could hear water trickling into a drain on the floor. Crumpet was nowhere in sight.

"Doris?"

She didn't so much as look around in acknowledgement, and my irritation spiked. I'd been scooping poop at the dog show all morning, getting peed on and sunburned, and Doris couldn't even acknowledge me?

"Doris, they've been asking for you up at the podium. The breed competitions are about to start."

When Doris still didn't respond, I took a step forward — taking in the odd angle of her torso and how she seemed to be draped across the steel lip of the tub. Water was sloshing over the sides, running onto the floor and into the drain.

I looked down, and my stomach clenched. Her face was in the water.

"Doris?" My sneakers made loud slapping noises as I crossed the wet floor, jerking to a halt just behind her.

Doris's upper body was floating in the grooming tub, her face partially submerged. Her straw hat floated in the water beside her, and her shirt was completely soaked.

A high-pitched whine drew my attention, and I looked over to see Crumpet shivering on the floor under one of the tubs.

"Hey, boy. What are you doing down —"

I looked back at Doris, my heart thumping in my chest. She wasn't — I mean, she couldn't be — *dead*?

No sooner had the thought crossed my mind than the door to the shop flew open. "Doris, we need you up at the —"

I wheeled around at the sound of the voice and saw Santa Sweater Lady from the grant committee standing frozen in the doorway between the pet shop and the dog wash. Her brows scrunched together as she took in the sight of Doris, half floating in the tub. Then her gaze slid over to me.

"What on earth have you *done*?" the woman whispered, clapping a hand to her mouth.

"What?" I shook my head. "I didn't —"

But Santa Sweater Lady appeared not to have heard me. Huge, fat tears sprung to her eyes, and she began to shake uncontrollably. "Oh, my Lord. Oh . . . *oh*!"

She wheeled around, as if looking for help, and then her gaze snapped back to me. "Stay right — where you — are," she hissed, pinning me to the spot with an accusatory finger. "I'm calling the authorities."

"But I just found her like this two seconds ago!"

Santa Sweater Lady's nostrils flared as she looked me up and down. I realized then that my shirt was still wet from when the Colonel had knocked me into the kiddie pool. I grimaced. "It's *not* what it looks like."

But the woman's face had gone deathly pale, her bottom lip quivering with fear and righteousness. "Don't — move — a muscle!" she growled.

Dread and annoyance rose in my chest as she scurried back into the pet shop. Leave it to crazy Santa Sweater Lady to pin this all on me. I could hear her fumbling around behind the counter, and I took the opportunity to survey the scene.

Something seemed . . . off.

Ignoring the sick, shaky feeling I got being this close to a dead body, I scanned the immediate area and tried to commit every detail to memory.

Doris's body was draped at a diagonal across the lip of the tub, her head bobbing toward the far-right corner. She was wearing her same volunteer outfit that she'd had on earlier, and she seemed frailer up close.

Bending over to get a closer look at the body, a line of scratches caught my eye. They were etched along the inside of the tub, just below the lip. Weird.

Shuffling to my right, I examined the empty tub beside the one Doris had been drowned in. This one didn't have any scratches.

Before I could work out what that meant, I heard Santa Sweater Lady punching in numbers on the shop telephone and her low, hurried voice. "Yes, this is Martha Mayberry. Please send Officer Hamby to The Pampered Pooch at once. Tell him it's an emergency. I need to report a murder."

CHAPTER SEVEN

As small-town police stations went, The Mountain Shadow Police Department was nothing special. The entire building was decked out with hideous faux-wood paneling, and the puke-colored tile in the lobby was broken and missing in places. Today it smelled like old coffee, microwave popcorn, and whatever cheap body spray the pack of teenaged miscreants in the lobby had doused themselves with.

The one thing the station had going for it, apart from Officer Will, was that it was air-conditioned. The cool air was a relief after sweating out in the sun all day, and after a few minutes sitting on the metal folding chair in the interrogation room, I was actually shivering.

Will was attractively sunburned after directing traffic all morning — a light pink burnishing the angular lines of his nose and cheekbones. I was sure I looked like a tomato by comparison, but at least I'd thought to ditch the hideous hat.

"Take me through what happened at the dog wash one

more time," he said, leaning back in his seat and clicking a pen with his thumb.

"I already *told* you," I said. "Daphne sent me to go look for Doris, since the competitions were about to start. I came in through the pet store, said hi to the dog, and called out for Doris."

"You said hi to what dog?"

"The shop dog."

"Okay . . ." Will squinted at a spot just over my shoulder, as if trying to make sense of it all. "Why didn't you come in through the door to the dog wash?"

"It was locked."

Will made a noise that sounded like "hmmph" and pushed his chair back onto two legs. "Go on."

"Like I said . . . I walked into the dog wash, and there she was."

"Did you move or touch the body?"

"No!" I said emphatically, shuddering at the thought. I still couldn't believe I'd been that close to Doris Ashcroft's corpse.

Will chewed on the end of his pen. "Did you see anyone leave the dog wash before you went in?"

"No."

"How about on the street?"

I rolled my eyes. "There were people everywhere today. I don't remember anyone specific."

"Did anything seem strange to you when you came in?"

"Besides the dead woman floating in the tub?"

Now it was Will's turn to roll his eyes. "Besides that."

"I thought it was weird that I didn't see Crumpet. He was hiding under the other tub."

"He must have been scared."

I nodded. "There were also some scratch marks along the inside of the tub."

Will's eyes narrowed in suspicion. "I thought you said you didn't move the body."

"I didn't," I said. "I just sort of leaned over, and I saw them."

"Huh." I wasn't sure if Will believed me, but he didn't press the issue. "Anything else?"

"No."

He regarded me for a moment, still leaning back in his chair and clicking the pen in his grip. "What was your relationship with the victim?"

"With Doris?" I shook my head. "I barely knew her."

"But you *did* know her."

"Yeah," I said slowly. "She was on the committee for the Main Street revitalization grant I applied for. *And* she was in charge of the volunteers today."

"And how would you describe your interactions with Doris? For the official record."

I sighed and shot him an irritable look. He knew very well what our interactions were like. "You were there. You saw Drill Sergeant Doris in action. All of our conversations have gone just about like that."

"So . . . not friendly?"

"Why does it matter?"

Will dropped his weight so that his chair slammed back down on four legs. He leaned toward me, planting his elbows on the desk, and tilted his chin down to meet my gaze.

This close, I could practically count the golden-blond lashes that fanned his blue eyes, and I had the sudden urge to reach out and brush my hand up his strong tanned forearm.

"It matters because I have a hysterical Martha Mayberry in interrogation room one, telling my partner and anyone who will listen that *you* killed Doris Ashcroft."

A perverse chuckle bubbled up from my throat at the absurdity of that statement. "But —" I broke off with a scoff. "You can't possibly think I had anything to do with this!"

Will's gaze drifted to the side, and he opened his mouth wordlessly.

"Will!"

His eyes snapped back to mine. "It's Officer Hamby in here."

*Oh.* Awk-ward.

He shifted in his seat and ran a frustrated hand through his hair, clearly thinking of the voice recorder in front of us that was capturing every syllable.

"Okay. Personally, I don't think you had anything to do with this. But I have to tell you it doesn't look good. Word travels fast in this town. I heard all about the way Doris treated you at your presentation the other day, and I saw how she was riding you at the dog show. You needed Doris's vote to win the grant to restore your hotel. Doris opposed the project. You're the one who discovered the body." Will was ticking off each point on his fingers as he went. "And, in case that weren't enough, when Martha found you at the scene, your clothes were soaking wet."

I opened my mouth to respond, but Will cut me off.

"And before you tell me it was from the hose, I know very well that you weren't that wet."

My eyebrows shot up, and Will's cheeks flushed a

deeper shade of pink. Had he just *admitted* to checking me out? And it was on record!

"I can explain," I said quickly, my own cheeks burning. "Your partner's dog attacked me right before I went to check on Doris. He knocked me into one of the kiddie pools, and I lost my hotdog."

The last bit came out sounding like a whine, and Will arched an eyebrow. "I would have loved to see that."

"Yeah, well, you might be the only one who *didn't* see," I mumbled.

Will's glorious blue eyes twinkled with mirth, but then he looked away and cleared his throat.

Just like that, his professional demeanor returned. "It doesn't change the fact that you had motive and opportunity to off the victim."

I shook my head, clinging to the life raft of rational thought that seemed to be missing from all Mountain Shadow Police Department investigations. "I can't be the only person who had issues with Doris. She wasn't exactly a sweetheart."

"No," Will agreed.

"And the whole reason I volunteered for the dog show was to get on Doris's good side. Why would I even bother if I'd planned on killing her?"

"People don't always plan on committing crimes, Caroline."

I crossed my arms, stewing in frustration. I knew Will had a job to do here, but I'd thought he *liked* me. He'd flirted with me more than a few times, and then he'd acted all jealous when he'd found Gideon helping me move my stuff into the hotel. Why was he acting as though I could have actually killed that nasty old bat?

I decided to try another tack. "Aren't there, like, security cameras that would show exactly what happened at The Pampered Pooch?"

"This is Mountain Shadow," Will said with a sigh. "Half our residents don't even lock their doors." He looked frustrated by this fact, and it occurred to me that Will might not be as much of a local as I'd always assumed.

I rolled my eyes. Only in a small town. Back in Chicago, the killer would have been caught red-handed on at least six separate security cameras.

I was beginning to worry about the lack of evidence in this case and what would happen if Will decided to arrest me. Would any new evidence come to light that exonerated me as the killer?

But my curiosity about Will was enough to cut through my sudden burst of panic. "How long have you been doing this?" I asked.

Will looked taken aback. "Doing what?"

I gestured around the interrogation room. "How long have you been a cop?" Will wasn't exactly wet behind the ears, but he couldn't have been much older than thirty.

He frowned. "I went into the army right out of high school, did four years there, and then entered the police academy right after that. I started out as a beat cop in St. Louis."

*Ah-ha.* So my instinct about him being in the military was correct. "When did you come here?"

Will hesitated. "I started here at the end of May."

Suddenly, it all made sense. Officer Will wasn't a new cop, but he was new to Mountain Shadow. Maybe that was why he'd been so "by the book" — first on the Jay Mathers investigation and then on this case. He was the new guy on the force. He had a lot to prove.

That familiar crease appeared between Will's brows. "Why do you ask?"

"Just curious."

"Listen," he said, leaning closer and speaking in a low voice. "I don't think you had anything to do with Doris Ashcroft's death. I think you were just in the wrong place at the wrong time, which is why I'm not going to arrest you."

I let out a breath I didn't know I'd been holding. Mountain Shadow PD might have been a podunk police station, but they didn't keep you in a little cell with the key hanging on the wall. They sent you down to Colorado Springs, which had its fair share of real criminals.

My relief must have shown on my face, because Will's expression turned stony. "This is serious, Caroline. We have you dead to rights on Doris's homicide. I hope for your sake that more information comes to light soon. Otherwise . . ."

Will trailed off, but I didn't need him to spell it out for me. If more evidence didn't surface — and soon — I'd be on the hook for Doris's murder.

"Call me if you think of anything, will you?" He produced a card and slid it across the table. "I might have more questions for you later. Stay where I can find you."

CHAPTER EIGHT

As I pulled up in front of the sprawling blue Victorian, my stomach curdled with dread. Despite the charm of the white-picket fence, the garden bursting with roses, and the cute rocking chairs crowding the porch, the inn immediately repelled me.

There was one other person who might be able to tell me who'd had a beef with Doris, but I really, *really* didn't want to see him.

Bellamy Broussard was the owner and innkeeper at The Wind Chime Inn Bed and Breakfast. He also happened to be on the committee for urban renewal with Doris and an infamous busybody.

I'd come to Bellamy for information once before, and I'd left feeling about two feet tall. It wasn't that Bellamy was outright rude, but he had this way of cutting people down to size with seemingly little effort. I thought perhaps he didn't want me to succeed in renovating the hotel, since that would make me a direct competitor to his little B&B.

"Wish me luck," I mumbled to Desmond, who was curled luxuriously in the front seat of Gran's Pinto.

Desmond gave two quick flicks of his tail, and I could have sworn he raised an eyebrow as if to say, "This is a dumb idea."

Ignoring him, I climbed out of the car and forced my feet to walk up the garden path toward the front door of the inn. A riot of flowers burst from pots on either side, and a tasteful sandwich-board sign out front read, "The Wind Chime Inn Welcomes Guests of the Lemmons-McDaniels Wedding."

As I pushed the door open, I heard the sharp edge of Bellamy's voice cut across the house like a knife. "Get those linens out of here, Karen! The bride *specifically* requested ivory. Not cream. Not off-white. *Ivory*. This arrangement is much too tall for this table. And is that . . . Is that a *raisin*? Please tell me I'm not seeing raisins."

Even though the reprimands weren't directed at me, I still felt my insides constrict. I was contemplating turning around and hightailing it back to my car when Bellamy appeared as suddenly as one of my hotel's ghosts.

"Can I help — Oh, Miss McCrithers." Bellamy's tone changed at once from fake-pleasant to annoyed. He drew himself up to his full height and pulled a tight smile that didn't meet his eyes. "To what do I owe the pleasure?"

The question was polite enough, but with the tone he was using, he might as well have asked where he'd stepped in a pile of dog poo. He was dressed in a pair of crisp eggshell slacks paired with boat shoes and a cobalt linen shirt. Somehow, the man always managed to look as though he'd been modeling for a *GQ* photo shoot.

"I-I'm sorry to drop in like this," I stammered. "It sounds like you're very busy."

"Yes, well, we are hosting a wedding here this weekend. It's always a perfect storm of chaos and disillusionment just before the party arrives . . ." He trailed off in a way that told me to get to the point, so I decided to skip the pleasantries.

"Uh, right. Well, this is a little unusual . . ."

"Isn't everything in this town?" Bellamy rolled his eyes as he held up a wooden sign in the shape of a dog bone that read, "It's More Than Puppy Love." "A dog-themed wedding. Can you imagine? The best man is a Weimaraner."

"That's . . . interesting," I said, unsure of the correct response.

It was just then that I noticed the decor. Dalmatian-spotted fabric hung in swaths over the windows and accented the little round table at the front of the parlor, welcoming guests to the inn. The scones and pastries were labeled with little bone-shaped placards, and the box for receiving cards for the couple was a miniature doghouse. A huge photo of a man and woman in matching turtlenecks hugging their Weimaraners dominated the gift table.

"They met at Dog Days three years ago," said Bellamy. "It's the classic dog-show-competitors-to-lovers story."

I wasn't sure if I was supposed to laugh or not, so I kept my expression carefully blank. "I'm sure you still have a lot to do, so I won't take up much of your time . . ." I took a deep breath, trying to decide how much I wanted to tell Bellamy about my predicament. "How well did you know Doris Ashcroft?"

A flash of suspicion streaked through Bellamy's keen

brown eyes, and for a second I wondered if Martha Mayberry had already told him about her discovery at the dog wash. "Not that well," he said in a carefully neutral tone.

"Oh." I bit my lip. Maybe coming to see him had been a bad idea.

"Why do you ask?"

"Well, uh . . ." *Should I tell him?* There was really no way around it. And if I knew Bellamy, word would reach him in no time. "The police seem to think she was murdered."

"*Really?*" Bellamy's tone wasn't one of shock or distress. On the contrary, he seemed to be vibrating with the knowledge that he'd picked up a juicy bit of gossip.

I nodded. "I was wondering if you knew of anyone who might have had a problem with Doris. Any other candidates for the grant who were upset with how their presentations were received, or someone at the dog show?"

Bellamy narrowed his eyes. "Are you running around playing detective again?" he asked. "Our local law enforcement not doin' it for you?"

The way Bellamy waggled his eyebrows told me I wasn't the only one who'd noticed Officer Will's good looks.

"It isn't that." I took a deep breath and wiped my sweaty palms on my shorts, wondering how long it would take Bellamy to tell everyone in Mountain Shadow that I'd been at the dog wash this afternoon. "*I* was the one who found Doris — found her body, I mean."

"You *did*?" Bellamy clasped a hand to his chest and looked at me askance. "That's morbid."

"Yeah," I agreed. "Anyway, I guess Martha Mayberry told the police that Doris wasn't a fan of my proposal."

"Ugh." Bellamy made a face. "That woman is absolutely vile."

I raised my eyebrows at his blunt assessment. "Well, that, combined with how the body was discovered, makes me a suspect, apparently."

"But you didn't kill her, right?"

"Of course not."

"Not that I would blame you if you had," Bellamy added hurriedly. "Doris could be . . . harsh. But I always admired her honesty. I can't talk about the other applicants' proposals," he added in a breezy tone. "Not until the committee has reached a decision. However, I will say that none of them got quite the . . . verbal lashing that you did."

I pulled a queasy half smile. So I was the only candidate who had motive to kill Doris. *Perfect*.

"Is there anyone else who might have had reason to kill her?" I asked.

"I mean, the list of people who have probably *fantasized* about killing Doris would have to include just about everyone in town. But the number of people who would actually follow through?" He shook his head. "I didn't know her well enough to say."

I sighed. I was more than a little disappointed that the town busybody didn't have any more leads on Doris. Going there had been a complete waste of time.

"You might check with her daughter-in-law, though," he added as an afterthought. "Well, I guess Maria wasn't *officially* her daughter-in-law, but she and Doris's son had a kid."

I perked up. This sounded promising. At least this Maria would be able to tell me more about Doris. "Do you know where I could find her?"

"She lives in the pink house on Second Street," said Bellamy. "She has a son with special needs. I don't know how old." He leaned forward, though he didn't bother lowering his voice. "Between you and me, Doris was *horrible* to Maria. Doris's son died of some super-rare brain cancer a couple years back, but she refused to help Maria financially, even though Maria is the sole provider and her son needs round-the-clock care."

I frowned. "Did Doris have money?"

Bellamy cocked his head to the side. "Doris was *loaded*. She and her husband donated an entire wing to the middle school down in Colorado Springs before he passed. She could totally have afforded to help Maria out, but since Maria and Doris's son weren't married, Doris always treated her like dirt."

I raised my eyebrows. Talk about heartless.

"Well, thanks," I said. "That gives me a place to start."

"Don't mention it," said Bellamy, lifting his chin and sashaying over to the front desk to hang up the sign he was holding. But before I could take a step toward the door, he turned and fixed me with a hard look. "Really — don't. I'll deny it if you tell *anyone* what I said about Doris."

CHAPTER NINE

With everything that had happened that afternoon, I'd almost forgotten that I'd had a roofing contractor coming out to inspect my leaky roof. His truck was still parked in front of The Grand when I pulled up, but the moment I climbed out of the car, I saw the roofer rushing out the open front door.

Sturgess was a tall, rail-thin man with a thick gray mustache and eyebrows like caterpillars. He was strong and wiry, the way lifelong construction workers were, and wore faded blue jeans, scuffed leather boots, and a T-shirt with his company emblem on the chest.

"Hey, Sturgess!" I called, waving as he strode down the walkway.

Sturgess hardly spared me a glance as he ripped the truck door open, tossed in his clipboard, and began to climb inside.

"Everything all right?" I asked, taking in Sturgess's pale pallor and shifty gray eyes.

"That's some place you've got there," he mumbled, casting a furtive glance back at the hotel.

I swallowed. "How's she looking?" I asked. "The roof, I mean."

"Not good," said Sturgess in a gruff tone. He still wouldn't meet my gaze.

My heart sank. "Yeah, I kind of figured that when I found the water damage."

"Roof's caving in," he barked, sticking his key in the ignition and fiddling with his sunglasses.

I shifted my weight from one foot to the other. That was sort of why I'd called a roofer. "Well, that doesn't sound good . . . Can you fix it?"

"Needs a lot of work," he grumbled as the engine roared to life. "I don't think I'm gonna be able to help you out."

I frowned. "Why not? Is it that bad? When we spoke on the phone, you said —"

"I know what I said!" he snapped.

For a moment, I just stared at him, taken aback.

Sturgess's eyes softened. "Sorry, kid. I just can't." He tossed me an apologetic look but didn't offer an explanation for his outburst — or his sudden change of heart. He just cast another glance back at the hotel, shook his head, and slammed the door in my face.

I watched in shock as he pulled away from the curb, his truck rumbling loudly as he hit the gas.

Puzzled, I opened the passenger door for Desmond and let myself into The Grand. The moment I walked through the door, Aunt Lucille's ghost swooped down from the ceiling. I cringed as her semitransparent form passed through me, causing my whole body to seize with chills as though I'd been doused in icy water.

There was an uncomfortable moment as Lucille peeled back to put an acceptable distance between us. "Ooh! Sorry, darling. Still figuring out how to work this thing." She held her arms out to her sides to indicate her ghostly form.

"It's okay," I whispered through chattering teeth, still recovering from the collision.

"Did he leave?" Lucille asked.

My shoulders sagged. "Yeah."

"Oh, dear. I should have known. Roy is incorrigible!"

A streak of panic flared through me at the mention of our least friendly ghost. "Roy?" I repeated. "What did *Roy* do?"

"Only about every nasty ghost trick you can think of — locking him in the stairwell, walking through the poor man so he felt a chill, making pictures fall off the walls . . . Well, not to mention Roy's *usual* stunt."

A cold vise clamped around my stomach. "What *usual* stunt?"

"Well, obviously I haven't been here as long as the others, but apparently when the hotel was still up and running, Roy would wait until guests were asleep and then lie down over top of them."

I put a hand over my mouth.

"From what I've been told, it makes the mortal feel as though he's drowning in a pool of icy water. Your friend had shimmied into the crawlspace over the fourth floor to inspect the roof, and Roy pulled that little trick. The poor man had no idea what was happening!"

I closed my eyes and shook my head. I could only

imagine the panic that must have caused. No wonder Sturgess had been so anxious to leave.

I couldn't even bring myself to ask Lucille about the "others" who called The Mountain Shadow Grand their home.

"I'm very sorry, darling," Lucille fretted. "I've tried talking to Roy, but he won't listen. He's never said a single word to me, and to be perfectly frank, I'm not even sure he can."

"What do you mean?"

"It's hard to explain." Lucille shook her head. "It's very strange being trapped over here — in this realm, I mean. Things feel a bit . . . *foggy*. Disconnected. Which is why it's so refreshing when you come to visit! You almost make me forget that I'm dead."

At those words, I felt a little stab of pity for Aunt Lucille. I'd never considered what it must be like to be a ghost — let alone a ghost whose spirit was tied to the hotel.

"Anyway, I can't speak to Roy," she finished. "I'm not sure anyone can. It's almost as if he sees us but is trapped on the other side of some invisible wall. Philip believes that his spirit has grown so weary of clinging to the earthen plane that he cannot concentrate on anything other than simply *existing*."

A little shudder rolled through me at that thought, but it took a moment for my brain to catch up. "Wait, who's Philip?"

"At your service." A young male voice rang out on my right, making me jump and whirl around.

I turned to find the spirit of a bellhop standing at the foot of the stairs. He couldn't have been a day over sixteen, with a ruddy complexion and a shocking number of freckles speckled across his nose and cheeks. Judging by the cut of the burgundy uniform he wore and the style of his carrot-colored curls, I guessed he'd died sometime in the late thirties or forties.

"W-who is this?" I asked Lucille, looking from her to the young man's ghost.

"Oh, silly me," said Lucille with a wave. "You haven't been introduced. Philip, this is my great-niece, Caroline McCrithers. Caroline, meet Philip — the most attentive bellhop ever to grace these halls."

Staring at the boy before me, I couldn't help wondering how young he'd been when he'd started working at The Grand. I guess they hadn't had child-labor laws back then, which led me to wonder how he'd died.

"It's nice to meet you," I said, suddenly weary. I didn't know if I could handle yet another ghost on top of everything else that had happened that day.

"The pleasure's all mine, ma'am," said Philip, tucking a hand behind his trim waist and offering a slight bow. He had a thick accent that sounded vaguely Cockney to me, but he was clearly well trained.

A grin twitched at the corner of my mouth. Somehow I couldn't imagine any of the teenaged miscreants I'd crossed paths with in Chicago *bowing* — just giving me the middle finger.

"Philip has been here nearly as long as Roy," Lucille explained. "He knows him better than anyone."

It took me half a beat to realize that Lucille was referring to how long he'd been a ghost rather than his tenure at The Grand.

I swallowed. What did it say about me that I'd seen not

one, not two, but *three* ghosts at my hotel? Ghosts that Jinx, the purported medium, claimed not to have seen . . .

Then there was the incident that morning with the hose and the mini earthquake that had brought down that wall — an event that was becoming harder and harder for me to ignore.

I thought back to my conversation with Aunt Lucille about the unique abilities that ran in the Blackthorne family. Was it some supernatural "gift" that allowed me to see not just Aunt Lucille but the ghost of Roy Wilkerson and an old-timey bellboy?

I decided I didn't want to think about it.

"Do you know how to keep him from chasing away my contractors?" I asked weakly.

Philip's mouth twitched into a grimace, but he hid it quickly. "Ah. No, ma'am. Can't rightly say I do."

"Because at this rate, *I'm* going to be a ghost before renovations get underway. Once word gets around that the place is haunted . . ." I trailed off. I didn't actually know how much weight that rumor would carry with other potential contractors — at least until they came to work at The Grand. Most grown men would probably scoff at the mention of ghosts, but it was hard to deny supernatural activity after spending ten minutes at the hotel.

"Yes, ma'am. I understand." Philip cast a nervous glance at Aunt Lucille. "I don' mean to talk outta school, but . . . Well, I believe that's just what Mr. Wilkerson wants."

I rolled my eyes. "Yes, I know. Aunt Lucille mentioned that some of the other 'resident spirits' weren't too jazzed about the renovations." I sighed. "Change is hard at any age, but the world moves on."

"All due respect, ma'am, but . . . I don't fink it's as simple as that."

I frowned at him. "What do you mean?"

Philip's eyes crinkled, and he glanced around nervously, as though he were afraid to say more for fear of being overheard. Was Roy Wilkerson's ghost lurking nearby? Just because I could see Aunt Lucille and Philip didn't mean I could see *every* apparition all the time. I really had no idea how my newfound ability worked.

"It's all right, Philip," said Aunt Lucille in a cajoling tone. "You can speak freely here. It's just us girls."

Philip shook his head, clearly conflicted. "Oh . . . Ah shouldn't be running me mouth about Mr. Wilkerson's business. Mr. Masterson would tan me hide."

"Who's Mr. Masterson?"

"He was the manager at The Grand back when Roy died," said Aunt Lucille.

"It's all right," I told Philip. "Mr. Masterson doesn't work here anymore. I'm the new owner of The Grand. I promise you won't be in trouble."

I felt a little silly reassuring him that his old boss wouldn't come back to beat him for spilling the beans about Roy. Then again, maybe this Mr. Masterson was still banging around in ghost form.

That was a sobering thought — being stuck at work with your boss breathing down your neck for all eternity.

Either way, I was in charge at The Grand now. I was also apparently the resident ghost whisperer.

Philip nodded and took a deep breath. "I can't speak for Mr. Wilkerson, but I s'pect the reason he's hauntin' the place is that he doesn't want to be forgotten. H-he might be worried that if the hotel is renovated, the last bits of him that remain will be . . . erased."

In that moment, I wasn't entirely sure if Philip meant that Roy had left behind some physical trace of his existence or if he was referring to the fact that Roy's spirit seemed to be tied to the hotel the way Aunt Lucille's was.

A horrible thought occurred to me then. What if renovating the hotel *did* disrupt the spirits who lived there? Roy Wilkerson I'd be glad to get rid of. But what if removing parts of the old structure caused Aunt Lucille's ghost to go *poof*?

"Can that happen?" I asked, suddenly frantic as I turned to Aunt Lucille. "Will renovating this place erase you, too?"

"I shouldn't think so, darling," said Lucille, though she seemed to be turning the thought over in her mind. "I'm new to all this, but thinking back to my studies of the occult, I seem to remember that spirits of the dead always congregated in places where the veil was the thinnest. It could be that The Grand acts as a sort of . . . limbo." She let out a trill of laughter. "I shouldn't think a little drywall and paint would have any effect on that."

I smiled wanly and looked to Philip.

"It's the worst fing about havin' one's spirit trapped on this side," he mused. "You can't ever find rest. You can't just . . . let go."

"Because you don't want to be forgotten."

Philip tilted his head from side to side in a noncommittal gesture. "Because most of us lef' things a bit . . . unfinished. It's like when you're about to fall asleep, but ya know you have to get up and let the cat in."

"Any idea what Roy left unfinished?"

Again Philip looked nervous, and I couldn't be sure if he was worried about Roy overhearing or if his discretion was simply an old habit from his bellhop days. "I shouldn't say, ma'am."

I shook my head and let out a breath. "Well, it doesn't matter. I can't deal with this right now — not with everything else going on."

"What's wrong, darling?" asked Aunt Lucille, blinking at me in concern.

"Do you remember Doris Ashcroft? That woman on the historical society committee for urban renewal who flat-out rejected my proposal?"

"Yes."

"Well, she's dead."

"*Dead*?"

I nodded. Philip was watching our conversation like a tennis match — seen but not heard, as the old expression went.

"The problem is that it looks as though Doris was murdered, and right now *I'm* the prime suspect."

"Oh dear!" exclaimed Lucille, clasping a bejeweled hand to her breast. "Another murder? In Mountain Shadow? And what do you *mean* you're a suspect?"

I proceeded to explain how I'd stumbled upon Doris's body at the dog wash — and how Martha Mayberry had come in and accused me of murder. I also filled them in on my interrogation with Officer Will, leaving out how incredibly sexy I found him when he was in full cop mode.

"I can't *believe* that Officer Hamby was so quick to peg you as a suspect!" Lucille fumed. She was practically vibrating with indignation.

"In his defense, I'm really the *only* suspect."

"But you're too pretty to be a murderer!"

I fought the grin that was tugging at the corners of my mouth. "Thanks." As ridiculous as that sounded, it felt nice to have Aunt Lucille in my corner. "But I *was* the one who discovered the body, and I had a reason to want Doris dead."

"That business with the grant?"

I nodded.

"Well, who do you think did it?" asked Lucille.

"That's what I have to find out."

CHAPTER TEN

It was bright and early on Saturday as I pulled up in front of the pink house on Second Street. It was a small craftsman bungalow not unlike the dozens of houses that crowded the hillsides of Mountain Shadow — one story with steps leading up to a cute little porch and a yard bursting with sunflowers.

Shifting a to-go cup to the crook of my arm, I hissed as a spurt of hot coffee shot out and trickled down my front. I wasn't sure why I'd thought I could manage two hot lattes *and* a bag of donuts. I had no free hand left to knock.

While it might have been weird to bring coffee and donuts to a woman I'd never met, it hadn't seemed right to come barging up to Maria's house empty-handed. I wasn't sure what Maria liked, but I figured all moms needed coffee. And if she didn't like donuts, well, then at least I'd know she'd killed Doris. Only total psychopaths didn't like donuts.

I could hear the pitter-patter of little feet on the other side of the door, followed by a high-pitched scream and a crash. Swallowing down my own awkwardness, I knocked and heard what sounded like "uh-oh" in the cutest toddler voice.

There was some general shushing, followed by the sound of footsteps, and I arranged my face in what I hoped was a friendly, not-accusing-you-of-murder-or-anything-type smile.

The door opened, and a pretty thirtysomething Hispanic woman stuck her head out. Her gaze drifted from me to the coffee to Gran's orange Pinto parked along the curb. "Can I help you?"

"Uh . . . hi," I said, my throat sticky with nerves. "My name is Caroline McCrithers." I took a deep breath. "This is kind of awkward, but I was hoping I could ask you a few questions about your —" I broke off. I'd been about to say "mother-in-law" but remembered that wasn't right. "About Doris Ashcroft."

"Are you with the police?" Maria asked, suddenly wary.

"Uh, no. Not exactly . . ."

As I fished for something I could add that wouldn't make me sound like a weirdo stalker, a little boy who looked as though he had Down's syndrome appeared at Maria's feet. "Mama! Mama!"

"Shh! Just a second. Mommy's talking."

The boy continued to tug at his mother's pant leg, but Maria just held him close to her side as she turned her attention back to me. "Why are you asking about Doris?"

I swallowed. "It's sort of . . . hard to explain."

It wasn't actually that hard to explain. I just didn't want to come out and say that I was a suspect in Doris's murder. Desperate to buy myself time to make up an excuse for why I was being so nosy, I held up the latte I hadn't spilled and the white paper sack. "I brought coffee. And donuts."

"Doh! Doh! Doh!" the little boy parroted, his eyes growing round in anticipation.

Maria smiled down at him in a half-indulgent, half-irritated way, and I realized I'd probably just hijacked whatever healthy breakfast she'd been planning for her son.

"Come on in," she said, shuffling back and opening the door wider — shuffling because the little boy was stuck to her leg like Velcro.

Maria's house was small but homey with a lot of natural light. Brightly colored toys were scattered across the living-room floor, and a kid's cartoon show was playing on the TV with the volume turned way up.

Maria led me through the main area of the house to the small kitchen and dining area near the back. Sunlight streamed in through a huge window, bathing the little table in warm light.

I set the coffees and donuts in the center of the table as Maria wrestled her son into a high chair. While she went to retrieve a bib and a couple of plates, I took a seat at the table.

"I wasn't sure what you liked to drink," I said when she returned. "So I just got you a mocha."

"Anything with caffeine is good," said Maria, reaching into the donut bag and taking an appreciative sniff. "Oh, these are from The Filling Station. They have the best donuts."

"That's what people tell me," I said. "I'm new in town."

Maria nodded, her mouth full of donut as she ripped a chunk off and fed it to the toddler.

I could tell she still felt awkward having breakfast with a total stranger, but she had a natural warmth about her that immediately put me at ease.

"How did you know that Doris was Teddy's grandmother?" she asked after she'd finished her bite.

I glanced at the little boy, who was wolfing down a chocolate donut and getting frosting all over his face. "Bellamy Broussard told me."

"Who?"

I cringed. Bellamy had known so much about Maria that I'd just assumed the two of them were friends. How was it that she didn't even seem to know who he was?

"Uh . . . he owns The Wind Chime Inn," I said, hoping that would jog her memory.

Maria had been frowning as she ate another bite of her donut, but at the mention of the B&B, recognition lit her face. "*Oh*, Bellamy. He goes to Dr. Michaels's practice. I'm a dental hygienist there." She rolled her eyes. "Bellamy sure likes to talk, huh?"

"Yep," I said, feeling guilty that I'd gleaned all this information through gossip.

"Listen, I know this is weird," I said. "Me showing up at your door . . . But I was actually the one who found Doris's body, and I'm sort of . . . looking for answers."

"Oh." Maria's eyes crinkled with sympathy. "I'm sorry. I didn't know."

I nodded, cupping my hands around my drink and trying to work out a way to launch into my questions without making Maria feel as though I were interrogating her. "Bellamy said that Teddy's dad passed away a couple years ago," I murmured.

"Yes."

"That must have been really tough."

"It was," said Maria, her lips tightening into a thin line as she straightened in her seat. I got the feeling that she was trying to put on a brave face for her son. "It's still hard. I miss him every day. But I have Teddy." She smiled at the boy, whose face was covered in chocolate. "That's what gets me through it."

I nodded, guilt licking my insides. I shouldn't have come here. There was no *way* she killed Doris, but I figured I might as well learn what I could.

"Bellamy said that you and Doris weren't on good terms, but I was hoping you might be able to . . ." I shook my head, searching for the right words. "Tell me more about the type of person she was."

"I'm sorry," said Maria, her voice turning cold as she fed Teddy another bite. "But I can't do that. It's not right to speak ill of the dead."

"Oh." I grimaced. "Was she that bad?"

Maria pursed her lips, shaking with silent anger. "Did Bellamy tell you about Casey?" Her voice broke on the name, and I assumed he was Doris's son.

"No."

"Casey and I were high-school sweethearts." She smiled sadly. "We had plans for after graduation. Casey was going to UMass in Boston, and I was going to go to a community college there to earn my associate's degree. We were planning to get an apartment together. Then, once we both had jobs, we'd get married and start a family." Maria's face became stormy. "But two weeks before we were supposed to leave for Boston, Casey broke up with me out of the blue."

I raised my eyebrows.

"I was heartbroken, but I figured it was just one of those things." She pulled a bitter smile. "People say puppy love doesn't last — that no one who marries their high-school sweetheart stays married. Anyway . . . Casey went off to Massachusetts, and I stayed here. Got my degree, got a job . . . bought this house . . . all on my own.

"We ran into each other at a party years later, and we got to talking again. Casey told me his mom had made him break up with me — told him that I would get pregnant to baby-trap him and ruin his chances of graduating. Doris threatened not to pay for his college if he stayed with me. Casey told me he'd been young and stupid — that he'd always regretted it. After that, we started seeing each other again."

Maria glanced over at the little table against the wall, where there was a photo of her and a man I assumed was Casey. It was difficult to tell at first, because the bump was so small, but it looked as though Maria was pregnant in the photograph.

"That was our engagement photo," she said, following my gaze. "Casey was diagnosed a few weeks after those were taken." She took a deep breath and let it out heavily, staring down at her left ring finger, where she wore a small diamond on a thin gold band. "When Casey got the diagnosis, we planned to do a courthouse wedding. But he just got so sick that . . ." She trailed off. "It doesn't matter. I never needed to call myself Mrs. to belong to him. I'm just sad he never got to meet Teddy."

I sat back heavily in my chair, completely at a loss for

words. I didn't think I'd ever heard such a sad story — or met a woman as courageous as Maria.

"And Doris?" I prompted. "How did she take it?"

"By the time Casey and I got back together, he and his mother hadn't spoken in years. He said he didn't want her in his life — that she was too controlling. The two of them made amends after he got sick, but Doris still hated me." Maria shook her head, and I could read the anger in her eyes. "When Casey was lying in a hospital bed, mostly out of his mind, do you know what Doris said to me?"

I shook my head, dreading the answer.

"She said she was glad her son would never learn what a user I was — that I was an unfit mother who'd used the pregnancy to manipulate Casey into proposing."

"That's awful."

Maria nodded.

I took a deep breath. "Did you ever . . . see Doris again after Casey passed away?"

Maria's brows scrunched together, and she bit the inside of her lip as though she were trying not to cry. "Teddy's Down's syndrome diagnosis was a surprise to me. When he was born, he needed three heart surgeries. Between the medical bills and having to take time off work, I got behind on my mortgage. I didn't know what else to do, so I asked Doris for help. I thought that since Teddy was all she had left of her son, she might be willing to . . ." Maria shook her head. "It was a stupid thing to do."

"No," I said, my heart aching for Maria. "It wasn't stupid at all."

"Doris told me that since I'd baby-trapped Casey, I

deserved this." She nodded at Teddy, and my stomach curdled with disgust.

Maria shook her head and lifted her gaze to the ceiling, eyes shimmering with unshed tears. "I decided right then that I didn't want her money — not after what she'd said about Teddy." She swallowed and met my gaze. "I knew that if I took money from her, I would have no choice but to let her into our lives. I wasn't going to subject my son to that . . . *woman*. Casey and I might not have planned on getting pregnant so soon, but he was just as excited as I was. I never want Teddy to think his dad didn't want him — or that he was somehow a burden."

I nodded. I couldn't help but admire Maria's strength — both the strength to walk away from any possibility of help from Doris and her strength in raising her son on her own. And though it seemed that Maria of all people had reason to wish the old woman dead, I truly didn't believe that she'd had anything to do with Doris's murder.

"Well, thank you for telling me about her," I said quietly. "Doris sounds . . ." I wanted to say "awful," but it didn't seem right, given that the woman was dead. I sighed. "I don't think her death will haunt me quite so much after hearing your story."

Maria chuckled.

"I should get going," I said, getting to my feet and ruffling Teddy's hair. "I've taken up enough of your time. Thank you for . . . sharing that with me."

"Sure," said Maria, studying me thoughtfully. A small crease appeared between her brows, as if she were still trying to figure me out. But she led me to the door like the good hostess she was and thanked me for the coffee.

I opened my mouth to reply, but the words died on my

lips as the door swung open. Will was standing on Maria's front porch, dressed in his full police uniform.

"Caroline?" He cleared his throat and glanced at Maria before turning his gaze back to me. "W-what are you doing here?"

"I, uh . . ." I swallowed a few times, but I didn't know what to say. I didn't want to tell Will that I'd come there in the hopes of clearing my name — even if that was true. After everything Maria had shared, I no longer viewed her as a potential suspect. I felt as though we could be friends, if I hadn't been trying to solve Doris's murder.

Maria looked from me to Will and then crossed her arms over her chest. "Can I help you, officer?"

Will's gaze lingered on me for another moment before he turned his attention to Maria. "Maria Gomez?"

Her frown deepened, and her shoulders waggled back and forth as she adjusted her stance. "That's me."

"My name is Officer Hamby. I'm looking into the murder of Doris Ashcroft, and I'd like to ask you a few questions."

CHAPTER ELEVEN

My mind was buzzing as I walked up Main Street toward the town square. It worried me that Will had shown up at Maria's house to question her about the murder.

According to Bellamy, Doris's husband was dead. If Doris didn't have any living family besides her grandson, Teddy could end up inheriting all her money. My gut told me that Maria was innocent, but the police could see that as a motive.

The one advantage to being stuck on piddle patrol was that it gave me an excuse to return to the dog show and poke around a bit. As much as I wasn't looking forward to adding a layer of sunburn to my tight, itchy skin, I needed to question anyone else who might have had a connection to Doris.

As I crossed the square to reach my station, a loud, shrill voice caught my attention.

*"Adopt! Don't shop! Say 'no' to puppy mills and forced breeding! Bring home a stray today!"*

I stopped and turned toward the familiar refrain to see the same hippie woman from the day before standing on the corner. She was brandishing the same poster, which showed a sad white pit bull, along with a photo of some Labrador puppies stuffed together in a rusted cage.

The hippie woman was almost as sunburned as I was, and I noticed that she wore a wide-brimmed hat as she paced along the street. Seeing her there waving that sign thrust me back to the day before when Doris had made her leave.

An animal activist like that woman probably hated people who put on dog shows. And after Doris had sent her away . . .

I realized that I didn't remember seeing the hippie woman when I'd gone to get lunch that afternoon. If she'd disappeared around that time, she would have had ample opportunity to corner Doris at The Pampered Pooch and drown her in that tub.

Murder seemed an extreme reaction to a little disagreement over picketing, but if the hippie woman thought that people like Doris contributed to the unnecessary deaths of animals, that might make her angry enough to kill.

"Excuse me!" I called, turning on my heel and striding toward the hippie woman.

She turned at the sound of my voice, and a dour crease appeared on either side of her mouth. I remembered then that I was wearing my blue volunteer T-shirt. She probably thought I was coming over to ask her to leave.

"This is a public sidewalk," the woman bit out once I was within earshot. "I'm not blocking foot traffic, or —"

"I know," I said, managing to sound friendly despite

my nerves. "I, uh . . ." I swallowed. "I just wanted to let you know that I admire what you're doing."

"Really?" The woman looked taken aback, and her expression instantly softened.

I nodded. "It takes a lot of courage to stand against something that, uh, seems so harmless."

"That's exactly the problem!" the woman gushed, and I knew I'd said exactly the right thing to get her to open up. "Dog shows like this one *seem* fun and harmless, but really they just provide a venue for people to show off dogs that have been overbred to the point that they have health problems. Not to mention the cost of life! Millions of dogs are abandoned or given up to shelters every year. Why do we need to breed more?"

I nodded emphatically. "I agree."

"Why don't we have dog shows dedicated to mutts? The cutest, the most obedient, the most agile . . ."

"Yes!" I said at once. I couldn't imagine what that kind of show would be like, but it sounded cute.

"I'm Meghan, by the way," she said, putting down her sign and extending a hand for me to shake.

"Caroline."

Meghan pumped my hand enthusiastically. "It's so good to meet a fellow animal advocate — someone working to enact change from the inside." She nodded at my T-shirt, and I felt my stomach bubble with guilt.

First I question the single mom with the sweetest toddler in the world, and now I was interrogating an animal rights activist? I felt like a terrible person.

"Do you have fur babies of your own?" Meghan asked.

"Oh, well . . ." I swallowed. I had a hard time thinking of

Desmond as my fur baby. "I have a cat that I inherited from my aunt, but he's really more of a fur *demon*." I gave an uncomfortable chuckle, but Meghan let out a full-belly laugh.

"I totally get it! My cat Kirby is a complete maniac!"

I smiled. I was actually starting to like Meghan. The guilty feeling in my gut intensified.

Sure, I was an animal lover at heart, but I wasn't dedicated enough to picket a dog show. That certainly wasn't why I'd volunteered, and it felt disingenuous to let Meghan think that that was what I was doing.

*She could be a killer,* I reminded myself. *A cold-blooded killer who drowns old ladies.* Not to mention the fact that if I didn't get to the bottom of this, *I* could be on the hook for murder.

"You know, if you're really interested in social action, some fellow bark-tivists and I have a rally planned for the dog show in Denver next weekend."

I blinked. "*Bark*-tivists?"

Meghan grinned. "It's what my friends and I call people like us — animal activists."

"Oh, uh . . ." I trailed off guiltily. As much as I didn't want to see any innocent animals end up in shelters, I sort of had my hands full — what with renovating the hotel, dealing with Roy's behavioral issues, and being the prime suspect in Doris's murder. "I'll think about it."

Meghan nodded in satisfaction. She didn't *seem* like a killer, but I knew the line between passion and fanaticism was a thin one. I decided to try another tack. "I, um . . . I'm sorry Doris made you leave the other day."

"Eh, I'm used to it," Meghan said with a shrug. "It sort of comes with the territory."

"Still," I said, watching her face closely. "Doris was pretty harsh."

"Nah, I've had it way worse. At least she didn't call the cops."

I squinted at her, trying to think of another way to get her to show her true feelings. Meghan hadn't reacted at all when I'd brought up Doris's name. Either she was innocent, or she had an amazing poker face.

"But you must *hate* people like Doris," I pressed. "Putting on these dog shows . . ."

"Hate's a strong word. I used to get more fired up about handlers parading their ten-thousand-dollar purebreds around a ring. But actually, all the proceeds of Dog Days go to the shelter down in the Springs."

I raised my eyebrows. This was news to me. It also made me doubt her motive for killing Doris. With Doris out of the picture, who knew if Dog Days would even *happen* next year?

"I always make a showing to let them know that I disagree with what they're doing, but honestly, more dogs will probably be saved *because* Dog Days exists."

I bit my lip. I'd never thought of it like that. "Did you and Doris . . . have it out? After she told you to leave, I mean."

Meghan shook her head. "I had to leave before the first round of competitions to get back to my fur babies. I live down in the Springs, and I'm fostering a litter of puppies. Their mom was abandoned behind Safeway, and she had a huge litter. I have to rotate the puppies to make sure they all get a chance to nurse. Look."

Meghan whipped out her phone and proceeded to take me through the cutest miniature slideshow I'd ever seen.

While it was hard to be upset when gushing over photos of tiny little puppies, my heart sank when I realized that Meghan couldn't possibly have killed Doris. She hadn't even been in town.

Once she'd finished showing me the pictures, I thanked her and returned to my station. There were no "deposits" in need of cleanup at the piddle pads, so I wandered over to the rings, where the group competitions were already underway.

What kind of dog was Doris's dog Crumpet? A whippet?

Following my hunch, I walked over to the ring, where the hound group was getting ready to compete. To my surprise, there was a little gray whippet who could have been a carbon copy of Crumpet preparing to enter the ring.

I couldn't tell whether the dog in question looked like a champion or not. It had a tiny head on a long neck and a skinny, athletic body.

Its handler was the exact opposite of his animal. He had a soft face, chubby cheeks, and a bit of a gut. A widow's peak of dark hair accentuated a receding hairline, and he was dressed in a flamboyant Hawaiian shirt.

When it was his dog's turn, the handler jogged into the ring, and the whippet ran along beside him. As I watched the little whippet glide around the ring with his ears flapping in the breeze, I couldn't help but think that the dog *moved* like a champion.

His handler beamed as they came to a halt at their platform, and a hush fell over the crowd.

In addition to the whippet, there was a beagle, an Irish wolfhound, a basset hound, a dachshund, and a bloodhound — all champions that had beat out the other dogs of their breed. Everyone seemed to hold their breath as the judge inspected each dog, getting up close and personal to look at their teeth and coat.

Then, without any fanfare, the judge called out the winners. When he pointed to the whippet and called out first, the handler was so overcome with joy that tears sprang from his eyes. He snatched up the dog and walked out of the ring, where he was engulfed by friends and admirers.

As I watched him parade his little dog through the crowd, Amber's words rang in my ears: *I guess Crumpet is a world champion or something. He's won best in show, like, three years in a row.*

To win best in show, Crumpet would have had to beat out this other little dog in the breed competition. He and his handler certainly benefitted from Doris's death.

Struck by sudden inspiration, I started making my way through the crowd of onlookers toward the victorious man.

"Congratulations," I said as soon as the cluster of people around him had thinned enough for me to approach.

"Thank you, thank you. It was really all Mr. Bittles here." The man wagged the paw of the tiny whippet, who was shivering from all the attention.

"Is this his first big win?"

"It's his first best of group title," said the man, gushing like a proud father.

I nodded. "Yeah . . . I guess Crumpet typically dominates the hound group."

"That's true," he said, his voice rising half an octave.

He turned to look around, as if searching the crowd for Crumpet and Doris. "I'm surprised he's not competing this year."

I studied the man's face for a long moment, trying to decide whether or not he was truly surprised that Doris wasn't at the competition. He seemed completely swept up in the joy of Mr. Bittles's victory, but maybe a cold-blooded killer could murder an old lady one day and then show up smiling the next.

"I'm Jeffrey Hanover, by the way," he said, holding out Mr. Bittles's paw for me to shake.

"Caroline," I said, awkwardly taking the eensy-weensy paw between my fingers and pumping it once for good measure. "I guess you didn't hear . . ." I said, keeping my tone carefully neutral.

Jeffrey leaned in, his eyes lighting up with what I could only assume was a hunger for gossip. "Hear what?"

I glanced around as if checking to be sure that no one was within earshot. "Doris Ashcroft is dead."

"What?" The man gave a theatrical gasp and leaned back in horror. "How did she die?"

"The police think she was murdered."

Jeffrey's eyes widened. "*Murdered*? But . . . how?"

"I don't know," I lied.

His eyebrows rose, and he let out a slow breath. "Well, I can't say I'm surprised."

I cocked my head. That wasn't the usual reaction I got when telling people Doris was dead. "Why not?"

Jeffrey shook his head. "You didn't hear it from me, but Doris was *not* well-liked on the show circuit."

"Oh, no?"

"No." Jeffrey's brows inched higher, and something

about the expression struck me as familiar. "Crumpet was a champion, but Doris fought dirty."

Little alarm bells went off in my head. "Dirty? How do you mean?"

Jeffrey glanced around, pulled Mr. Bittles closer, and lowered his voice to a whisper. "Well, a few years back, Crumpet was up against Minnow — the dog who held the championship title. None of us thought that Crumpet would be able to usurp him, but then, all of a sudden, Minnow came down ill. Like, *deathly* ill. He almost didn't make it."

"Seriously?"

Jeffrey nodded. "Meanwhile, Crumpet took home the blue ribbon."

"You think Doris *poisoned* Minnow?" I asked, simultaneously doubtful and horrified.

"I don't know what I think," said Jeffrey darkly. "But I wouldn't put it past her. We all take these competitions so seriously. I mean, they *are* our babies —" Jeffrey tightened his hold on Mr. Bittles, whose eyes bugged out a little. "I don't know what I'd do without him. We were both adopted, and he just gets me, you know?"

"I do," I said, nodding emphatically.

Jeffrey sighed and began caressing one of Mr. Bittles's long paws, massaging between his toes. "Sometimes I think it's his fear of abandonment that keeps him from going all the way. But I tell him, 'I love you as much as or more than your biological mother could have.'"

"Uh-huh." I honestly didn't know if he was being serious.

"I mean, I know he's a dog, but sometimes it's like he can see into my soul. Does that sound crazy?"

"No," I said, shaking my head in what I hoped was a convincing manner. I enjoyed snuggling up with Desmond at night, but I didn't think he had the power to see into my soul.

I chewed nervously on the inside of my cheek, weighing the risks of questioning Jeffrey further. I didn't want him to get wind of what I was up to, but the fact that Doris had died just before showing Crumpet did seem a bit fishy.

"Did you happen to see Doris before the breed competitions yesterday?" I asked, hoping my question came across as casual and not an interrogation.

"No," he said. "I didn't even know she was here. Usually, Doris gets to registration early so she can scope out the competition. I think she runs this show just so she can lord her position over everyone," he said with an eye roll.

"How does one normally prepare for a show like this?" I asked, hoping I could get him to tell me where he'd been just before the breed competition.

"Well, Mr. Bittles is a hard-core introvert. He likes to have his quiet time before a big competition. After grooming, I try to find somewhere out of the way where he can put on his eye mask and take a nap."

I tried not to laugh as I pictured the little whippet wearing an eye mask. "And ... yesterday?"

"Yesterday we went by The Pampered Pooch for a little bath and blowout. Then we went back to our camper for some rest and relaxation." Jeffrey gestured over his shoulder, where a huge white camper van was squeezed into a spot along the street. It was one of those deluxe models they have on movie sets — the kind with an onboard generator to run the air conditioning and a flatscreen TV.

Mr. Bittles traveled in style.

"What time were you at The Pampered Pooch yesterday?" I asked, trying and failing to make the question sound casual. If he'd been there at the same time as Doris, then I could catch him in a lie.

"Around lunch, I guess. Why, do I need an alibi?" he asked around a bubble of nervous laughter.

I joined in chuckling, though my heart was racing. He *had* to have been at The Pampered Pooch when Doris was bathing Crumpet.

"No," I said, rolling my eyes to keep the mood light. "But you must have seen Doris at the dog wash yesterday. That was the last place she . . ." I trailed off, purposely neglecting to mention that she was murdered *at* the dog wash — and that I'd been the one to find her body. I figured if I gave Jeffrey as few details as possible, he might slip up and say something that only the killer could know.

Instead, Jeffrey shook his head. "No. No, there were several handlers and volunteers at The Pampered Pooch, but Doris wasn't there. The owner came in and cleared everyone out before the first round of competitions. Mr Bittles's fur was still wet."

Huh. That fact was easily verifiable, so it didn't make sense that he would lie. Maybe the others left the dog wash before Doris arrived. "So after that, you took Mr. Bittles back to relax — just the two of you?"

"Yep," said Jeffrey with a bracing smile. "It's just the two of us."

I could tell from his tone that he thought my questions were weird, but he was too polite to say so.

While my intuitive alarm bells weren't going off, I couldn't ignore the facts: Jeffrey and Mr. Bittles were among those who directly benefitted from Doris's death. He'd been at the dog wash just before the murder — even if he claimed not to have seen her. The man was definitely strong enough to drown Doris in that tub, and he didn't have an alibi.

CHAPTER TWELVE

I was exhausted by the time I left the town square late that afternoon. My feet ached, my sunburn itched, and based on the way my fellow volunteers seemed to be avoiding me, I was fairly certain Martha Mayberry had been telling the whole town that I killed Doris.

After the day I'd had, I wanted nothing more than to get back to Gran's and take a long hot shower. The couch and my PJs were calling to me, but the black storm clouds gathering overhead promised rain.

Since my roofer had fled, I needed to figure out a way to temporarily patch my leaky roof. I also had to deal with the small matter of Roy's disgruntled ghost.

Cold, fat raindrops were splattering the sidewalk by the time I reached The Grand, and there was a definite chill in the air. I scurried into the lobby, shivering in my damp clothes. Dilapidated loveseats and wingback chairs loomed in the darkness, and the grand staircase directly across from me seemed to vanish into the inky blackness.

Fighting an intense case of the heebie-jeebies, I flipped

on a light switch and stared around at the crumbling grandeur of it all.

"Caroline! Thank *goodness*! I was afraid you'd been arrested!"

Aunt Lucille materialized a foot in front of my face, and I clapped a hand to my chest. It didn't matter how much I loved my great-aunt's ghost. I would *never* get used to her doing that.

"No, not yet," I sighed, forcing a shaky smile as my heart rate returned to normal.

Aunt Lucille was dressed in a gorgeous floor-length evening gown that dipped dangerously low in the front and flared out along the bottom. Her slender arms were swathed in white silk gloves, and the whole ensemble was set off with thick diamond cuffs.

I still didn't understand how she always seemed to be wearing a different outfit. Apparently, being trapped in the earthen realm didn't limit her access to a seemingly infinite wardrobe.

"I questioned several potential suspects, but I don't feel like I'm any closer to figuring out who might have killed Doris."

"You'll get there," said Aunt Lucille. "The killer won't be able to hide for long — not with Caroline McCrithers on the case!"

I smiled. Even though I knew she was only saying that to make me feel better, it cheered me up nonetheless. True, I'd managed to clear Gran's name when she'd been accused of murdering Jay Mathers, but I chalked that up to a combination of beginner's luck and sheer desperation. I wasn't a detective.

"Well, hit me!" said Lucille. "Who are our suspects?"

I gave a noncommittal groan and trailed across the lobby, poking my head into a closet as I searched for a bucket. The leaks in the roof weren't getting fixed that night. The best I could do was catch the water to prevent any further damage.

As I poked around behind the front desk, I recounted my earlier conversations with Maria, Meghan the barktivist, and Jeffrey Hanover — Mr. Bittles's handler.

"The problem is that there seems to be no shortage of people who might have wanted Doris dead," I huffed. "And I like them *all* better than Doris."

"Well, where are your markers and sticky notes?" Aunt Lucille asked. "We need to start our murder board!"

I snorted at her enthusiasm and stacked the grimy five-gallon buckets I'd found in a housekeeping closet. "I suppose it wouldn't hurt to start one — after I find the source of these leaks."

Rain was pattering on the roof, and I could practically see the dollars draining out of my bank account as the water found its way down from the attic and into the ceiling and floors below. I forced my stiff legs up the three flights of stairs as Aunt Lucille trailed behind me, railing on about work ethic and flaky tradesmen.

I was huffing and puffing by the time I reached the fourth floor, and I realized I had no idea how to access the attic crawlspace above the guest rooms.

"Aunt Lucille . . . Do you remember there being an attic access up here?"

"Perhaps I may be of assistance," came another voice from directly behind me.

I gave a cartoony jump worthy of Scooby Doo and the

gang and wheeled around to face Philip, the ghostly bellhop.

"Yes. Thank you," I huffed, struggling to breathe through the tension in my chest.

Since Philip had made himself known only the day before, I hadn't yet come to think of him as a permanent feature of the hotel. Apparently, I just made friends wherever I went.

Philip beamed and led the way toward a suite at the end of the hall, which was a mirror image of Aunt Lucille's preferred room. He led me into the filthy bathroom and showed me a tiny door that blended so perfectly into the wainscoting that I might have overlooked it.

A huge poof of dust greeted me as I pried the cover off to reveal a slender opening. The scent of dirt and decay wafted out, and I hesitantly shined my pocket flashlight into the cramped dark space.

A narrow shaft just wide enough for me to stand in waited on the other side. A ladder formed by two-by-fours nailed to the wall led up as far as my flashlight would reach.

"We'll meet you up there, darling," said Aunt Lucille, not sounding at all concerned that I had to climb up the creepy dark shaft all alone.

I smiled weakly and shimmied into the tiny opening, wincing as I felt a giant spiderweb adhere to the side of my face. I spit and swiped at my cheeks and brow, cringing as I pulled away the sticky gossamer threads.

Dragging the buckets into the shaft, I pulled off my belt and looped one end through the handle of the bottom bucket so I could pull them up behind me.

Bracing myself to be grossed out, I straightened up and

tried to ignore the spiderwebs and creepy crawlies lodging themselves in my hair.

*It's fine*, I told myself. Most spiders aren't venomous. And I needed a shower anyway.

Sticking the flashlight between my teeth, I started to climb the rickety ladder. Each time the boards creaked, I braced myself for the inevitable fall, but miraculously they held.

My eyes were itching from the dust by the time I reached the opening at the top. I shined my flashlight into the attic, taking in the maze of joists that seemed to go on forever.

Swirling motes of dust floated lazily in the beam of my flashlight, and I searched along the ceiling until I found a tattered cotton string. I gave it a tug, and a single dusty lightbulb illuminated the cramped crawlspace. I could stand hunched at its tallest point, but the roofline slanted sharply down, rendering the far end inaccessible.

My ghostly sidekicks materialized in front of me. Aunt Lucille perched on a small stack of lumber, while Philip crouched beside a pile of broken crates.

"I didn't know that this was up here," I said, listening to the now-deafening patter of rain on the roof as I took in my surroundings.

"Only the help ever came up here," said Philip, his gaze taking in what appeared to be discarded liquor bottles and smashed cigarette boxes.

Moving unsteadily over the thin plywood flooring nailed over the ceiling joists, I shined my flashlight into the dark corners of the attic. The shape of steamer trunks and old suitcases loomed from the shadows, along with a box of what looked like bellhop uniforms like the one Philip was wearing.

"Back in my day, this was sort of a catch-all for forgotten fings," Philip mused, the corner of his mouth lifting in a small smile.

I recognized that wistful look, and it made me wonder what the hotel must have been like in its heyday. I imagined a lively, luxurious place bustling with an army of servants, ready to deliver five-star service to the rich and famous.

"Quite a few amorous young couples used to sneak up here as well, if memory serves," said Aunt Lucille.

Philip's cheeks reddened beneath his freckles. "I-I wouldn't know anyfing about that, ma'am."

"No, I'm sure you wouldn't."

Stifling a snicker, I moved into a dusty corner, searching for any telltale signs of a leak. I found an area where the plywood was waterlogged and squinted up at the roof. I placed a bucket beneath the leak and backed out of the corner on hands and knees.

My gaze snagged on a cardboard box with the word "Misc." written across one side in a familiar untidy scrawl.

I paused. I recognized that handwriting. It was the same handwriting I'd seen on the boxes of bank duplicates I'd dug out of Aunt Lucille's armoire at the nursing home.

"Is this . . ." I scooted closer to the box, glancing at Aunt Lucille.

"Oh, yes. That was mine." She shook her head. "I forgot that was up here."

Truth be told, I'd spent so much time going through Aunt Lucille's personal effects that I wasn't that interested in another trip down memory lane. But since she'd downsized before moving into the nursing home, it struck me as odd that this box was up there.

Curious, I opened up the cardboard flaps and shined my flashlight inside. A bunch of yellowed notebooks were piled at the bottom, along with several small pamphlets whose covers were faded and torn.

But there was one book that wasn't like the others nestled in the middle of the stack. It was as thick as a phonebook and bound in leather, the pages worn and slightly uneven.

Fingers tingling, I pulled it out and rubbed my hand over the dusty leather cover. The coffee-colored leather was embossed with a pattern of sinister-looking flowers, and the name "Blackthorne" was engraved in huge trippy-looking letters near the very center.

"What's this?" I asked, turning it over in my hands and looking up at Lucille.

"Oh. Oh, that." Aunt Lucille looked suddenly sheepish, and she waved a dismissive hand. "I'd forgotten that old thing was up here."

"Aunt Lucille . . ." I prompted, grinning at her. I didn't think I'd ever seen her this flustered.

"Do you remember me telling you how I studied the occult?"

"Yeah."

Aunt Lucille nodded and pointed at the book. "That is a compendium of all I ever learned. At least, that was what I *intended*. There are many questions I never could answer, but everything I know is in there."

My eyebrows rose. Aunt Lucille had been holding out on me. "Can I have it?"

"What for?"

"I-I don't know," I mumbled, swallowing to wet my parched throat. "I guess I'm trying to figure out why I'm seeing ghosts." I traced the raised edge of an evil-looking lily that was embossed in the leather. "And why weird things keep happening to me."

Aunt Lucille brightened. "Well, it certainly won't do *me* any good, though I'm not sure if it will do you any good, either. It's not a spell book. There's no exact science when it comes to using our abilities — at least none that I ever encountered. I learned to hone my skills through trial and error. But the theory is what I studied."

"It's gotta be better than the diddly squat *I* know about magic," I said, my hands trembling as I flipped through the yellowed pages.

For some reason, just holding this book in my hands felt dangerous. If I tried to brush off the fact that I could see ghosts — if I denied that there'd been anything out of the ordinary about the brick wall crumbling before my eyes — I could go on pretending that there was no such thing as magic. But if I took this book back to Gran's and read it, I'd have to acknowledge the possibility that the supernatural world existed.

"Well, you're welcome to it," said Aunt Lucille brightly. "It would make me very happy if that book was some use."

Pulling a shaky smile, I walked over to the attic entrance and set the book down by the ladder. Then I shined my flashlight along the roofline, scanning for additional leaks.

In one corner, a wooden crate overflowing with junk sat discarded beneath a blanket of cobwebs. Thinking it might be another box of Lucille's things, I scooted across the plywood floor to see what was inside.

Thick tendrils of cobwebs and grime told me this box had been up there a lot longer than the magic book. I recoiled as something brushed my arm, but it was only another cobweb. I pulled back a threadbare drop cloth that was acting as a lid. Tucked in the folds was a metal comb, an old tin of chewing tobacco, and a battered cigar box.

"Ah," said Philip, looking suddenly uneasy. "Them must 'ave been Mr. Wilkerson's personal effects."

The way he said it, I got the feeling that Philip wasn't thrilled about me going through the dead handyman's belongings.

"Were you and Roy friends?" I asked quietly.

"Me and Mr. Wilkerson?" Philip laughed. "I wouldn't say that. Mr. Wilkerson, he — well, he weren't really the friendly sort. I was always in his way — always trippin' over meself."

I smiled, and — ignoring the feeling that I was doing something I shouldn't — opened the cigar box and peered inside.

"What is it?" asked Aunt Lucille anxiously, leaning forward for a better look.

I fought back a smirk. Gran didn't talk about her sister much, but she always did say that Aunt Lucille was a hopeless busybody.

"Letters," I murmured, reaching inside and pulling out the thin stack. The paper was thin and yellowed with age, and when I peeled open the topmost letter, the two halves of the paper almost fell apart.

The letters had been opened and read so many times that the creases had become threadbare. This particular piece of paper was penned on hotel stationery and nearly falling apart. The words were scrawled in a loopy cursive that was undeniably feminine.

"What does it say?" Lucille demanded.

I glanced from my aunt to Philip, who looked very tense.

*Can't stop thinking about last night. Even now I can feel your hands on me — the touch of your lips on my skin. No one has ever made me feel the way I do when I'm with you, R. To be near you each day and unable to touch you is the worst torture imaginable. Meet me tomorrow evening — our usual place.*

When I finished, Lucille was hanging on my every word. Her eyes were as round as silver dollars, and her fake lashes looked in danger of popping right off her eyelids.

"*Well*?" she said. "Who is it from?"

"It isn't signed."

"Ooh, a secret lover!" Lucille clapped her hands excitedly, looking even more delighted by this turn of events.

"Miss McCrithers, I really don't fink we should be readin' Mr. Wilkerson's personal correspondence," said Philip.

"I have to get to the bottom of why he's haunting the hotel," I said. "These letters might be the key."

Philip pursed his lips but didn't say anything as I fished out another letter.

*I wish I could spend every evening lost in your arms. It doesn't matter who I'm with or what I'm doing. Your presence haunts me everywhere I go. It's your face I see as I fall asleep — your touch I crave in the dark. I yearn for more than stolen moments . . .*

"Oh, *Roy*. Who knew?" Lucille quipped, fanning her face with one gloved hand.

"Miss Lucille, I really don't fink —" Philip began, but Lucille shushed him before he could finish.

"This one isn't signed either."

"Well, of course it isn't," said Aunt Lucille. "Our mystery woman couldn't risk being discovered!"

"And there was probably a reason for it," Philip put in.

"Oh, pish posh!" said Aunt Lucille, waving away his objection. "If she didn't want someone reading her letters, she shouldn't have written them in the first place."

I picked up the next one and continued to read despite the slightly icky feeling in my stomach.

*Can't meet tonight. He is growing suspicious, and I must play the role of the devoted wife. Will miss your touch.*

"Roy was sleeping with a married woman?" gushed Lucille, looking scandalized but no less delighted. "Oh, this is *too* good!"

"There are only a couple of letters left," I said, my stomach twisting with dread and that pesky sense that I was intruding on another person's private thoughts.

"Well, what are you waiting for?" Lucille demanded. "Open them!"

Even though I knew I probably shouldn't, I shifted the other letters to the bottom of the stack and opened the next.

*I'm so sorry to do this, darling, but we simply can't continue this way. The risks are too great, and there is much at stake. I will always cherish our time together.* —C

"C?" Lucille's ghost was practically vibrating with excitement, and I wondered if it was possible for a spirit to cause some sort of electric surge. "Our lady's name begins with 'C'?"

"Either that, or it's the first letter of a nickname." I turned to Philip. "Any idea who this 'C' person was?"

Something like panic flashed in the bellboy's eyes, and he quickly shook his head. "No, ma'am."

I wasn't convinced. The kid was a *terrible* liar.

"Philip . . ." The reprimand died on my lips at the look on the bellboy's face. Beneath his freckled, accommodating countenance, Philip was a human fortress who gave new meaning to the phrase "my lips are sealed." I had the feeling that he wouldn't have given up Roy's lover on pain of death — especially since he was already dead.

"There's one more letter," Lucille reminded me, gesturing to the stack in my hands.

She was right. I'd almost forgotten about the final letter, but something told me it wasn't a love note.

Taking a deep breath, I unfolded the last piece of paper. Like all the others, this note was penned on hotel stationery, but of all the letters Roy had saved, this one seemed to have been read the least. The crease in the paper was still intact, and the edges were crisp and perfect.

*I told you to stay away — away from me and especially my family. This is my final warning.*

"*Yeesh*," I said, lifting my eyebrows. "Quite the change in tone."

"It sure is," said Aunt Lucille, looking confused and a bit put out.

Reading these letters made my heart ache for Roy, but this last one made it sound as though he'd overstepped. Had he been threatening his former lover? *Stalking* her, perhaps?

It was a sobering thought, but that wasn't what bothered me. It was the tone of the final letter that chilled me to the bone. *This is my final warning.*

"Philip," I said slowly, following that train of thought. "Were you at the hotel when Roy died?"

"Yes, ma'am, I was."

Okay — this was progress. Perhaps Philip knew something that would help me piece together what had happened. "What do you know about the *way* Roy died?"

"Oh, it was awful, ma'am." The bellhop looked acutely distressed by the memory, but he swallowed and continued. "I, uh . . . I was the one that found him."

"*You* found him in the elevator shaft?" I asked. I couldn't even begin to imagine how awful that must have been.

Philip nodded, and a haunted look came over him. "I, eh . . . heard him moanin', you see."

"Moaning?" That explained the weird noises I'd heard when Roy had trapped me in the fourth-floor stairwell with Will and Gideon the other day. I shook my head. "But that means . . . He was still *alive*?"

"Yes, ma'am. He was hurt somefin' awful. I sent for a doctor straight away, but . . ." He swallowed. "The good Lord called him home, I suppose."

My stomach churned. "Did he . . . say anything?"

Philip smiled sadly. "Mr. Wilkerson was in a lotta pain, so he didn't say much. I asked him who'd done it — who'd pushed him down the shaft — and he got rather upset. Made me swear to tell everyone that he fell. I wasn't supposed to have seen anyfing."

"But you *did* see something," I pressed.

Philip clamped his mouth shut.

"What did he say when you asked who'd pushed him?"

"I told you, ma'am. He got angry with me. Told me I'd better not breathe a word of that to anyone, or Mr. Masterson would sack me straight away."

"But he didn't deny he was pushed."

"No, ma'am."

I sat back on my heels, my head spinning from this new information. "So Roy didn't fall. He was pushed."

"All due respect, ma'am, but no one who knew Roy would believe he fell."

I exchanged a glance with Aunt Lucille. If Roy *had* been pushed, why would he want to protect his killer? "You think it was the woman from these letters?" I asked.

"It certainly seems like a romantic gesture," said Aunt Lucille. "One last way to show the woman he loved that he still had feelings for her."

"I wonder why she pushed him."

"Maybe he threatened to tell her husband," Lucille suggested.

"Or maybe he wouldn't take no for an answer." I turned to Philip. "If you can't tell me *who* killed Roy, can you at least tell me what it was about? The affair or . . . something else."

"I've already said too much, ma'am."

"Philip . . ." My voice trailed off in exasperation, but before I could lean on my bellboy some more, the single bulb dangling overhead flickered and went out.

I sucked in a breath that tasted like mold, and for a moment, nobody said a word. The steady patter of rain on the roof drowned out everything else, but then a low, throaty groan reached my ears, followed by a string of angry curses.

Goosebumps rose up all over my arms, and my heart began to race.

"Roy?" I called, flipping on my flashlight and shining it around the attic. There was no one else there. "Roy?"

Still no answer. But then my flashlight began to fade, its beam growing weaker and weaker. I gave it a shake, illuminating the ghostly faces of Philip and Aunt Lucille before the light went out.

## CHAPTER THIRTEEN

After crawling down a dusty, spider web–infested shaft to reach the relative safety of the fourth floor, it was a relief to get back to Gran's, peel off my clothes, and jump into the shower. The steady stream of water felt amazing on my stiff muscles, but I was too anxious to look through Aunt Lucille's magic book to linger under the hot spray.

I was practically shivering in anticipation as I pulled on my pajamas, which had realistic cartoon drawings of cat heads printed all over them. I set Lucille's book on the bedspread and used a clean washcloth to dust off the leather cover, cracking it open with trembling hands.

Just inside the cover was a family tree drawn in several different colors of ink. Its branches were twisted and prickled with thorns, which seemed appropriate, given Lucille's surname. The names of Gran, Lucille, and their two sisters were scrawled at the very bottom. Some of the names had little black flowers drawn next to them, including Lucille's.

Fascinated, I turned the page, where she'd listed out various family members and made notes beneath each name.

I spied my great-grandfather's entry — Gerald Blackthorne. Underneath, Lucille had written *"Precognition — otherwise known as the Sight."*

Lucille's entry bore a laundry list of supernatural abilities, including precognitive dreams, clairaudience, retrocognition, and something called psychometry.

The book was part diary, part family history, and part encyclopedia of the supernatural abilities Lucille had learned about — either through her studies or in practical application. I was fascinated to read Lucille's account of the psychic dreams she'd had as a child and how she'd developed her other abilities.

The account mentioned various spiritual masters she'd studied under, as well as breakthroughs she'd experienced in psychometry — which, I discovered, was the ability to learn things from physical objects simply by touching them. Updates were noted beneath this narrative, the first dated nineteen fifty-two.

*I saw my aunt Betty today after laying hands on a platter that had belonged to my great-grandmother. All the others have only come to me in flashes, but Betty was clear as day. She stood and walked across the room, smoothed out the tablecloth, and took up her knitting.*

Underneath that was another entry dated the year before my dad was born.

*I finally found Hopper tucked in a box with Mother's wedding veil. The instant I touched him, I saw through his eyes — watched Midge pretend to pour tea from a broken china cup. The sight brought tears to my eyes.*

Apparently, psychometry was easier with objects that were used heavily by a person — or objects that held special significance.

Lucille's compendium got more technical the further I read, and I knew it wasn't the sort of text I could skim. For one thing, Lucille's handwriting was atrocious — the letters all jammed together and sentences tilting downward as if they were slipping off the page. It was the type of penmanship that became harder to read the longer you looked at it, and my head started to ache after just thirty minutes.

The other reason I needed to take the book slowly was the fresh dose of skepticism that came rushing to the surface every time Lucille made a new claim. Although I knew my aunt to be perfectly sane, the entries sounded like the ravings of a lunatic.

Still, it was worth wading through the supernatural gibberish to get more insight into family members who'd died long before my time. I'd known Gran had a younger sister called Midge, though I'd never realized Midge had passed away when she was six.

Lucille's account mentioned their littlest sister sitting in the garden having an enthusiastic and drawn-out conversation with their deceased grandfather — whom Midge had never met.

A chill raced down my spine. Maybe I wasn't the only Blackthorne who could see ghosts, I thought. Maybe Midge had been like me.

Feeling shaky and excited, I closed the book and set it carefully on the dresser. I could hear the TV chattering from the living room and the sound of Snowball pawing at his bed.

When I emerged from my room, the house smelled like freshly baked cookies. I could see Gran's shock of white hair over the back of her chair as I padded into the kitchen. A fresh tray of chocolate-chip cookies was waiting for me, hot out of the oven.

I stuffed one in my mouth, did a little happy dance, and piled three more on a plate. After my long day of interrogating suspects and delving into Roy's past, I deserved *all* the cookies.

I put on the kettle and joined Gran in the living room, flopping down on the couch. In the short time I'd been living there, I'd come to realize that Gran had a bit of a Home Shopping Network addiction. That was where my cat PJs had come from. Gran claimed she only watched HSN because there was nothing else on after nine, unless one wanted to listen to what she called the "constant catastrophe report" that was cable news. The shopping network was what was playing as I settled against the pillows and pulled a knitted blanket over my legs.

The second I was comfortable, Desmond came tearing into the room. He leapt brazenly onto the couch, scooting behind my legs.

Gran narrowed her eyes at the cat but didn't object to his being on the couch as he started making biscuits along the folds of the blanket. Snowball was curled up in his usual spot at Gran's feet, his eyes growing heavy as a man on the TV showed off a collection of life-sized busts modeled after dead celebrities.

"Long day?" Gran asked as I stuffed another warm, delicious cookie into my mouth.

"You have *no* idea." My words came out all garbled

around the cookie, so I finished chewing my bite. "Tell me about Midge."

Gran whipped her head around to look at me, her thick eyebrows knitting together in shock. "Midge? Why the sudden curiosity about her?"

I shrugged, trying to pass it off as casual interest. "I was just thinking . . . I've heard a lot about Lucille and Cordelia, but you never talk about Midge."

"She died very young," said Gran by way of explanation. Her voice was even, but I could have sworn I saw a flicker of pain in her expression before her mouth became a thin line. "She was six."

"How did she die?" I asked quietly, suddenly needing to know.

"Leukemia. They didn't have the sort of treatments then that they do now, and even if they had, my parents never could have afforded it."

I swallowed. "And Midge was . . . the baby of the family?"

Gran nodded. "Two years younger than me."

It must have been awful for Gran to watch her little sister die with her being so young herself.

"You never told me about her," I murmured.

"Sure I have."

I shook my head. "What was she like?"

Gran eyed me for a long moment, and I thought she might tell me to shut up and mind my own business. But then her eyes softened, and a small smile cracked her lips. "She was a funny little thing — always outside, talking to the animals. She had names for all the cows. Never could figure out how she could tell them apart." Gran shook her head. "We had this cat, Cookie — meanest thing you ever saw, but he had a soft spot for Midge. Used to let her carry him around in a flour sack. Anyone else would have lost an eye. Then one spring, a coyote came by and killed Cookie. Midge cried for a week. And for an entire year after that, anytime she had a tea party, she'd say Cookie had come for tea." Gran chuckled. "She and Cookie and that stuffed rabbit she carried everywhere."

At the mention of the rabbit, something I'd read in Aunt Lucille's account jiggled free from my memory — Midge pretending to pour tea from a broken china cup. "Hopper?"

The name slipped from my mouth without so much as a thought, and I instantly realized my mistake. Gran's brow furrowed, and she turned to look at me. Her face was as white as a sheet. "Yes. Hopper. How did you know?"

"You must have told me this story before," I said with a shrug. "Hopper just stuck in my brain."

But Gran was still staring at me as though I'd just told her pigs fly. "I'd forgotten what she used to call him all these years later," said Gran slowly. "I don't know how *you* knew . . ."

I swallowed, casting around for a change in topic. I couldn't tell Gran that I'd learned about her dead sister's tea parties from an entry in Lucille's book of the occult. That would be a bridge too far for my shrewd, practical gran.

"Thanks for telling me about her," I said, forcing a shaky smile. "I know it's probably hard to talk about."

Gran grunted and turned back toward the TV, though I was pretty sure she wasn't riveted by the celebrity busts on offer.

"How did Snowball do today?" I asked tentatively.

"He did really well," said Gran, nodding her head. Clearly she was more comfortable talking about Snowball than ancient family history. "I don't want to count my chickens, but I think there might just be a blue ribbon with our name on it this year."

Grateful to have landed on a topic that Gran was happy with, I launched into telling her about the dog show and everything I'd learned that day. When I told her of Jeffrey's suspicions that Doris had poisoned a fellow competitor, Gran didn't look surprised.

"I wouldn't put it past her," Gran muttered. "Doris was a conniving, mean-spirited woman. But that Jeffrey's not much better. He's worse than those mothers on that horrible TV show. Oh, what is it called?"

"*Dance Moms*?" I offered.

"No, that's not it."

I snorted and went into the kitchen as the tea kettle began to whistle. Normally, I much preferred coffee, but I knew I wouldn't be able to sleep if I guzzled down a bunch of caffeine after the day I'd had.

"Did Jeffrey have an alibi?" Gran called from the living room.

"Not really." I pulled the kettle off the fire and poured hot water into two mugs. "I asked him where he was just before the competition, and he said he was in his camper. Before that, he was at the dog wash, though he claimed Doris wasn't there."

Gran made a harrumphing sound, and I carefully carried our tea into the living room and set Gran's on the coffee table. I was just contemplating how to peel

Desmond out of the warm indent I'd left on the couch when Snowball's eyes flew open.

I jumped as he let out a sharp yip, sloshing tea all down my arm.

"Snowball! Quiet!" Gran snapped. "It's probably just —"

A loud knock at the door cut her off, and I stiffened in surprise. "Who's that?" I asked, glancing at the clock. It was almost nine thirty.

"Oh, probably that poor delivery driver. He's always mixing up my house with the house down the way. Those hooligans are always ordering pizza and Chinese food at all hours of the night."

"The house with the Broncos flag and the Jeep with the flat tire always parked out front?"

"That's the one."

I raised an eyebrow. I'd seen the "hooligans" to which Gran was referring. They were just a couple of twentysomething guys who looked as though they spent most of their time watching football and drinking beer.

Taking pity on the poor driver, I set down my tea and shuffled into the entryway to point him in the right direction. But when I opened the door, I found myself staring at a very handsome police officer holding a ceramic bird bath.

"I can fix it," said Will by way of greeting, and I saw that the bird bath he was clutching like a bouquet of flowers had a giant chunk missing from one side. "I . . . didn't see it as I was coming up the walkway, and —"

Will broke off as he caught sight of what I was wearing, and a grin tugged at the corners of his mouth as he took in every inch of me in my orange flannel cat pajamas.

"My eyes are up here," I said, pointing two fingers toward my face, which was no doubt bright red.

First piddle patrol, and now *this*? Was I doomed to live the life of a crazy cat lady?

Amusement danced in Will's eyes, but he cleared his throat and schooled his expression. "Right. Well, I wish I was here on a social visit, but . . ." He set the bird bath down on the porch, a crease working between his brows. "That's actually not why I'm here."

"You wanna come in?" I asked, hitching a thumb over my shoulder and wondering if I was making a huge mistake allowing him and Gran in the same room.

"Sure," he said, glancing behind me with clear apprehension before following me inside.

Will was tall — at least six two, I would have guessed — but I'd never noticed just how tall he was until he stood crowding Gran's entryway.

"Caroline?" came Gran's concerned voice. "Was it the delivery driver?"

"No," I called. "It was Officer Hamby."

"*Ooh*, goodie." Gran's voice inched up at least half an octave, and I braced myself for shenanigans. "Well, you kids have fun. Don't do anything I wouldn't do."

I winced. "We're not going anywhere, Gran."

"Well, all right . . . but keep those hands where I can see 'em. That means you, *detective*."

I stared at the ceiling and took a deep breath as my face burned with embarrassment. Cancún was probably nice this time of year. I'd just flee to Mexico — it was where my phony liar of a fiancé had disappeared to.

"I'm afraid I need to ask you some questions," said Will, his face all business.

My stomach dropped. This did not sound fun or romantic at all. "Okay . . ."

Shuffling into the living room, I shifted Desmond over a few inches and earned an annoyed little nip. I wiggled my butt back into my spot, ignoring Desmond's glare.

Snowball bounded up to sniff Will's shoes as Will pulled out his phone. He flipped through to find something and then turned the screen to face me. "Do you recognize this hat?"

I squinted at the photo he'd pulled up. It showed a plastic evidence bag labeled with permanent marker, and inside was the hideous straw Dalmatian hat.

"Where did you find this?" I asked in confusion, trying to remember when I'd last seen it.

Something shuttered behind Will's eyes, and the uneasy feeling in my gut intensified. "It was recovered at the crime scene where Doris Ashcroft was murdered. We found it behind the tub."

"*What?*"

My mind was racing. If the police had recovered it from the scene of the crime, that meant it was considered evidence. And since they'd found it behind the tub, they might assume that the killer had been wearing it.

I swallowed. How many people had seen me wearing that stupid hat on Friday? Detective Pierce, for one.

My heart started to race as I thought back to the day's events. I knew without a shadow of a doubt that I'd left my hat behind before I'd gone to find Doris. Either the killer had bought the same exact hat from the vendor at Dog Days, or someone was trying to frame me.

"Caroline," said Will in a serious tone. "Do you recognize the hat?"

"Y-yeah," I choked. "It looks just like the one I was wearing at the dog show. But I didn't have it on when I discovered Doris's body."

Will blinked once, and his mouth became a hard line. "That's what I was afraid of."

I shook my head. Come again?

He sighed and ran a hand through his short blond hair. "I don't think you killed Doris Ashcroft, but —"

"Of *course* she didn't!" Gran broke in.

Will's eyes swiveled over to her, though he continued to address me. "*But* . . . I think the real killer is trying to make it look as though you did."

I let out a long breath of relief before the onslaught of emotions hit me. I was oddly flattered to have Will on my side, but I was terrified the other officers working the case wouldn't share his conviction. I was also miffed and a little insulted that someone had tried to frame me for murder.

"Just a sec," I said, getting to my feet and padding down the hall. I made a beeline for the guest room and started tearing through my belongings like a tornado. I could hear Gran talking to Will, and I didn't want to leave them alone for long.

Finally, I located the tote bag I'd been carting back and forth to the dog show. The hat wasn't inside. I racked my brain, trying to remember if I'd unpacked it Friday night or if the hat had been gone before I'd even left the show.

"The hat's gone," I told Will as I rejoined them in the living room.

Will nodded. "The tech team recovered a few blond hairs from the hat and sent them off to the lab for testing." He grimaced. "I'm pretty sure they'll come back a match for you."

Scratching the back of my head, I started to pace in front of the couch. It gave me all the warm fuzzy feelings that Will believed in my innocence, but that didn't change the fact that all the evidence pointed directly to me as the killer.

"The team didn't find the hat until today," Will mused, leaning forward in his seat and resting his elbows on his knees. "The problem is that the crime scene has been sealed since Friday afternoon when Martha Mayberry called in the body. I'm not sure how someone could have gotten in and planted it."

"Are you here to arrest me?" I asked. Maybe Will would at least allow me to change out of my cat pajamas first.

"I probably should," he admitted. "And if it were anyone else, I probably would."

I sucked in a breath.

"But I don't think you killed Doris. I'm interested in flushing out the real killer."

"O-*kay* . . ." I wasn't sure where he was going with this.

"I have an idea," Will continued. "I'm not sure it'll work, but it's worth a shot." His eyes flickered up to meet my gaze. "Do you trust me?"

My stomach was doing all kinds of crazy backflips as I nodded, my throat suddenly very dry.

"All right then," he said, giving Desmond a nice pat before getting to his feet. "Be at the town square tomorrow morning — and be ready to put on a bit of a show."

CHAPTER FOURTEEN

By the time Will left Gran's that night, I was too queasy to finish my cookies. I liked his plan in *theory*, but I wasn't certain that it would work.

If someone was trying to frame me for murder, I needed to act fast. I couldn't wait for the killer to make a mistake — or hope that Will would solve the case. I would have to gather my own clues and figure out who'd murdered Doris before Will was forced to arrest me.

"Snowball and I are going to bed," Gran announced from the living room as the TV shut off.

"Goodnight," I called, squeezing into a chic black turtleneck and lamenting when it rolled back up over my stomach. I hadn't worn this thing in months, and I'd been indulging in a few too many donuts since coming to Mountain Shadow.

Luckily the material was stretchy. Extra lucky was that I'd hauled all the wardrobe boxes over to Gran's — even my off-season stuff. I'd paired the turtleneck with a pair of black skinny jeans and found gloves and a thin black balaclava with my cold-weather gear. I was already sweating in my cat burglar ensemble, but I wasn't taking any chances.

"You look like someone who's up to no good," Gran observed as I met her and Snowball in the hallway.

I tucked the ski mask behind my back and propped a hand on my hip to cover the gesture. "Says the woman who brings her own Tupperware to an all-you-can-eat buffet."

"Don't throw stones, Caroline. Glass houses and all. And you know a woman my size can't possibly get her money's worth at one of those things."

"Goodnight," I said, waggling my eyebrows and slinging my purse over my shoulder.

Desmond skittered after me with a little yowl, and I didn't try to stop him as he slinked out the door.

Fortunately, it was a moonless night, and I stuck to the shadows as I made my way up the street. I'd found Doris's address in the phone book, which had seemed almost too easy. There was an official-looking notice on the front door — probably saying that the place was off-limits due to an ongoing police investigation or something.

Glancing behind me to make sure I was alone, I caught the flash of Desmond's yellow eyes in the orange glow of the street lamp. He followed me around the back of Doris's house, and my heart sank when I saw the shiny brass deadbolt securing her back door.

I whispered a curse. I was something of a novice lockpicker, and I was certain that a modern deadbolt was far beyond my skill set.

Circling the house, I squinted in through the wavy glass panes that had to be the original windows. The house was dark, but I didn't dare shine my flashlight inside in case any of the neighbors happened to be awake and looking in this direction.

Finally, I found what I'd been hoping for — a window along the back of the house that had been left unlatched. I dragged a heavy lawn chair over from the patio to give myself a boost and grabbed the letter opener I'd stashed in my bag for this very purpose.

Wedging the blade through the crack at the bottom, I managed to wedge the window open wide enough to get my fingers underneath and push it all the way open.

I wasn't an idiot. I'd spent enough time yelling at the TV screen to don a thin pair of black gloves, lest I leave any prints behind.

"Stay here and keep a lookout," I whispered to Des — more to make myself feel better than anything else. "If you see anyone coming . . . meow or something."

Desmond didn't reply — not that I'd expected him to. I might be the type of person who talked to my cat, but I wasn't *that* nutty. Des stared back with those huge yellow eyes, and I had the strange niggling feeling that he'd gotten the message.

It took some effort, but I managed to haul myself through the little window and slide out onto a washing machine. The lid gave as I transferred my weight, and I grimaced at the loud *thwang* of metal as it sprang back into place.

My heartbeat was a dull throb in my throat. I'd never done any breaking and entering. It was both nerve-wracking and exciting, but mostly I just wished I'd stretched first.

Doris's sprawling Queen Anne had that typical old-house smell, mixed with the artificial fragrance of some heavy floral air freshener. Deciding to take a chance on the light shining through the windows, I flipped on my flashlight so I could see where I was going.

Unsurprisingly, Doris's house was immaculate. There wasn't a single dirty dish in her sink — not even a coffee cup or a spoon. The kitchen didn't have a dishwasher either, which meant the woman must have washed every single dish by hand and put it away when she was done.

The home was comfortably furnished but lacking in the typical old-house charm. There were no knickknacks on the end tables, and the only art on the walls were pressed flower arrangements and generic prints of garden-themed paintings. The only real sign that the house had been lived in were the fluffy dog beds scattered around.

My first stop was Doris's home office, where an antique Chippendale desk dominated the space. Two diplomas hung on the wall — one from Druxton University and another from Colorado College. Two neat stacks of papers lay on the desk. One was bills — paid, of course — and the other was a stack of grant applications.

Resisting the urge to snoop and see who my competitors were, I tried Doris's desk drawers. Inside I found her medical records, income taxes from the last seven years, and what looked like a paper copy of every bill she'd ever received.

Doris might have been a nasty woman, but I couldn't help admire her filing system. Every folder was neatly labeled and filed in alphabetical order, and there didn't appear to be so much as a receipt out of place.

Thumbing through her files, I realized I didn't even know exactly what I was looking for. I'd come there to find something that might point me to the killer, but so far all I'd learned was that Doris was a type-A neat freak. It may have been annoying to those around her, but it didn't seem like a strong enough motive for murder.

Feeling defeated, I turned to the bookcase, which was filled with nice leather-bound copies of all the classics. I'd never read *Moby Dick* or *Northanger Abbey*, but the sight of all that rich, buttery leather embossed with gold text made me wish I could just kick back with a hot cup of coffee and read to my heart's content.

I chewed on my bottom lip as my gaze drifted down to a short row of leather photo albums. Running a gloved hand along the spines, I racked my brain for inspiration. I just needed *something* to point me in the direction of the killer. Some tiny clue that could —

Suddenly, I heard a soft scrape, and one of the albums slid out a few inches. It was bound in soft red leather and looked about a million years old.

I gaped, heart pounding against my ribs. Did *I* do that?

I'd barely brushed the spines with my fingers. I hadn't done anything to force the album out. So what in the world had just happened?

Maybe my eyes were playing tricks on me. It was dark outside the beam of my flashlight. The thing couldn't have moved on its own, right?

Hands shaking, I tugged the album off the shelf and let it fall open in my lap. The photos were all in black and white, but I recognized Doris immediately. Even as a twenty-year-old, the girl in the photo wore Doris's trademark dour expression.

She stood in the back row with six other girls between a dark-haired woman and a pretty young blond with a cleft chin. They all wore twin-set cashmere sweaters and the same style of gold pendant necklace.

I squinted at the photo, wishing for a magnifying glass. I was pretty sure the pendant formed the letters ASA. Greek letters, perhaps?

Had Doris been in a sorority? I wondered. Somehow, I couldn't picture it.

I kept flipping through the fragile pages and found a photo from Doris's wedding. She wore a long-sleeved white gown with a lace yoke that went all the way up to her neck. Even on the happiest day of her life, Doris was still scowling.

I still couldn't wrap my head around how this album had seemed to jump off the shelf at me — nor did I understand why. Doris's husband was dead, so *he* couldn't have killed her. This album was nothing but ancient history.

I must have been imagining things, I told myself firmly — sliding the album back onto the shelf. I wasn't going to find the answers I was looking for snooping through photos that were half a century old. I needed something current.

Turning back toward the study door, I saw a framed bulletin board hanging on the wall. A flyer for Dog Days was neatly pinned in one corner, along with a schedule of events and a list of what looked like refreshments.

*Peanut-butter-oat biscuits*
*Pumpkin-spice puppy pies*
*Elk jerky, plain*
*Beef jerky, seasoned*

It was a catering menu for Dog Days, I realized. Then something clicked in my brain.

The ugly dog hat. I hadn't picked it out myself. Daphne had given it to me Friday morning.

When I'd first learned about Dog Days, Daphne had complained that Doris was difficult to work with. She'd also been the one who'd sent me to find Doris.

As that last little detail crystalized, my insides turned to ice. Daphne had been nothing but sweet to me and Gran. She wasn't a cold-blooded killer.

And yet, she was the one who'd made sure I put on that hat *and* that I'd gone to find Doris at The Pampered Pooch.

I swallowed. I didn't want to believe that Daphne had set me up, but it sure looked as though she had.

CHAPTER FIFTEEN

I awoke the next morning sunburned and defeated. Birds were chirping merrily outside my window as they gorged themselves at Gran's feeders, and Desmond was curled in the crook of my legs. It was the perfect Colorado summer day, and yet all I wanted to do was pull the blankets over my head and stay under the covers for another two hours.

I'd come in late the night before with a leaden weight in my stomach. Daphne *couldn't* be the killer. It didn't make any sense. She'd seemed to take Doris's prickliness in stride, and her kindness toward me had felt . . . genuine.

But maybe Daphne had everyone fooled. Maybe that made it the perfect crime.

Then there was the incident with the photo album. In the cold light of day, it seemed impossible that it could have jumped out on its own. Inanimate objects didn't just *move*. And yet I'd been so shaken back at Doris's house — so convinced by what I'd seen.

*Nope,* I thought. Not gonna go there — not this morning, at least.

My mind drifted back to my conversation with Will, and I pulled the sheet over my head with a groan. I was about to make a spectacle of myself in front of the entire town, and I still didn't have the money to begin renovations at the hotel. To top it all off, I'd lost my roofer, and I was no closer to figuring out how to keep the ghost of Roy Wilkerson from running off everyone who came to work at The Grand.

After my talk with Jinx, I was pretty sure that learning what unfinished business Roy had on earth was the key to putting his spirit to rest. But if Roy didn't want me to get to the bottom of things, I was destined to be a broke hotel heiress and soon the pariah of Mountain Shadow.

As if he sensed my descent into self-pity, Desmond extended his front claws and dug into my leg through the sheet.

"Ouch! Watch it, demon cat, or I'll tell Gran you've been sleeping on the bed."

Des blinked back at me with those bright-yellow eyes, and I knew he was calling my bluff. I was more afraid of Gran's wrath than he was.

"Fine," I grumbled. "I'm up. I'm up."

With a few more grunts and groans, I scooted over to the edge of the bed and stuffed my feet into my slippers. I could hear the TV blaring from the living room, along with some rhythmic, shuffling stomps.

Bracing myself for another morning on piddle patrol, I went out to find Gran in a swishy teal tracksuit with a matching teal sweatband. She was moving along to a grainy VHS tape of Richard Simmons, who wore a red unitard with tall white tube socks.

"You're up early," she huffed, pivoting in a circle as she spread her arms overhead like a rainbow.

"It's the last day of the dog show."

"It's a blue-ribbon kind of day," said Gran with relish. "I can feel it."

I cast around the living room for Snowball, but he wasn't in his usual bed by the couch. "Where is our champ?"

"Out on the sunporch."

Gran didn't offer any further explanation, so I padded out onto the enclosed porch to say good morning. I found Snowball lounging on what appeared to be a dog-sized couch. An odd buzzing sound was emanating from the doggie bed, but I was distracted by a recording of Gran's dulcet tones, which were coming through an old boom box positioned near Snowball's head.

*I am a champion. I am a winner. I am the best dog there is. I choose to live each day to my fullest potential . . .*

"Gran?" I called, slightly alarmed that she'd finally gone off the deep end.

"Yeah?"

"What *is* this?"

"Snowball's massage bed," she called over the music and Richard Simmons's shouts.

"I meant the tape player."

"Oh! Snowball's just listening to his affirmations."

"His *what*?"

"Positive affirmations, Caroline. It's backed by science — and Oprah."

"Oh." I made a face. "Well, if *Oprah's* dogs listen to affirmations . . ."

"If you're not going to be positive, Caroline, then leave Snow alone. He needs to get in the zone for the finals, and you are *oozing* negative energy."

"I am not!" I protested. I might not have been feeling my best that morning, but I wasn't *oozing* negativity. Still, I knew better than to argue with Gran before I'd had my coffee, so I left Snowball to his affirmations and shuffled into the kitchen.

Once I'd choked down some eggs on toast, I donned my volunteer uniform and walked up to the dog show. It was the final day of competition, and the air was buzzing with anticipation.

I'd nearly reached my station when I heard — or rather sensed — something watching me from the grass. I turned, but there was no one there. Then my gaze drifted down.

Desmond was crouched beside a tree, his long tail swishing in the grass.

"Des!" I hissed. "What are you *doing* here? This is the last place you want to be!"

Desmond gave a half-impetuous, half-wounded *ree-arr*.

Glancing around to see if there were any dogs nearby, I quickly crossed the distance between us and scooped him into my arms. "I have to take you home. Now. You shouldn't be —"

But before I could even finish that sentence, I heard a desperate voice from behind me. "Mr. Bittles! Mr. Bittles?"

Wheeling around, I saw Jeffrey Hanover crouched beside his little gray whippet, who seemed unable to stand. The dog's legs were stiff and wobbly, and he was shaking uncontrollably.

"Help! Help me!" Jeffrey called, holding his dog, who stared helplessly at his owner.

"It's all right," came a reassuring voice from behind me. Selma Lewis appeared wearing a blue volunteer shirt over a long-sleeve white blouse, a red emergency bag over her shoulder. "Let's get him on his side."

Selma's face and neck were flushed from the heat, and her voice was calm and businesslike as she bent to help maneuver Mr. Bittles.

A small crowd had started to gather, and I felt Des go stiff in my arms. Several dogs were edging closer, and a low growl reverberated in Desmond's throat. I could feel the annoyed looks the dogs' owners were throwing my way. Yes, I was the girl who'd brought a cat to a dog show — or at least that was how it looked.

While Jeffrey fretted and rubbed Mr. Bittles's head, Selma rested her right hand on the whippet's shoulder and peeled his eyelid open with her left. Her examination was quick and professional, and her hands were certainly steadier than mine would have been.

"He's having a seizure," she informed Jeffrey.

"A seizure?" Silent tears were streaming down his face, and my heart went out to the guy.

"Has he had them before?"

Jeffrey shook his head.

"Let's get him out of the sun and try to cool him down," said Selma. "The greatest risk with a dog having a seizure is that he'll become overheated."

Jeffrey nodded and scooped Mr. Bittles into his arms. As he did, his story about the dog who'd been poisoned came floating back, and a dark feeling settled in the pit of my stomach.

What caused seizures in dogs? I wondered. Was it possible that someone had poisoned Mr. Bittles to keep him from advancing in the competition?

My mind raced through the sinister possibilities as I crossed the town square. Rather than heading for the piddle station, I wandered over to the doggie refreshments area. Daphne stood at her table, passing out treats to canine contestants.

"Looking sharp, Butterscotch," said Daphne, beaming down at a silky brown shih tzu as she handed the dog's owner a bone-shaped treat. "Good luck today! Break a paw!"

She chuckled at her own joke, and my stomach clenched at the very thought that Daphne had murdered Doris.

"Any idea where I could find an extra kennel?" I asked, nodding at Desmond, who was digging his claws into my arm. "Someone followed me from the house."

"Oh, poor kitty!" Daphne laughed. "Hang on . . . I'm sure somebody's got one they're not using."

She disappeared for a moment to talk to the other volunteers. After some back and forth, she returned with a small plastic crate and held the door open while I shoved Des inside.

I breathed a sigh of relief as I slid him into the crate. Desmond might have been smarter than the average feline, but a dog show was no place for a cat.

"Scary, isn't it?" I said to Daphne, nodding toward the medical tent where Mr. Bittles had disappeared.

"Oh, yeah." Daphne made a sympathetic face. "The dogs get so stressed at these things. It hardly seems worth a blue ribbon."

I nodded. "It sort of makes you wonder if one of the other owners had anything to do with it — especially after what happened to Doris." I lowered my voice. "Jeffrey told me that one of the dogs ended up getting poisoned at a show he and Doris attended."

Daphne's eyes went wide. "You're *kidding*."

"That's what he told me."

Daphne scoffed. "Some of the owners take these things *way* too seriously — Doris included. She started Dog Days, you know — way back in the nineties. Say what you want about the ol' girl, but she was always giving back to this town."

"Yeah, but . . . the way people talk about her, Doris sounds like she was . . ."

"Horrible? Mean-spirited? Tyrannical?" Daphne chuckled. "Doris *was* all those things. She even made me cry once — at the first event I ever catered for her."

"She *did*?" Now things were getting interesting.

"I swear, nothing about that event was to her liking. There were smudges on the glassware, the soup was too hot, the iced tea was too cold. I swore up and down that I would never work for that woman again. But then she took a bite of one of my scones and declared that they weren't half bad. She booked me again just a few weeks later for an event with the historical society."

"And you took the job?"

Daphne quirked a brow. "Honey, I run a restaurant in a small town. I don't say no to business. Doris booked me for that event, and she's kept me busy ever since."

I nodded in understanding. It sounded as though Daphne was indebted to Doris, no matter how much she might have disliked her.

"You said Doris was being difficult when you were getting ready for Dog Days," I said, still trying to suss out any potential motive.

While it didn't seem likely that sweet Daphne could have killed Doris, I didn't dismiss the possibility. Maybe they'd gotten into an argument over dog biscuits and Daphne had just snapped.

"No more than usual," Daphne mused. "She was actually a bit preoccupied, since Crumpet had been throwing up the morning of the breed competition."

"He had?"

Daphne nodded. "Luckily, he hadn't eaten any of my treats. Doris only ever feeds him this special grain-free diet she buys online from a company in Canada."

"Any chance the owner of the dog wash had a beef with Doris?"

"Katy?" Daphne chuckled. "Maybe. Why? You think she killed Doris?"

"I don't know."

"She didn't. I know Katy. She hasn't got a mean bone in her body. Besides that, she wasn't even *at* the show when Doris was killed."

"No?" It struck me as odd that one of the main event sponsors would be absent from the dog show.

Daphne shook her head. "She got a call Friday that there was a gas smell outside her house and had to run and deal with it. She closed up shop around noon."

I chewed on the inside of my cheek. That seemed fishy, to say the least. It also gave me a definitive window for Doris's murder. "Any idea who called her?"

"No. But you sure have a lot of questions. If the thing

with The Grand doesn't work out, I think you'd make a decent PI."

I snorted. "Thanks. Maybe I *should* be thinking of a fallback. I don't know how I'm ever going to come up with the funds to renovate the place. I applied for the Main Street revitalization grant, but I don't think the committee was terribly impressed."

Daphne's eyebrows scrunched together. "Aw, I'm sure you're just being overly critical of yourself. The Mountain Shadow Grand has been vacant for decades. I know everyone on that committee would love to see it restored."

"I'm sure they would," I said glumly. "I'm just not the person to do it."

"Don't you say that about yourself," Daphne chided. "If you want something bad enough, there's always a way."

I let out a slow puff of air. "I suppose. I just haven't found it yet. I was really counting on that grant to get me started, and now . . ."

"Now that Doris is . . . at rest," said Daphne, "maybe you stand a better chance."

So Will wasn't the only one who'd heard about my humiliating pitch. I would have bet money Bellamy Broussard was the leak.

"Doris wasn't wrong about my proposal," I admitted. "I *am* inexperienced. I don't know the first thing about renovating historic buildings or running a hotel."

Daphne seemed to consider my point. "Well, you know, I didn't know the first thing about running a restaurant when I opened Fireside."

"You didn't?"

"Lord, no! I mean, I *thought* I did, which was probably

even more dangerous. I'd been waiting tables since I was fourteen years old. As a teenager, I hosted, I bussed, I prepped . . . Then, after culinary school, I got a job cooking at a really high-end restaurant down in Colorado Springs." She laughed. "*That* didn't last long."

"Why not?"

She sighed. "Well, I got pregnant, and once I had my daughter, I couldn't be at work until two every night. So I quit and became a stay-at-home mom. I sort of lost confidence in myself, I think."

"So what happened?"

Daphne smiled. "Mike and I — Mike's my husband — we didn't have more than a few thousand dollars in the bank. But he had the idea that I should open my own restaurant right here in Mountain Shadow. We had to take out a second mortgage on our house to afford it, but he believed in me." A wistful look came into her eyes. "Piece of advice? Opening a restaurant when you have an infant and an almost four-year-old at home is *not* a good idea. It was touch and go there for a while, but we've made it work."

"You sure have." I couldn't even imagine what that must have taken — to build a business completely from scratch with two young children.

Daphne gave me a bracing smile. "Nobody starting a new business really knows what they're getting into. You may think you do, but trust me. The reality is never *quite* what you imagine."

Those words probably should have scared me, but for some reason, hearing that Daphne had struggled despite her experience made me feel suddenly lighter.

"Maybe Selma was right," I mused. "Maybe I just need

a partner — an investor with some experience in commercial renovation or something."

"Yes! A partner!" Daphne clapped her hands together. "I think that's a *great* idea."

"You do?"

She nodded. "You should ask Gideon Brewer. He's part-owner of Chumley's, and he managed the renovations of the Phantom Canyon Boulevard building."

I frowned. "Gideon?" I shook my head. "I thought he was the bartender."

Daphne snorted. "Well, he does tend bar there, but no. Gideon is one of the owners. He's done very well for himself, flipping commercial real estate."

I thought back to the first time I'd met the surly, tattooed bartender. There'd been little employee-of-the-month plaques hanging behind the bar — all with Gideon's name on them. He's said the owner did that to annoy him. But why would he lie about being one of the owners?

As though she'd read my mind, Daphne said, "Gideon doesn't like to throw his weight around. I used to babysit him as a kid, and he's always been the modest type. Plus, he probably thinks he'd have to hand in his tattoos if people started thinking of him as some fat-cat business owner."

I snorted. That sounded like Gideon. I was about to ask her more about him when I heard the bloop of police sirens behind me. I closed my eyes as dread washed over me and turned slowly on the spot.

When I opened them, I saw Officer Will climbing out of his cruiser, looking so handsome that it should have been illegal. Our eyes met across the colorful cluster of tables and booths, and that adorable little crease appeared between his brows.

Daphne glanced from me to Will, and a knowing smile curled her lips.

"Caroline McCrithers?" said Will as soon as he was within earshot.

"Yes?" I said, suddenly annoyed that he was approaching me as if he didn't know my name.

"You're under arrest for the murder of Doris Ashcroft."

"What?" cried Daphne, clapping her hands to her mouth. She looked utterly devastated that this interaction between me and Will was not going as she'd imagined.

Will ignored her and pulled a set of cuffs from his belt. "Please turn and face the table."

Cheeks burning, I did what I was told. I could feel the eyes of all the volunteers glued to us and knew this was all anyone would be talking about for days.

"Put your hands behind your back," said Will, his voice gentler than before.

Fighting the growing lump in my throat, I did as I was told. A little shiver rolled down my spine as his fingers brushed my wrist, but the feel of the cold metal cuffs on my skin doused whatever fire had been burning in my belly.

"You have the right to remain silent. Anything you say can and will be used against you in a court of law."

The first cuff clicked shut, the hard edge digging into my wrist.

"You have the right to an attorney. If you cannot afford an attorney, one will be appointed for you."

Will's fingers encircled my other wrist, and I felt the second cuff click into place.

"Let's go," he rumbled, placing a warm hand on my shoulder and steering me gently toward his cruiser.

"Wait!" I said, jerking around. "My cat!"

"Your cat?" I could hear the frown in Will's voice.

"Des, he . . . followed me here. He's in the crate." I nodded toward the plastic pet carrier sitting in the grass.

Will sighed and bent down to grab Desmond's carrier before guiding me toward his cruiser.

"Officer," Daphne choked, nearly tripping over her own feet as she scrambled after Will. "Is this really necessary? Caroline isn't a killer. I'm sure there's just been some sort of mistake."

"No mistake, ma'am," said Will in a weary voice. "I'm just as shocked as you are."

At those words, I thought my face might combust. Even though Will and I had cooked up this plan the night before, the reality of being led away in handcuffs in front of half the town still made my insides burn with shame.

The worst part was the look on Daphne's face as Will marched me toward his cruiser. I felt as though I'd just made a new friend, and now the sweet chef was always going to think I might have killed Doris Ashcroft.

"Sorry, Caroline," Will rumbled softly as he opened the back door and placed a hand on my head.

I didn't like to admit that I enjoyed his touch — even if this was how he treated every perp. I swallowed as I scooted into the back seat, not saying a word as he shut the door.

Through the bars on my window, I could still see the gleam of Daphne's flaming-red hair as she watched us pull away.

CHAPTER SIXTEEN

"Sorry about that," said Will once we turned off Main Street. My face was still painfully red, and I could practically hear the giant wheel of the gossip mill beginning to turn.

Desmond was yowling miserably from the front seat. He was not a fan of crates.

"It's fine," I croaked, my throat dry and scratchy. It *would* be fine, wouldn't it? Once we learned the true identity of Doris's killer and cleared my name.

"You want me to take you back to your gran's place?" he asked.

I hesitated. I couldn't exactly be seen hanging around town — not since I was supposed to be in police custody. Then again, Gran would be at the dog show, and I didn't want to spend the day milling around the house.

"Could you take me to the hotel?" I asked. At least then maybe Aunt Lucille and I could put our heads together on the case.

"Sure thing."

It was strange. Under any other circumstances, I would have been thrilled to score some alone time with Will. But since he was chauffeuring me through town like a common criminal, it was a little awkward.

"Did you know why the owner of The Pampered Pooch wasn't at her store on Friday?" I asked — mostly to break the unbearable silence.

"Katy?"

I nodded, frowning out the window. "Daphne said Katy got a call from someone who smelled gas outside her house."

In the rearview mirror, I saw Will's eyebrows shoot up. "That's strange. Most gas leaks happen in the winter due to all the freezing and thawing."

"Yeah. I think it's pretty convenient that she got the call just before somebody drowned Doris at her dog wash."

Will nodded. That crease between his eyebrows was back. "I'll look into it. If we can figure out who placed that call, we might just find our killer."

He pulled up in front of The Mountain Shadow Grand, threw the vehicle into park, and climbed out to open my door.

"Thanks for the ride," I said, realizing as I said it that I was essentially thanking Will for fake-arresting me.

"Thanks for playing along," he said, opening the passenger door and extracting Desmond in his carrier. "Hopefully, after that little show, the real killer will think he can relax . . . That's when people make mistakes."

"I hope so," I said, bending down to let Des out. He slinked out of the carrier with his tail tucked, turning to glare at me over his shoulder.

"Could you do me a favor?" I asked.

"Anything."

My stomach gave a funny little leap at the enthusiasm in Will's voice. "Could you return the crate to the volunteer station at the show? It's a loaner."

"Sure thing." He bent down, closed the door of the crate, and set it back in the front seat. He started walking toward the driver's side door, turning to look at me over his shoulder. "Take it easy, Caroline."

I smiled, but my chest ached as I watched Will drive away. Then I caught a flicker of movement out of the corner of my eye. Gideon was taking a bag of trash out to the bar's dumpster.

I narrowed my eyes and crossed the street, entering through the front door of Chumley's as Gideon walked in through the back. The leather booths along the right side of the bar were completely empty this time of day, as was the long oak bar. I took a seat at a creaky stool and drummed my fingers on the scuffed wooden bar top as I waited for Gideon to appear.

He strode in from the back, and his eyebrows shot up in surprise. "Caroline." Gideon cleared his throat, and his broad shoulders tightened. "W-what can I get you?"

"Why didn't you tell me you were one of the owners of this place?" I asked.

Gideon frowned and crossed those strong tattooed arms over his chest. "You never asked."

"When I pointed out your employee-of-the-month plaques, you said the owner just did it to bug you."

The shadow of a smirk flickered across Gideon's face. "Gladys has an odd sense of humor." He gestured around. "She's the one who owns the building. When we decided to go into business together, I managed the renovations for a percent of ownership. I run the bar and work here seven days a week, and Gladys and I split the profits."

"And now that the building has been sold?"

I decided not to mention how the back wall of the tearoom next door had crumbled in a miniature earthquake — a miniature earthquake that *I* might have caused.

Gideon shrugged. "I have to decide whether I want to sell the bar or start paying rent to the new owners."

"You must have made a tidy profit when the building sold."

Gideon quirked his dark eyebrows, which was as good an answer as any.

"Are you . . . looking to reinvest your capital?" I asked, feeling my throat tighten with nerves.

"It would depend on the investment," said Gideon with a slight frown.

Ignoring the fact that I was dressed in shorts and my volunteer shirt, I drew myself up and lifted my chin. "Well, as it happens, The Mountain Shadow Grand is looking for investors."

The corner of Gideon's mouth twitched. "*Is* it now?"

"Oh, yes. We are one of the finalists competing for the Main Street revitalization grant." The use of "we" was an old business-speak trick I'd learned in the ad industry. I figured since I was already lying about being a finalist, I should go big or go home. "Once the funding comes through, renovations will be underway. We hope to be open for private events by early next year."

Gideon fidgeted and flexed his crossed arms. "I'd . . . need to see some numbers," he said, his voice rumbling with amusement.

A victorious warmth spread through my chest, and I

jammed a hand into my bag. I just so happened to have one of the faux-leather folders I'd used for my presentation with me. I'd been lugging it around just in case the opportunity ever presented itself — the analog equivalent to the "pitch deck" that all my entrepreneurship podcasts insisted one should have at the ready.

"It's all in there," I said, feeling a little tingle of pride as Gideon opened the folder to reveal the glossy full-color photo spread. The whole package looked pretty sleek, if I did say so myself.

"I've already gotten a bid from Miles Briggs, and I'm currently in the process of securing two competing bids."

This wasn't a total lie. I'd left messages with six other contractors, though none of them had returned my call.

"Briggs is good," said Gideon approvingly. "He usually comes in a little high, but that's better than someone who shoots low and then ends up two mil over budget."

*Two mil.* As in two *million*? Was that a thing that could happen?

Just the thought made me queasy, but Gideon threw the number out there as if it were no big deal — as though he negotiated multimillion-dollar deals all the time.

I nodded sagely, as if that was why I'd chosen Miles in the first place — and not just because he'd had the best online reviews.

"He's saying five on the renovations alone?" Gideon's eyebrows crept higher, and he rubbed his upper lip. "That's before you've even bought a single piece of furniture, ice machine, or appliance."

"I've factored in those costs," I said, my throat suddenly very dry. *Mostly.* I pointed to another line item, and Gideon glanced up at me. "That's a little optimistic, don't you think?"

"They're just rough figures," I choked.

Ice machines! Why hadn't I thought of that? Every hotel had ice machines!

Gideon sighed and set the folder down on the bar. "I'm not gonna lie to you, Caroline. It's gonna be tricky to pull this off." He gestured up and down the street. "The location's not bad, but this is Mountain Shadow, not Breckenridge. Not to mention that consumers are gravitating more toward short-term rentals than full-service hotels these days. You can't compete with the budget motels down in the Springs, and —"

"We're not *trying* to," I said, the excitement bubbling up inside of me. *This* — the branding, the market positioning — was where I shined. "Consumers are turning to short-term rentals because they want to create unique memories. They're tired of cookie-cutter chain hotels. The rooms aren't clean. The staff isn't accommodating. The whole place reeks of chlorine . . . it's not a great experience."

Gideon stroked his chin. "I suppose . . ."

I started to pace in front of the bar. I could feel my pitch mojo returning.

"People don't just come to The Grand for a place to stay on vacation. They come for an *experience* — a meticulously restored nineteenth-century hotel with an antique birdcage elevator, sheets that feel like butter, and a staff that is there to ensure comfort and luxury at every turn."

My mind went to The Grand's current shabby interior, and then I got a stroke of inspiration. "Picture bellhops in traditional bellboy uniforms," I said, the thoughts tumbling out of my mouth. "Brass buttons . . . little pillbox hats. Impeccable manners. You pull up, and a valet takes your vehicle as the bellhop carries the bags to your room. You check in at the front desk, and the concierge hands you a real room key, not a plastic card. During your stay, the staff calls you by your name and anticipates your every need. I'm talking turndown service, pillow mints, live entertainment, and the most delicious breakfast you've ever —"

"Whoa, whoa!" Gideon chuckled. "All right. I get it."

I pressed my lips together to keep from babbling anymore. Once I got in the zone during a pitch, it was really hard to shut me up. My heart was pounding in my ears, and for the first time since I'd inherited the hotel, I could truly envision it.

"It sounds like you have it all figured out," he said. "With the right marketing, I think it could be a viable idea."

My heart gave an excited jolt. Gideon thought my idea was a good one.

But my delight was quickly engulfed by panic. I'd been so caught up in the flow of the pitch that I'd sort of blacked out. I wasn't sure I'd be able to remember everything I'd said.

"I'm in," he said, spreading his hands on the bar top.

I blinked. "But you haven't even seen my projections," I spluttered. "I have a graph and everything."

Gideon chuckled. "First lesson of pitching investors? *Never* try to talk them out of it after they've agreed."

Heat bloomed on my cheeks, and I nodded.

"I don't need to see your projections. Most first-time

business owners are way off on the numbers. Anyway, I'm not investing in a hotel. I'm investing in you."

My eyes widened at his words, and my breaths came a little faster. I was flattered, shocked, and scared out of my wits. No pressure or anything . . .

Gideon seemed not to notice my reaction. "I'm in for two and a quarter."

My stomach flipped over. "Two and a quarter *million*?" I squeaked.

Gideon nodded, his expression serious. "In exchange for forty percent of the business."

I let out a hard exhale. Forty percent of the business? Between Gideon's money and the grant, if we got it, I'd have nearly half of what I needed. We'd still have to bring in other investors, though, and by the time I'd finished dividing up my hotel, I wouldn't own the majority share.

"Twenty," I countered.

"Thirty-five," said Gideon.

I was so shocked that he'd countered at all that it was a good four seconds before I responded. "Twenty-five."

"Thirty, and that's my final offer."

I swallowed and blinked like a complete idiot. Had I just negotiated my first big business deal?

"Thirty I can live with," I said, sticking my hand out as though I did this sort of thing all the time.

Gideon tilted his head to the side, his eyes dancing with . . . amusement? Attraction? I honestly couldn't tell.

"I can have my attorney draw up the paperwork," he said. "Unless you'd rather use R.P. Stein."

I shook my head, completely lost for words. "No. Your attorney's fine. I'll, uh . . . have R.P. look it over once we have something on paper."

"Great." Gideon waggled his eyebrows once, and I honestly found myself wondering if I'd fallen asleep in the back of Will's cruiser and this was all a dream. I'd been banging my head against the wall for weeks trying to figure out how I was going to fund the renovations, and the first person I'd approached to invest had said yes.

Had I gotten the raw end of the deal? Should I have negotiated harder? I decided not to think about it.

Slowly, I picked up the presentation folder and slid it back into my bag. I wasn't sure how one exited after the deal was done, but fortunately, Gideon beat me to the punch. He rapped his knuckles on the bar top and turned to go into the back room. "It's a pleasure doing business with you."

CHAPTER SEVENTEEN

"Aunt Lucille! Philip!" I called as I crested the second-floor landing. "I just secured our first investor! This is happening! This is hap—"

The ghosts flickered into existence so quickly that I stumbled backward and nearly fell down the stairs. I caught myself on the railing, my heart hammering in my throat.

Lucille was dressed in a gorgeous off-the-shoulder number and a white fox-fur stole. Giant gemstone earrings glittered at her lobes, and her jet-black curls tumbled down her back.

"An *investor*? My word! Oh, that's *terribly* exciting."

"Congratulations, Miss Caroline," said Philip with a slight bow of his head. At least *he* didn't seem opposed to the renovations. What the heck was Roy's problem?

"Who is it, dear?" Aunt Lucille asked.

"Gideon Brewer," I huffed, struggling to catch my breath. "He owns the bar across the street."

Aunt Lucille's painted lips jutted out in a smug little

pout. "That strapping fellow with the tattoos who helped you move all those heavy boxes?"

"That's the one."

"I must say, he doesn't *look* like a Rockefeller, but looks can be deceiving."

I nodded. Who would have thought the bartender at Chumley's was secretly a millionaire? Daphne had said he'd made his money flipping commercial real estate, but I planned to online stalk him later.

"Any progress on the case?"

"No," I sighed, shoulders slumping. I'd momentarily forgotten about the murder — and that I was still a key suspect. "I'm calling a meeting to review what we know so far. Right now, we have an advantage in that the killer thinks I've been arrested for Doris's murder. He or she might slip up, and we need to be ready when and if that happens."

"Well, let's get to it," said Lucille, leading the way up to her preferred suite on the fourth floor. Philip followed a few paces behind me, which sort of gave me the creeps.

I wasn't sure if I'd inadvertently summoned Philip or if he simply had nothing better to do than hang around and help me solve a murder. I found I didn't mind his company; I just didn't like being followed by a phantom bellboy from the nineteen thirties.

The fourth floor was hot and stuffy that time of day, and sunlight was shining weakly through the grimy windows of Aunt Lucille's suite. Desmond alighted onto the bed with a satisfied *reeow* and stretched out in the sunbeams.

Tossing my purse onto a chair, I struggled with a few of the old windows to let in a light breeze. Fishing a hair tie out of my purse, I swept my sticky curls off the back of my neck and gathered them into a ponytail. I also located a pink dry-erase marker and jotted down everything we knew on the largest window.

*12-1 p.m. — Approx. time of murder*

*1 p.m. — Body discovered*

*Doris drowned*

*Door left unlocked, owner of The Pampered Pooch called away*

*Doris murdered before Crumpet's event — cleared the way for competition*

Beneath my notes, I wrote out a list of potential suspects, along with any motive I could think of.

*Meghan (bark-tivist) — Hates dog shows*

*Maria (daughter-in-law) — Inheritance? Revenge?*

*Jeffrey (Mr. Bittles's owner) — Eliminate the competition*

*Daphne —*

I faltered as I finished writing Daphne's name on the list. Not only did it feel incredibly disloyal to include her as a suspect, but I couldn't help but think that Doris's death would hurt Daphne's business more than it helped it.

"I guess I'd better include myself," I said, adding my own name to the bottom.

"But we know *you* didn't kill Doris," Lucille protested.

"You know that and I know that, but I'm trying to look at the case objectively."

Since Meghan had an alibi, I went ahead and crossed out her name. I also made a note of the big question marks in the case that seemed important.

*Mysterious gas leak call*

*Stolen hat*

"I think we need to consider who else was competing that day," I mused as I took in everything we knew so far. "With Crumpet out of the running, Mr. Bittles won best in breed, but that might not have been the way the killer saw things going."

"You *really* think someone would commit murder over a silly dog competition?" Lucille asked.

"I don't know." Most of the proceeds went to charity, but I knew the grand prize was five thousand dollars. People had certainly killed for less.

I shook my head and let out a long breath through my nose. "We have to be missing something," I murmured. "This feels bigger than a dog show."

"Agreed," said Philip. "This was a crime of passion."

"Most murders are about sex, money, or revenge," I said as I started to pace. "Those high-waisted pleated khakis Doris wore might appeal to some, but I think we can probably take sex off the table."

Philip looked as though he'd swallowed a frog. I glanced at Aunt Lucille and snickered.

"Knowing Doris's personality, revenge seems most likely, but what could be bad enough that it would drive someone to murder?"

"You wrote down that the woman Maria might inherit Doris's money," Lucille offered. "Maybe she was after the inheritance?"

"Maybe," I said. "Her son was Doris's only living relative."

"There's nothing stronger than the love for a child," said Philip. "People will go to extraordinary lengths to give their children a better life."

I nodded. Maria had seemed completely devoted to her

son, and as the sole provider, it was probably difficult to give him the care he needed while working full time.

"Maria just doesn't strike me as a murderer," I said, scratching the back of my head.

"I know you liked her, dear, but that doesn't mean she didn't do it."

"I know, but —"

Just then, a gust of cold air shot through the room, and the door to the suite slammed shut. Goosebumps sprang up all over my arms, and I instinctively went to open the door. But when I tried to turn the tarnished brass knob, it wouldn't budge. The door was stuck.

Thinking the draft must be to blame, I went to close the windows. But before I'd even reached them, the windows slammed down — causing a few of the panes to shatter.

I jumped as a feeling like static electricity crackled over my skin, raising the hairs on my arms and along the back of my neck.

"Roy?" I called, staring up at the ceiling as if his ghost might suddenly materialize.

Another draft blew through the room, rustling the sheets that still covered the furniture. The fabric rippled in the lingering breeze, throwing shadows over the floor. That electric feeling in the air intensified.

"He's here," said Lucille, glancing to one side. I wasn't sure what she saw, but she looked simultaneously spooked and annoyed.

"I fink maybe you should go, miss," said Philip uneasily.

"This is *my* hotel!" I cried. No spirit was going to run me off.

I jumped at the sound of breaking glass, and when I turned, I saw that the mirror over the vanity had shattered.

"Roy," I growled, my irritation getting the better of me. "Stop — breaking things — in my — hotel!"

Another round of cracks drew my attention, and I looked up in time to see a hundred hairline cracks spreading across the plaster ceiling.

A huge chunk of plaster fell through the air, and I jumped out of the way just in time. It landed with a thud and broke apart exactly where I'd just been standing.

Looking up, I saw a spiderweb of cracks spreading from the center of the room. More pieces of plaster were breaking off, falling from the ceiling at random. I covered my head and ran for the door, which opened on the first try. A feeling like icy water shot down my spine, and I knew that Roy had just blazed right through me.

I let out a growl and stormed down the hallway — straight toward the haunted birdcage elevator. The crackling plaster seemed to follow, and I winced as a chunk landed on my head. "Roy!"

"Don't yell at him, dear!" Aunt Lucille called. "We don't want to get on his bad side!"

"I have to agree with Mistress Lucille," Philip added hastily, trailing after me down the hall.

"That's where you're wrong," I growled as Desmond streaked past me. The lights in the sconces were starting to flicker like some low-budget haunted house. "It's *him* that doesn't want to get on *my* bad side."

As soon as the words left my mouth, I got a sudden stroke of inspiration. Rusty the elevator whisperer had said that Roy tended to act up whenever there was an overflowing toilet or leaky faucet to be fixed.

Either he just had that much pride in his hotel, or he was a bit of a control freak. Whichever it was, I had a feeling my plan might work.

A small closet lay to my left. I ripped open the door and tugged a thin cord to turn on the single bulb hanging from the ceiling. An old mop was propped in one corner of the closet, and an industrial-sized plunger sat in another. A few rusted tools were scattered about, half-covered in cobwebs. A huge monkey wrench lay on the floor behind a boiler, and I grabbed it in both hands.

"You don't want me to get a contractor involved?" I bellowed at the aether, not caring that I was acting like a crazy person. "Then I'll do the renovations myself!"

Gripping the monkey wrench in both hands, I slammed the end of it into the wall. It made a slight dent through the peeling wallpaper, and I swung again.

This time, I knocked loose some plaster and sent a pocket of white dust issuing down the wall.

"Caroline!" exclaimed Lucille.

Philip looked as though he might faint, but I ignored them both as I continued to beat at the wall. After a few good swings, my shoulder ached, but it was strangely satisfying to watch as I knocked chunks of plaster loose.

In that moment, it did occur to me that it was a bit eccentric to be causing damage to my own property. But Roy's antics weren't the innocent hijinks of a bored ghost. Roy was out of control.

To my relief, the cracks in the ceiling stopped spreading, and I felt the charge in the air abate. The hall lights stopped flickering, and I sensed that Roy was gone. Well, maybe he wasn't *gone* gone, but he'd at least toned down the ghostly theatrics.

"There," I panted, lowering the monkey wrench.

"Well done, darling!" said Aunt Lucille, looking shaken but impressed.

I shrugged. "You just have to be willing to set firm boundaries."

I was new to this whole ghost-whisperer thing, but hey — it seemed to have worked.

Silently lamenting the damage Roy and I had caused, I trudged back to the closet and tossed the monkey wrench down where I'd found it. I lingered for a moment in the dim, cramped closet, which smelled like turpentine and mildew. Across from the door were several hooks screwed into a board, with the initials REW etched into the wood.

I turned to find Philip standing in the doorway behind me, and my heart gave an involuntary leap. I was *never* going to get used to this kid. "Was this . . ."

"Yes, ma'am." Philip swallowed and glanced around nervously. "This 'ere was Mr. Wilkerson's broom cupboard."

"Did he live at the hotel?"

Philip shook his head. "He lived in an outbuilding behind the 'otel, but that was torn down many years ago."

"Right." I swallowed to wet my parched throat and ran a finger over the letters REW, which appeared to have been scratched into the wood with the tip of a nail. My gaze drifted to the left across the unfinished lath walls, and the corner of something caught my eye on the other side of a warped two-by-four.

There, tucked behind the board, was a tiny black-and-white photograph. The edges were crumbled and ripped in a few places, probably from being handled.

Carefully, I gripped the photo and eased it out one

millimeter at a time to avoid causing more damage. As I did, I got that feeling of icy-cold water shooting down my spine and knew Roy was standing practically on top of me.

Swallowing down my discomfort, I turned to look at Philip. His expression was unreadable as he stared at me, and I glanced back down at the photograph.

It showed a little boy dressed in a sailor's outfit, high socks, and leather shoes. He couldn't have been more than three years old. His chubby legs dangled over the bench he was sitting on, and he held his hands clasped in front of him.

I turned over the photo and stared down at the faded cursive handwriting on the back: *Charles — Age 3.*

"Who was Charles?" I asked, looking up at Philip.

The bellboy swallowed but wouldn't meet my gaze, and my mind flashed to all sorts of possibilities. But there was something about that loopy handwriting. I knew I'd seen it before.

*The letters.* Whoever had written Roy those letters had written on the back of this photograph. Thinking back to what the author of the love notes had said, something clicked into place.

"Charles was Roy's son," I said aloud.

"What?" Aunt Lucille crowded past Philip into the small closet and stared down at the boy in the photo. "How can you be sure?"

"The handwriting is the same as the letters," I said, watching the bellboy's face. "This boy . . ." I pointed at the photograph. "He was Roy's love child."

Philip cleared his throat and looked down at his shoes.

I knew he didn't want to say anything out of some sense of loyalty to Roy, but he wouldn't lie to me.

"Is that why Roy was murdered?" I asked, my mind racing to connect the dots. "Did this boy's mother push Roy down the elevator shaft so that no one would ever find out?"

"It's more complicated than that," said Philip in a scratchy voice. "Mistress Cecille was just scared —" He broke off, and a look of horror came over him.

"Mistress Cecille?" I repeated.

I recognized that name. Where had I seen it before?

Then I thought back to the day I'd asked Jinx to come out to deal with Roy. He'd knocked a framed photograph off the wall — a photo of Ernest and Cecille Bellwether.

"Cecille *Bellwether*?" I said. "As in the hotel owner's *wife*?"

Philip grimaced, clearly upset that he'd revealed his former mistress's indiscretion.

I raised my eyebrows. "Philip — *spill*."

"I beg your pardon, miss?"

"Tell me what happened, and don't leave anything out."

Philip sighed, a pained expression rumpling his otherwise smooth, youthful face. "I swore to Mr. Wilkerson and Mistress Cecille that I would take it to my grave."

"And you did," I said, gesturing at his ghostly form. "You kept your word, Philip. And now as the new mistress of The Mountain Shadow Grand, I demand that you fill in the details."

Philip still appeared reluctant, so I started going through everything I already knew. "Roy and Cecille were having an affair. Cecille was worried that her husband — her much older, *rich* husband — would find out, so she tried to break things off. But when Roy found out Cecille was pregnant, he wouldn't leave her alone. Does that sound about right?"

"That's about the long and short of it, ma'am."

I nodded, satisfied that I'd connected the dots. "Roy wanted a part in his son's life. As the child grew older, Cecille would leave photos for Roy to try to satisfy his need to know the boy. But the pictures weren't enough. Am I on the right track?"

"It's uncanny, miss," said Philip miserably.

"Roy finally got fed up and threatened to tell Cecille's husband about the affair if she didn't let him see his son. Cecille was worried that Charles wouldn't inherit the Bellwether fortune if Ernest learned his son was illegitimate. Cecille and Roy argued . . . She panicked and pushed him down the elevator shaft."

"I don't fink she meant to kill him, miss!" Philip cried.

"You didn't hear Roy moaning," I guessed. "She ran to get you, because you already knew about the affair. She regretted what she'd done and wanted you to help get Roy out of the elevator shaft, but there was nothing you could do for him."

"No, ma'am." Philip's voice was slightly stuffy, and his eyes looked red around the edges.

Then it hit me. If Philip had known about the affair, he probably felt as though he were partly to blame for Roy's death. That was why he defended the crotchety old handyman. Philip still carried that guilt.

"There was nothing you could have done," I said in a low voice.

Philip sniffed and swiped hurriedly under his eyes. "I knew it wouldn't end well, miss. I should've —"

"What could you have done?" I asked, shaking my head. "Roy wouldn't have broken things off, and Cecille probably would have fired you."

He nodded.

"Roy told you not to tell anyone, didn't he? That's why there's the story of him falling down the elevator shaft. He didn't want to incriminate the mother of his child."

Philip sniffed and mopped under his eyes with the sleeve of his uniform. "Mr. Wilkerson said his greatest regret was that his son would never know who his real father was."

I blinked. "That's it."

"What's —"

"*That's* Roy's unfinished business!" I could only imagine how great a pain it was to father a child you could never have a relationship with. I turned to Aunt Lucille. "You think it's possible his son is still alive?"

"I suppose it's possible, darling, but . . ."

Ticking off decades on my fingers, I did some quick math. "If he was born in the early- to mid-thirties, that would make him about ninety."

Maybe if I could track down Roy's son . . .

I dismissed the idea as soon as it had formed. If the son was still alive, I couldn't blow up a ninety-something-year-old man's life by telling him that the father he'd grown up with wasn't his biological dad. I'd have to think of some other way to put Roy's spirit to rest.

"Maybe if Roy could just *see* his son one last time," I mused. I wouldn't have to tell him about his parentage — just get him to the hotel.

"Oh, what a great idea!" exclaimed Lucille, clapping her hands together.

The single overhead bulb flickered again, but I didn't detect any menacing energy.

I lifted my eyebrows, feeling a faint tingle of hope.

"A father-son reunion." Two fat tears sprang to Aunt Lucille's eyes. "Oh, it's just so *wonderful*."

"We don't even know if he's still alive," I reminded her.

"Oh, he *must* be. I'm sure of it! Fate demands it!" Aunt Lucille was melting into a full-on puddle of emotion, but I was thinking of practical matters.

I sure hoped that Roy's love child was still alive. The future of my hotel depended on it.

CHAPTER EIGHTEEN

Cecille and Roy's son, Charles Bellwether II, was very much alive. He was residing at a retirement home down in Colorado Springs, and I wasn't proud of the way I'd found him.

Charles's daughter Penelope was in the phonebook. I'd called and told her I was restoring the hotel that Charles's grandfather had built and that I was putting together a historical record of The Grand. When I'd said that I was hoping to interview her father, she'd been all too happy to put me in touch with him.

Bending Pine Estates was much nicer than the "estates" where Aunt Lucille had spent her final years. Despite the hotel shuttering its doors sometime in the eighties, it seemed the Bellwethers had managed to hold on to at least some of their considerable fortune.

A smiling woman greeted me at the front office, and I recited the same story I'd told Penelope. It was a little scary how easily the lie rolled off my tongue, but I desperately needed to get Charles to the hotel so that Roy's spirit could finally rest.

The woman led me to Charles's suite, and I stood awkwardly outside the door, trying to think of what I would say. Part of me hoped that he wouldn't answer, but within a few seconds of me knocking, I heard slow, shuffling footsteps on the other side of the door.

It opened a crack, and a man's face appeared. Charles Bellwether II was stooped and gray. His eyes were watery and a bit tired-looking, and he wore a gray Dartmouth sweatshirt with a pair of loose-fitting khakis.

Despite his casual attire, he oozed money and class. A thick ruby ring gleamed from one finger, and a gold Rolex flashed on his wrist. And yet behind the rectangular glasses, I could see that he resembled Roy.

"Mr. Bellwether?"

"That's me." Charles's tone was brusk and businesslike, though he didn't seem annoyed by my visit.

I took a deep breath. "My name is Caroline McCrithers. I'm the new owner of The Mountain Shadow Grand. Your daughter Penelope told me where to find you. She said you might let me interview you about what you remember of the old hotel?"

"McCrithers, you say?" Charles blinked a few times and turned his head to the side to reveal a flesh-colored hearing aid.

I swallowed. How much of that had he heard?

"Yes, sir," I choked. "I'm the new owner of The Mountain Shadow Grand." This time, I raised my voice ever so slightly and tried to enunciate each word.

"Oh, you are?" Charles seemed to brighten at once, and a boyish spark of excitement lit those watery eyes.

"Yes." I hesitated. I was starting to worry that Charles *would* want to talk to me, in which case I'd have to decide whether or not to tell him that Roy was his biological father. "I-I was hoping I could ask you a few questions about the hotel. What it was like growing up there in the thirties and forties..."

"Oh." Charles lifted a pair of bushy eyebrows, looking surprised but not unhappy. "Well, I don't know how much help I'll be." He chuckled and tapped a wrinkled finger to his temple. "Memory's not what it used to be. But I can tell you what I remember."

Fighting the guilty knot in my stomach, I forced a grin. "That'd be great."

"Come in, come in," Charles said with a wave. "Pardon the mess. I'm not used to having many visitors."

I smiled uncomfortably and stepped inside the spacious suite, which was made to seem even more airy with tall ceilings and light-ivory walls. Modern cream fixtures hung from the ceiling, making the place look more like a swanky hotel room than a unit in a sad retirement home. Most of the furniture was the same tasteful dark wood, but there were a few more old-fashioned pieces that had probably come from Charles's own home.

Either Charles didn't understand the meaning of the word "mess," or his definition was just different from most people's. Every inch of the one-bedroom apartment was immaculately clean, and there wasn't a dish out of place in the kitchen. A newspaper was spread across the small dining-room table with a cup of coffee, a pill organizer, and a half-eaten Danish beside it.

"I'm sorry for interrupting your breakfast," I said.

"Don't be," said Charles with a wave of his hand.

"When you get to be my age, you tend to break your fast at a more leisurely pace than most. I'm not as sharp as I used to be, I'm afraid, and sometimes it takes me 'til noon to get through the morning paper." He chuckled and gestured for me to have a seat. "You drink coffee?"

"Yes, sir."

"How do you take it?"

"Cream and sugar, please."

"I don't take cream myself," he said, a self-conscious lilt to his voice. "Real cream spoils if you keep it too long. I only have the powdered kind."

"That's fine," I said quickly.

Charles nodded and shuffled into the kitchen, his hands shaking slightly as he carried a steaming cup of coffee in one hand and a canister of Coffee-Mate in the other. I got the impression that he wasn't used to having guests, which only made me feel worse about showing up under false pretenses.

I stirred in the Coffee-Mate as he refilled his own cup before lowering himself stiffly into a chair. Maybe I really could have some kind of historical placard made for the hotel lobby. Then at least I wouldn't be lying to Charles about the reason for my visit.

"So," he said, still in that businesslike manner that belied the boyish gleam in his eye. "What do you want to know?"

"Well, I . . ." I trailed off self-consciously, digging into my oversized handbag and pulling out my trusty Filofax. If I was going to turn my cover story into the real thing, I'd need to take some actual notes. "I was wondering if you could tell me what it was like growing up at The Grand."

"Oh, well . . ." Charles trailed off, a wistful smile

tugging at his lips. "I know it was a lot of work for my father — and it took a toll on Mother — but I remember those years quite fondly. It was a hopping place, you know. We had guests from all over the world . . . movie stars, oil men, titans of industry. Of course, I didn't care about all of that. I was always just sliding down the banister, looking to see what sort of trouble I could get up to."

I cracked a smirk at the thought of the old man in front of me sliding down the banister. "And did you get into a lot of trouble?"

"Oh, yes!" Charles chuckled. "I was always stealing those little chocolate mints for guests' pillows that the maids had in their carts. Masterson, the hotel manager at the time, used to think the *maids* were eating them. I think one of them must have told on me, and then Mr. Masterson told my mother." He shook his head. "Ol' Cook used to keep me in chocolate cake. She could make the most scrumptious German chocolate cake — but only if she was in the mood. If Cook was angry about something, well, you'd know about it. The food would come out just *terrible!*"

I smiled. "So you spent a lot of time at the hotel, then."

"I did. Well, we all did — my mother and father and I. Actually, my mother and I were there more often than my father. He was always away on business for one of his other ventures. Back when we had ol' Masterson, The Grand practically ran itself."

"So what happened?" I asked, hoping I wasn't being indelicate. It didn't make sense to me how the hotel had gone from being such a destination to having to shut its doors.

"Well, eventually, my father wanted to retire. I was

working for NASA at the time, so my younger brother took over the hotel. Things took a turn for the worse, and eventually we were forced to sell."

"I'll bet you were sad to see it go."

"Oh, yes. Yes, I was. But you know, every dog has its day, and The Grand's day was passed."

I sighed. "Well, I hope it's got a few good days left in it."

"I hope so, too."

We fell into a comfortable silence, and I chewed on my bottom lip. I didn't want to tell Charles about Roy. It just didn't seem right. But maybe I could still help Roy pass on. "Mr. Bellwether —"

"Call me Charles."

"Charles . . ." I hesitated, unsure if he'd even be allowed. "Would you . . . like to come see the hotel? For old time's sake?"

"Oh." Charles sounded taken aback, and for a moment, I was certain he was going to decline. But then that boyish twinkle returned to his eye, and all his ninety years seemed to melt away. "Why, I'd love to."

---

CHARLES DIDN'T DRIVE ANYMORE, which was one reason he'd moved to the retirement home. I'd been worried the nice lady at the office would try to stop us on the way out in case I was trying to kidnap the heir to the Bellwether fortune, but no one paid us any mind as we left the premises.

It was a short drive up the pass to Mountain Shadow. Charles alternated between ranting about the range of electric vehicles and regaling me with stories of his childhood at the hotel. He remembered Philip as an energetic young bellhop and something of an older brother figure. Apparently, Philip used to give him rides on the bell carts while the adults were dining in the grand ballroom — something that drove the hotel manager up the wall.

Based on the stories Charles shared, it sounded as though he'd led a lonely childhood, though he didn't seem to feel he'd been deprived. His mother was a busy socialite who spent the majority of her evenings entertaining wealthy guests. His father had been, by his account, cool to his wife and indifferent to Charles. From the way he made it sound, Charles was basically raised by hotel staff.

He fell silent as we pulled up in front of The Grand, and I watched as he surveyed the crumbling brick facade with a mixture of sadness and longing. I went around to help him out of the Pinto, and the two of us walked slowly up the concrete path toward the enormous front door.

The scent of mildew and stale cigarette smoke greeted me as I walked in, and Charles stood frozen in the doorway. I wiped my sweaty hands on my jeans and tucked them behind my back, unsure what to say.

I'd swept most of the dead leaves off the floor, but now you could see all the scuffs and scratches. The ceiling was cracked, the carpet runners were stained, and the furniture was all destined for the dumpster.

"It needs a lot of work," I said self-consciously, my voice echoing in the cavernous space.

"It's just how I remember it," said Charles.

I smiled. He didn't seem saddened by the cobwebs and dust. If anything, he looked delighted to discover that the hotel was practically unchanged.

"I want to keep as much of the original architecture as possible," I told him. "Most of the renovations down here will be cosmetic. The electrical's already been updated on the first three floors. I just need someone to come work on the elevator."

"You try Rusty Coleman?"

I nodded.

"He's the best. He worked on the elevator back in the seventies, and before him, it was his father."

"We've met," I said, unable to keep the edge of exasperation out of my voice. Rusty was the one who'd first told me the hotel was haunted. I hadn't believed him then, but I sure believed him now. "Can I . . . ask you something?"

"Shoot."

I sucked in a breath. *Here we go . . .*

"Do you remember a handyman who used to work here back in the thirties?"

"There was Roy Wilkerson," said Charles without missing a beat. "He died on the property when I was, oh, maybe four or five. Mr. Wilkerson wasn't like the bellboys or the maids — here one week, gone the next. He was sort of a permanent fixture here — lived on-site, as a matter of fact. He looked out for me when I was a boy."

I nodded, worrying my bottom lip between my teeth. I didn't know how to broach the topic of his mother's affair with Roy, and I still wasn't certain I should. Charles *appeared* to be in good health, but he was so old. I didn't want to kill the poor guy! And how would I even explain to him how I knew?

"Why do you ask?"

"No reason."

"No?" Charles turned to look at me, canting his head. "Because usually when someone asks about a man that history forgot, there's a reason."

I opened my mouth, but no words came out.

Charles made a noncommittal noise in his throat. "In my experience, when people ask me about Roy Wilkerson, what they're *really* asking about is how he died."

I raised my eyebrows. "H-how did he die?"

"Well, now that's a funny question," said Charles. "No, not funny. It's damn sad, is what it is. Mr. Wilkerson was found dead in the elevator shaft. Some say he fell . . . some say he jumped . . . a few claim he was pushed."

"Pushed?" I repeated, deciding to play dumb to see where this would lead. "Wh-who do you think pushed him?"

Charles stared at me for a long moment, and I could have sworn he was calling my bluff. Simple-minded people didn't end up working for NASA. Charles was still sharp as a tack, and he knew that I'd already heard the story.

"Now, there's no point in digging up old ghosts."

"Mr. Bellwether —"

"Charles, please."

"Charles." I let out a heavy breath. "This is going to sound strange, but the reason I asked you about Roy Wilkerson is because . . . there's a sort of *presence* at the hotel. Some people say it's his ghost."

"I'll bet they do." Charles smiled sadly. "It's funny how those types of rumors get started."

And even though I knew I was pushing my luck, I couldn't seem to stop the next words that tumbled out of my mouth. "Some people say that he and your mother were . . . that they may have had an affair."

Charles didn't say a word. He didn't even blink. For one desperate moment, I thought he might storm out in a fury and demand that I drive him back to the Springs.

Instead he asked, "Who told you that?"

I swallowed. I couldn't very well tell him that the ghost of Philip the bellhop had helped me figure it out. But since I'd already lured Charles to the hotel under false pretenses, I couldn't stomach lying to him anymore.

"My great-aunt mentioned something about it. She was often at the hotel in those days."

Charles made an agitated harrumphing noise and adjusted his grip on his cane. "Now, listen here, young lady. My mother was a class act. Never met a stranger, that woman. She was always so gracious. Now, I know my father wasn't around much, and I'm sure that was damn hard for her. He wasn't always faithful, and I don't think she was either. But I don't want that making it into your little history thing, you got it? Things were different back then."

I nodded emphatically. I'd forgotten that I'd actually been planning to erect some kind of historical placard, and it took me a moment to remember what Charles was talking about.

He sighed. "Mr. Wilkerson was always kind to me, and he was not the friendly sort. As I got older, I started to suspect that the man who raised me was not my biological father. But Ernest Bellwether gave me his name, fed me, clothed me . . . so I kept my mouth shut."

I swallowed. It sounded as though I didn't need to

drop the bomb on Charles at all. He'd always known the truth.

"And you never asked your mother about it?"

"I figured if she wanted me to know, then she would have told me," said Charles matter-of-factly. "If she sought the company of other men now and again, that was her business. All that matters was that she took care of me, and she stood by my father 'til the day he died."

I nodded.

Charles sighed and shook his head. "As for Mr. Wilkerson, I don't know how or why he died, but I was sure sorry to see him go. He was kind to me as a boy, and I never forgot that."

I swallowed down the hard lump in my throat just as I got the familiar feeling of icy-cold water shooting down my spine.

I caught a flicker of movement out of the corner of my eye, and when I turned toward the elevator, I saw Roy standing there in his shabby overalls, a large metal bucket in hand. He was staring at his son with a look I'd never seen from the miserable old ghost. Silvery tears glistened in his eyes.

Charles followed my gaze to the elevator and squinted. His face went entirely slack, and for a split second I worried he was having a stroke.

He stood and stared at the spot where Roy's ghost was. Then he pulled a sad smile and turned back to me. "It was real nice of you to bring me back here. I'm sure glad I got to see the old girl one more time before I go."

## CHAPTER NINETEEN

After dropping Charles back home at Bending Pine Estates, I parked the Pinto in Gran's driveway and walked the three blocks to The Pampered Pooch. Although the dog wash half of the store was blocked off by yellow police tape, the pet-supply shop was packed with dogs and their handlers, who were purchasing treats and supplies for the journey home.

A lady I assumed was the owner stood behind the counter ringing up customers. Katy was a fit-looking woman in her midsixties dressed in hiking shorts and sandals. Her straight salt-and-pepper hair was cut in a blunt bob, and she wore a pair of small rimless rectangular glasses over astute gray eyes. Her skin was that deep, wrinkly tan of people who spent a lot of time outdoors.

I wasn't exactly sure how to approach her and ask my questions, so I stood back and strained my ears for snippets of conversation as I browsed the wall of pet harnesses.

"They won't tell me when I can reopen the dog wash," she complained. "Apparently it's still a crime scene. But this is my busiest weekend of the year."

I could hear the strain of business-owner woes in her voice, though she didn't seem all that broken up about the fact that Doris had been murdered at her store.

"Such a shame," another woman tutted. "Another murder? In Mountain Shadow?"

My skin itched uncomfortably as the whisper of gossip buzzed around me. If any of the people in here had been following the case closely, they might remember that I was supposed to have been arrested earlier that day.

Figuring I'd better question Katy and get the heck out of there, I selected the harness I needed and went up to the counter to check out.

"Will that be all for you, hon?" Katy asked, not looking me in the eye as she rang up my purchase.

"Yep, that's it."

"Eighteen seventy-nine."

I took my time opening my wallet and easing out a twenty-dollar bill. "It's too bad about Doris Ashcroft," I said. "I heard she died over there." I jerked my head at the dog wash.

"Yes. It sure is," she said with a bitter shake of her head. "I can't help but think that if I'd just *been* here . . ."

"Was the dog wash closed that day?" I asked, deciding I'd learn more if I played dumb.

Katy nodded. "I had a whole crowd in here, but I had to close up shop and run home around lunchtime. Doris was *beside* herself. I guess Crumpet had been vomiting all morning, poor thing. He was just a mess. I told Doris to go ahead and finish bathing him and then lock up when she was through. I'd gotten a call from someone saying they smelled gas outside my house."

I raised my eyebrows. Something Katy had said didn't fit with what Jeffrey Hanover had told me. "Was Mr. Bittles's owner in here the same time as Doris and Crumpet?"

Katy frowned, thinking hard. "He might have been. I don't know. It was a hectic morning. And then that phone call . . . There *was* no gas leak, if you can believe it. I think maybe someone was pranking me." Katy shook her head. "Heck of a time for it. If I'd been here, I can't help but think . . ."

She bit her lip, and I realized that what I was picking up from Katy wasn't a lack of remorse. She felt guilty that she hadn't been at the shop to stop the killer. It hadn't even *occurred* to her that the murderer might have placed the call to get her out of the way.

"Do you know who was pranking you?" I asked.

"No," Katy sighed. "I thought it might have been a volunteer from the dog show needing something from me. That's the only reason I answered."

"They called the shop phone?"

"No. My cell."

I frowned. That meant the caller couldn't have just looked her up in the yellow pages. The killer had to know Katy personally. "What did the caller sound like?"

"I don't know, honey. It was a female voice, but there was too much background noise to hear her all that well."

I nodded, turning this new information over in my head. As Katy slid my purchase into a paper bag and handed me a receipt, I realized that her little shop dog hadn't come running up to the door to bark at me when I walked in.

"Where's the dog that was in here the other day?" I asked.

"Oh? Snickerdoodle?" Katy's mouth drooped. "I'm keeping him home right now. Ever since Doris was . . . well, you know . . . he's been a little on-edge with customers."

"Poor boy," I said. "I'll bet he's pretty shaken up."

"He witnessed a murder," said Katy sharply. "He and Crumpet are the only ones who know what truly happened."

I nodded. If only dogs could talk.

"Anyway, I'm having my dog sitter look in on him today. Hopefully, with a little R&R, he'll be back to his old friendly self."

I smiled in what I hoped was a reassuring way, but then something clicked in my brain. Katy hadn't said "*a* dog sitter." She'd said "*my* dog sitter," implying that she'd used this person before.

"Say . . . does your dog sitter have a card?" I asked. "I'm new in town, and I could really use someone to look in on my pup when I go camping on the weekends."

Katy's eyebrows knitted together, and those sharp gray eyes flashed suspiciously. "Your dog doesn't like to go camping with you?"

I swallowed, heart thumping. Was that something dogs liked to do? I'd never owned a dog — never been camping — and the fib had just tumbled out of my mouth. "He's, uh . . . afraid of the dark," I said quickly.

Katy raised an eyebrow but didn't question me further. "I think I do have some of her cards," she mused, rifling around behind the counter. She pulled out a couple of flyers for Dog Days and set them aside before producing a stack of business cards. "Ah. Here we go."

She handed over a crisp white card, which had a name, phone number, and a border of little blue paw prints. When I saw the name, my heart beat faster, and my mouth went very dry.

"Thanks," I said, stuffing the card into my purse and grabbing the paper sack. I backed toward the exit, my mind racing. "I'll . . . give her a call."

---

I WASN'T sure what had gotten into me since moving to Mountain Shadow. Breaking into someone's house was a new experience. Breaking and entering twice in one week . . . well, it was the start of a very bad habit. B&E was also much more difficult to pull off in the middle of the day.

I knew I needed a cover if I hoped to get back inside Doris's house, which was why I'd spent the last twenty minutes wrestling Desmond into the harness I'd bought. My arms were covered in angry red scratches, and, if looks could kill, I'd be spending the rest of eternity with only Aunt Lucille, Philip, and Roy Wilkerson for company.

Desmond was already irritated that I'd stuffed him in a pet crate at the dog show. Squeezing him into a harness so he could walk on a leash was an indignity he would not tolerate.

In truth, walking a dog around Doris's neighborhood would have attracted a lot less attention. But Snowball was with Gran at Dog Days, and walking a cat was such a bizarre thing to do that no one could *possibly* think I was up to no good.

Smiling and waving at Doris's next-door neighbor, I lingered in the shade of a locust tree as I waited for the man to finish weed-whacking his fence line. When the neighbor disappeared into his garage, I made a break for Doris's backyard.

Using the same point of entry I'd exploited on my first visit, I tossed a very angry Desmond through the laundry-room window before scrabbling over the sill after him.

When I emerged in Doris's laundry room, Desmond was glaring daggers at me. I cautiously unhooked the leash from his harness, and Desmond flounced off to explore the house.

This time, I didn't bother poking around. I headed straight for Doris's study and yanked the photo album off the shelf. I was working off a crazy hunch, and I needed confirmation before I took my theory any further.

Holding the album in my trembling hands, I tried not to think about the last time I'd been there. The album hadn't slid out on the shelf, right? That was impossible. And yet I couldn't quite shake the feeling that Doris's house had been trying to tell me something all along.

Starting at the beginning of the album, I was able to put together a picture of Doris's years at Druxton University — the college she'd attended. Apparently, she'd pledged ASA her freshman year and stuck with the sorority for her entire time at Druxton.

As I flipped back and forth between the photos, a familiar face caught my eye. It was the smiling young woman next to Doris.

In the photos from Doris's freshman year, the girl looked nervous and shy. In later photos, the blond had her arm around Doris and was grinning at the camera. I knew I'd seen that woman before, and when I flipped through the other pictures of the sorority, my heart pounded harder.

The blond woman was gone.

Chewing on my bottom lip, I closed the album and slid it back onto the shelf. I dug my phone out of my purse and searched for the university's directory.

I scrolled down until I found a link to the records department. It was a long shot, but it was the best lead I had.

Holding the phone to my ear, I waited breathlessly for someone to pick up.

"Hi," I said once somebody answered. "I'm calling about one of your former students. She would have graduated sometime between nineteen sixty-six and nineteen sixty-eight."

The college-aged receptionist told me they hadn't digitized student records spanning back that far. Apparently, she needed special permission to access the file room where those old records were kept.

I waited impatiently on hold as Desmond scratched at my leg, meowing loudly and swatting at my arm when I tried to ignore him.

"Ow, Des! What the —"

There was a crackle on the other end of the line. "Miss? Are you still there?"

"I'm still here," I said.

But just then I heard a door slam — followed by the

sound of heavy footsteps. I sucked in a breath and ended the call, rising to my feet.

Gathering Desmond into my arms, I tiptoed to the study door. Pushing it open, I stuck my head out and came face to face with Officer Will.

CHAPTER TWENTY

"Caroline!" Will sucked in a startled breath as all the color drained from his face. Surprise, confusion, disbelief, and anger flew across his face in quick succession. "You scared me. What are you *doing* here? This is an active crime scene."

"I was just . . . investigating."

"*Investigating?*" The color rose in Will's cheeks again, turning them an adorable shade of pink. If this was what he looked like when he was angry, I might have to let him stay mad at me. "That is not your job. I should arrest you for trespassing!"

"Should?" I squeaked in a hopeful tone. "Does that mean you aren't going to?"

Will breathed a frustrated sigh and dragged a hand through his hair. "I haven't decided yet."

"Anything I can do to sway you one way or the other?"

Will fixed me with a reproving look that sent all sorts of warm tingly feelings straight to my lower belly. "Why don't you start by telling me what you're doing here?"

"I told you!" I said, spreading my hands. "I'm investigating. I have a hunch, and I just need to follow it."

"No, you don't. That's *my* job."

I opened my mouth but then closed it again, not wanting to mention his less-than-stellar record of crime fighting. Will had only fake-arrested me, after all. I had to give credit where credit was due.

"What's your hunch?" he asked, sounding suddenly very tired.

"I can't tell you," I said. "I can't run around accusing people of murder without having all the facts."

"You mean the way you did with Jay Mathers's murder?"

Ugh. How rude to bring that up. "Live and learn," I said, jutting out my chin.

"What details did you need to confirm?" Will asked with a smirk. "Anything I can help you with?"

I considered for a moment. Will *did* have access to the medical examiner's report — something I'd never be able to get my hands on. "Maybe," I said. "Did the victim have bruising along her ribs from being drowned in the tub?"

Will frowned. "Yeah. Pretty nasty ones, too."

"And the bruising was way worse on her *right* side, correct?"

The little line between Will's brows deepened as he tried to remember. "I think so." He crossed his arms over his chest. "Why? What are you thinking?"

"I can't tell you," I said. "At least not yet."

There was still one piece of the puzzle that I needed to confirm.

"Well, get your cat out of here, will you? He's contaminating my crime scene."

I winced as I imagined Desmond's little black hairs lodging in every piece of upholstery and carpeting in this place. "Roger that."

"Don't let me catch you in here again," said Will. His voice was serious with the promise of trouble, but his eyes hinted at a *different* sort of trouble that made my stomach feel all funny.

I gave a little salute and slipped out of the study, fully aware of Will's eyes on me as I walked away. I put an extra shimmy in my stride, secretly delighting in our game of spy versus spy — or, in our case, cop versus murder suspect.

"Where do you think you're going?" he asked, stopping me halfway down the hall.

"I thought my cat was 'contaminating your crime scene.'"

Will arched a brow. "I can't let the neighbors see you prancing out of the victim's house. Half the town already thinks you had something to do with Doris's murder, and I could lose my job."

I crossed my arms. What was he suggesting?

"I know you didn't go through the front door," Will added. "You're gonna have to go back out the same way you came in."

Crap. Was he serious?

It was bad enough doing my acrobatics without an audience, but with Will watching, I very well might die of humiliation.

Pushing out a huff of air, I turned around and strode through the kitchen to get to the laundry room. Will followed a few paces behind, his tall frame filling the doorway between the laundry room and kitchen.

Feeling self-conscious, I opened the window and slowly lowered Desmond down. He hit the ground with a low *reeow* and sat back to wait for me.

Now for the embarrassing part . . .

Dangling one leg over the windowsill, I straddled the small opening. I ducked my head and then flattened my chest all the way to the sill.

Will snickered as I squeezed myself through the gap like ground sausage out of a tube. I fumbled gracelessly onto the chair below, nearly toppling it over in my haste to escape Will's amused gaze.

He didn't say a word as he shut the window behind me, and there was an audible *click* as he locked it. There went my secret entrance.

Desmond bared his teeth as I reattached the leash to his harness, but he didn't fight me. I smiled and waved as I passed Doris's neighbors, making my way toward the square.

Once we'd reached Main Street, I whipped out my phone and hit redial, praying I'd be able to reach the same person I'd been speaking with earlier.

Will's information supported my theory, but I still had questions that needed answers.

---

As it turned out, Alpha Sigma Alpha made it easy to track down its former members. When I called the chapter at Druxton University, the den mother put me in touch with a friend whose mother had been in the sorority in the years overlapping Doris's time there. I wasn't able to get ahold of the mother on such short notice, but when I pressed the daughter, she told me her mother usually had afternoon tea at the country club on Sundays.

Following my hunch, I drove down to Colorado Springs and pulled into the gated, tree-lined parking lot. I parked as far from the glossy Range Rovers and Mercedes as possible and lingered in the car, trying to come up with a plan.

I couldn't just walk into the club uninvited — not when the entrance to the dining area was guarded by a very bossy-looking maître d'. I had a feeling the club frowned on young ladies barging in during afternoon tea to harass their members, and I'd already had one brush with the law that day.

Thinking fast, I got out of the car and darted through a row of neatly trimmed bushes, skirting around the building to the very back of the club. The entrance to the kitchen was just beyond the dumpsters, which were hidden by a tasteful stone wall. I could hear voices and clanging drifting through the open door, and I held my breath as I approached the doorway.

At least four different staff members were clanking around in the kitchen, shouting instructions over the sizzle of the grill.

My heart pounded in my throat. If I ran in there and someone spotted me, would anyone buy that I'd wandered in by mistake? And if they didn't, what were the chances they'd just ask me to leave?

I didn't have any friends in the Colorado Springs PD, so I didn't think I'd be able to talk my way out of a trespassing charge. Still, I was so close to putting the final pieces of the puzzle together that I couldn't just walk away. Will might have believed in my innocence, but I needed to convince everyone else in Mountain Shadow if I had any chance of opening a successful business in town.

A few more burger patties hit the grill with a sizzle, and the line cook shouted something to a person I couldn't see. It was now or never.

Dashing through the door, I made my way around the perimeter of the kitchen. It smelled like charred meat and disinfectant, and the room was hazy with smoke.

I didn't stop to see if anyone had noticed me. I just kept walking with purpose in the direction of the dining room.

But as soon as I reached the swinging door that led out to the main area of the club, I realized there was absolutely no chance of blending in with the crowd.

Every single person in the dining room was dressed in what I would call Kate-Middleton-meets-the-Kentucky-Derby. Lampshade hats, fascinators, pastel blazers, and frilly blouses abounded as old ladies sipped tea and munched on cucumber sandwiches. Every garment looked as though the Easter bunny had thrown up all over it, and there I was without even my hideous Dalmatian hat!

I glanced down at my blue volunteer shirt and cut-off jean shorts. Maybe no one would notice?

But then the security-guard/maître d' sauntered by the kitchen, his hawklike gaze shooting over the tables, searching for anything that seemed out of place. Even if the ladies were too busy enjoying tea and scones to notice my attire, there was no *way* I was making it past that guy.

Just then, a waitress came flying toward the door I was hiding behind. I scrambled back, but there was nowhere to go besides back into the fray of the prep line.

The other workers were plating dishes. I was *so* busted.

But then the waitress pushed her way through the

door, calling into the back without so much as a glance at me. "Bill, can you bring the dessert cart out to table five?"

There was a grumble of assent from behind me, and the waitress closed the door.

Dessert cart? Hang on a minute . . .

Chancing a glance around the corner, I saw a large wheeled cart laden with cheesecake, tarts, chocolate cake, bread pudding, and at least three delectable items I didn't know the names of. The cart was covered in a crisp white tablecloth that nearly reached the floor.

Inspiration struck so violently fast that I didn't have time to question it. Glancing back at the prep line to be sure no one was watching, I dove for the cart, whipped up the tablecloth, and climbed onto the lower shelf.

I'd just managed to fluff out the tablecloth when the cart gave a lurch, and the delicate china plates above me clattered. Gripping one leg of the cart, I held my breath and crossed my fingers that the waiter wouldn't wonder why the desserts suddenly weighed a ton.

As we entered the dining room, I could see the silhouettes of people moving around through the thin polyester tablecloth and hear the rumble of polite chatter accompanied by the clink of spoons on china. The cart came to a sudden stop, and I heard the waiter demurely greet the people at the table before describing each dessert in rapid, mouth-watering detail.

I peered through a gap in the tablecloth, searching the table of older women behind the waiter's legs. They were all over the age of seventy, wearing such elaborate hats that I wouldn't have been surprised if they'd been lifted from Queen Elizabeth's personal collection.

Almost immediately, I spotted a woman who bore an

uncanny resemblance to the ASA daughter I'd tracked down online. Her honey-blond hair was cut short, but she had the same sharp brown eyes and beauty-queen smile as her forty-year-old daughter.

It had to be the woman I was looking for — the Alpha Sigma Alpha who'd gone to Druxton at the same time as Doris Ashcroft.

I waited for the server to move to the other side of the table before slinking out from under the cart and getting to my feet. The eyes of everyone seated nearby snapped on to me, but I ignored their confused stares and focused on my target. "Margaret?"

The old woman with the beauty-queen smile looked up, her heavily stenciled brows furrowing as she tried to place me.

"I'm Caroline," I said quickly, pulling out a chair and sliding up to the table as though we were old friends. I figured the staff wouldn't ask me to leave if they thought Margaret and I knew one another. "You were an Alpha Sigma Alpha at Druxton, weren't you?"

Margaret's confused look seemed to deepen. "Why, yes. Yes, I was . . . about a million years ago!"

The ladies around the table chuckled, all of them staring at me with polite curiosity and only a smidgen of judgement.

"I'm pledging ASA in the fall," I told her, hoping my twenty-nine-year-old face could still pass for a slightly dehydrated eighteen.

"Oh?" Margaret smiled politely, though I knew she was still wondering why I'd hijacked her tea.

"Yeah — me and my best friend Angie. Her mom and grandma were both Alpha Sigma Alphas. You were probably there about the same time as her grandma," I added, almost as an afterthought.

"If she was there from sixty-five to sixty-nine, then maybe she and I knew one another. What's her grandmother's name?"

I swallowed. I honestly hadn't expected my ruse to get me this far, and now I was drawing a blank. "Uh . . . Mary," I said. There was always an old lady named Mary, right?

"Mary McCubbins or Mary McKay?"

I squinted. What was this woman? Ex-CIA? "You know, I don't remember her grandmother's maiden name." I waggled my eyebrows conspiratorially. "She said there was *quite* the scandal at ASA back when she was at the house."

Margaret leaned forward and grinned like a minx — a look made all the more hilarious by her giant hat and white lace gloves. "You'd have to be more specific, dear. I don't mean to talk out of school, but we Alpha Sigmas *certainly* knew how to have fun."

The other ladies at the table giggled, and my heart sped up. This seemed like my big chance to ask Margaret anything I wanted to know. "Did you know Doris Frank?" I asked.

Doris's maiden name was one helpful piece of trivia I'd gleaned from snooping through her files.

"Oh, yes!" said Margaret. "I knew Doris and the girls she ran around with. Even —" She broke off. "Well, Doris and Selma were two years ahead of me, and by the time I came to Druxton, Selma was already on her way out."

I frowned, heart pounding against my ribs. "On her way out?"

"Well, yes. She was kicked out when —" Margaret broke off and waved a hand. "Well, I shouldn't say. Let sleeping dogs lie, as they say."

"No, I want to know," I said, scooting my chair closer to the table.

"I shouldn't gossip," Margaret said in a languid drawl — the kind that said I wouldn't have to twist her arm very hard to get her to spill her secrets.

"It's just us girls," I said encouragingly, propping my chin on my hand. "One Alpha Sig to another."

Margaret lifted her eyebrows, glanced at her tea companions, and leaned forward excitedly. "Well, as it turned out, Selma was going with Gary Grossman — this Beta Sigma on the football team. Gary was *quite* the catch. All of us girls were jealous when she sauntered into the stands for the homecoming game wearing his letterman sweater."

I raised my eyebrows. If this was Margaret's idea of a scandal, it wasn't going to get me anywhere.

"Anyway, young couples break up, as they do. And when winter formal rolled around, Gary Grossman had another girl on his arm. Well, as you can imagine, Selma was just heartbroken." Margaret waved this away. "We all went home for holiday break, and when we returned, Selma was gone."

"She left?"

Margaret nodded. "Packed her bags and left the university."

"W-where did she go?"

"I have no idea. But when I asked around, I learned that Selma had been asked to leave the university." Margaret lowered her voice. "Apparently, the final touchdown of the homecoming game was not *all* Gary Grossman scored that night."

The other ladies all chuckled, gloved hands over their mouths. It gave me flashbacks to every Regency-era mean-girl scene ever.

"She was in the family way," Margaret whispered.

My jaw must have hit the table. I'd expected to learn that Selma had been expelled for cheating on her midterms or underaged drinking — not for being pregnant.

But then I thought back to the online stalking I'd done on the historical society committee after my failed pitch. Something didn't fit.

"But . . . Selma doesn't have any children," I said, momentarily forgetting that I wasn't supposed to know who Selma Lewis was.

Margaret appeared not to have noticed my slip. "Well, Gary Grossman didn't *marry* her," she said, shaking her head and tsking at my apparent naivety. "Gary was the starting quarterback. He wasn't about to give all that up for *Selma*." She said Selma's name as if she were some kind of garden pest that Margaret had found burrowing into her prized zucchini. "No. In those days, girls did the respectable thing."

"Which was . . ."

"They went away to have the baby! Made up some story about a sick aunt in another state so they could *gestate* out of the public eye in a home for unwed mothers."

My stomach curdled at Margaret's blunt explanation, but I forced my expression to remain neutral. "So . . . what happened to Selma?"

Margaret arched an imperious eyebrow. "I haven't the faintest idea. We haven't kept in touch." Margaret wiped her mouth daintily on a cloth napkin and tucked it neatly back into her lap. "If she was smart, she would have got her figure back as soon as possible and found a nice husband to settle down with."

CHAPTER TWENTY-ONE

The final round was in full swing at Dog Days by the time I got back to town. I no longer had my hideous dog hat, so I'd stopped at Gran's house to borrow one of Gramps's wide-brimmed baseball caps.

Since half the attendees had seen Will arrest me, I needed to keep a low profile.

Pulling the hat down low over my face, I made my way toward the main ring, where the winners of the group contests were preparing. Gran's shock of white hair caught my eye. She was seated in a lawn chair wearing a lilac tracksuit and a matching purple visor. Snowball was perched attentively in her lap, watching the event proceedings as though he had a real stake in the outcome.

Slinking around to where Gran sat, I knelt down beside her chair. "Psst. Gran!"

"Caroline?" Gran turned to look at me in surprise. "I thought you'd been 'arrested' by that handsome policeman." She said it with a little twinkle in her eye that made my face grow hot.

"I escaped," I said impatiently. "Have you seen Daphne?"

"Daphne?" Gran frowned. "She's probably down at the café preparing for the winners' circle dinner this evening."

"Thanks." I got to my feet and headed across the street to the Fireside Café. From the outside, the restaurant appeared deserted, and a "closed" sign hung in the window.

I rapped on the door, intent on asking Daphne who else had known Doris was down at the dog wash that day, but no one answered.

I tried the door handle. It was unlocked.

For a moment, I just stood outside the café — silently debating with myself. I knew I should just wait to talk to Daphne after the show, but I had this uneasy feeling that I needed to act fast. Doris's killer might not be going anywhere, but the longer rumor of my involvement had to fester, the more people would continue to believe that *I'd* murdered Doris.

Dragging in a shaky breath, I let myself into the restaurant. The normally bustling café was empty, the tables made up with fresh white tablecloths.

Thinking Daphne might be in the back, I shuffled cautiously toward the kitchen. It smelled heavenly — a mix of lightly fried dough and melted chocolate. Something was simmering gently on the stove. Daphne couldn't be far.

"Daphne?" I called.

Again there was no answer, though a loud electric hum filled the small space. It was a wonder Daphne could hear anything back there.

I called her name again and opened the door to the

walk-in freezer, pushing aside the thick plastic curtain in search of the little chef.

It was dark and freezing inside the walk-in, and there was no sign of Daphne. A feeling of uneasiness crept over my body as I squinted at the boxes. I started to back out of the freezer, but then I heard a scuff of footsteps behind me.

"Looking for Daphne?"

For some reason, the sugary-sweet voice from behind made every hair on my body stand on end. I slammed the freezer door behind me as I came face to face with Selma Lewis. Her wrinkled face was crumpled in a smile, but it didn't quite meet her eyes.

"Uh, yeah." I swallowed to unstick my throat and forced an uneasy smile. "Have you seen her?"

"No," said Selma, her smile faltering. "I've been looking for her myself."

Her answer was innocent enough, but something in her tone left me cold.

"Ah, well," said Selma, pulling her smile tighter. "She must be helping with the final round of the competition."

"Shouldn't you be out there, as well? In case they need a veterinarian?" The words tumbled out of my mouth before I had a chance to stop them, and I immediately wished I could stuff them back in.

"I don't know what you mean," said Selma — still in that saccharine tone of hers that set my teeth on edge.

"I think you do," I said quietly. I took a deep breath. "The first time we met, you told me you were just a homemaker. But that wasn't your plan, was it? You attended Druxton University and majored in animal science, intending to go on to veterinary school."

Selma's eyes flashed. "How did you know that?"

"I called the university. Had them look up your records."

"Now, why would you do a thing like that?" Selma asked with an uneasy laugh.

The harshness of the sound in the empty café made my stomach clench with nerves. I knew I was treading in dangerous territory, but I couldn't seem to stop myself. "I was impressed that you knew exactly what to do when Mr. Bittles had that seizure."

"I used to have a dog who had seizures," Selma said dismissively.

"Maybe. But when I found Doris's body floating in the water —"

Selma made a noise of horrified disgust, but I kept going.

"I thought it was odd that her body was angled right, draped over the side of the tub like that. It would have been impossible for a right-handed person to drown her in that position, and when I saw that you were left-handed . . ." I trailed off.

I hadn't noticed it when Selma had handed me my presentation folder at my pitch, but I'd noticed when she was administering first aid to Mr. Bittles.

"I didn't put it together right away," I murmured. "But when I learned that you'd gone to Druxton with Doris back in the sixties, I wondered why you left."

Selma's mouth became a hard line.

"Not a lot of women went to college back then — and even fewer went to veterinarian school. You had to be serious about becoming a vet if you were on that path." I swallowed. "The woman in the records department didn't know what the note in your file meant: *Dismissed due to improper conduct unbefitting of Druxton University students.* She had to find someone who'd worked there a lot longer to interpret what it meant."

Selma's nostrils flared, and I could hear her breathing heavily.

"The thing is, before Title Nine, Druxton could just kick students out for becoming pregnant out of wedlock."

"My, you are a *nosy* thing," Selma huffed.

"I got in touch with Margaret Bealman. She was Margaret Mitchell then."

By then, Selma was full-on glowering at me, but I couldn't seem to shut my mouth.

"Doris told your den mother you were pregnant, who turned around and reported it to the university. You've hated her ever since."

"We were *children* back then," Selma gritted out, color rising to her cheeks. "I don't hold that against her anymore."

"Maybe not now that Doris is dead," I said matter-of-factly. "You might have lived with it all these years, but seeing Jeffrey set you off."

Selma shook her head, muttering to herself. I wasn't entirely certain she was listening anymore.

"Margaret said your parents sent you to a home for unwed mothers, where you were forced to give up your son. Most of those old records are sealed, but you found him, didn't you?"

"I don't know what you're talking about," Selma snapped.

"Jeffrey said he was adopted. You kept track of him all these years. That's why you volunteer for the dog show. It allows you to keep tabs on him."

Selma was still shaking her head, her arms folded over her chest.

"You were both at the dog wash when Doris showed up. She must have said something snarky to you, and you just . . . snapped. You got the idea to call Katy about a fake gas leak so she'd have to lock up and clear everyone out. You knew she'd let Doris stay behind to finish washing the puke off Crumpet."

"It isn't true," Selma growled, her eyes narrowing to slits. She was breathing hard and fast, and when she spoke, I got the feeling she was talking to herself more than me.

"After Doris's body was discovered, Martha Mayberry was telling everyone that *I* killed Doris. But you were terrified someone would discover the truth. You planted my hat at the crime scene to frame me. I couldn't figure out how someone had gotten back into the shop after the police had been there — unless it was Katy. But then she gave me your business card."

Selma blinked at me in surprise.

"You started a little dog-sitting business on the side," I said. "You watch Snickerdoodle sometimes, so you had Katy's house key. It wasn't hard to get your hands on her shop keys and let yourself in to plant the evidence."

"This is *absurd*," Selma hissed.

"And I'm guessing that you came here to silence Daphne. Her refreshments table was right across from the phone booth where you called in the fake gas leak. You were worried she might talk to Katy and put two and two together."

"You don't understand," said Selma in a shaky voice, her throat bobbing as she swallowed. "Back in those days, compassion was in short supply for girls like . . . like me. When I went into labor, the sisters at the home took me to the hospital and *left* me there all alone." She dragged in a breath. "It was a very difficult birth. If I'd had someone with me when the baby came — a husband or a family member — I might not have had to suffer alone for so long. I might have been able to have children of my own — a real family with a man who loved me. But after Jeffrey . . ." She shook her head. "I wasn't able to have children anymore."

"I'm sorry," I said, and I meant it.

Selma might have been a murderer, but my heart ached for her. She'd carried her secret — and her grudge — for decades. And now she was going to prison for murder.

"So am I." It took half a beat for her tone of calm resignation to hit me. A loud scraping sound drew my attention, and I saw her hand curl around a long knife.

"Selma . . ." I muttered, taking an automatic step back and staring at the blade.

"This is a small town," she said with a sad smile. "I've lived here for forty years without anyone discovering my secret, and I intend to keep it that way."

My stomach gave a nasty jolt. Selma lunged with a surprising amount of speed for a woman her age, and I staggered back on my heels until my butt hit the walk-in freezer.

"Get in," Selma hissed, jabbing the knife toward my stomach.

"What?" I threw up my hands in panicked surrender, sucking in my gut.

"Get in!" she yelled, her voice breaking. She sounded absolutely unhinged.

I'd never been held at knifepoint before, and I found myself obeying. I opened the door to the walk-in freezer, and Selma forced me inside.

My heart beat faster as the door slammed shut, throwing me into frigid darkness. I immediately threw myself against the door, fumbling for the handle. A second later, I heard the unmistakable *clink* of a latch being thrown.

"No," I breathed. What had I *done*?

I backed up a few paces and rammed my shoulder into the door, but I only succeeded in sending a shooting pain down my entire left side.

"Help!" I cried, pounding on the door. "Somebody help me!"

The thud reverberated inside the small space. I swore and fumbled for some kind of safety release. There had to be a safety release, right?

My hand brushed over what felt like a lever, but the layer of frost coating the inside of the freezer was so thick that it wouldn't budge.

I banged uselessly on the door for a few more seconds, the heel of my hand stinging in protest.

What was I doing? Selma was probably long gone, and no one was coming to let me out. I supposed I should have been grateful that she hadn't stabbed me.

Skimming my hands over my pockets, I felt around for my phone. Nada. I'd left it and my purse back at Gran's. All I had was a house key.

The winners' circle dinner was scheduled for later that evening, but I'd be a popsicle by then. There was a chance that Gran would come looking for me after the final round of the competition, but she'd probably assume I'd just gone home.

How long would it be before she grew concerned enough to look for me? Would she even remember that I'd gone to the café to look for Daphne?

Daphne. *She'd* come back. She was catering the dinner, and she had no idea that Selma was looking for her.

Feeling desperate, I rubbed my hands along my arms for warmth. Daphne was in danger. I had to find a way out of there.

It was pitch black inside the freezer, so it was with some trepidation that I made my way along the sides to the far back corner. I felt around for an "off" switch or some way to shut the freezer down, but my search came up empty. Worse, my teeth had begun to chatter, and my stomach was quivering from the cold.

Why hadn't I worn something with *sleeves*? Why had I worn shorts? Hypothermia would set in quickly. My best hope was to make enough noise that someone would come to investigate.

Feeling my way back to the front of the freezer, I banged on the door some more. The side of my fist quickly grew numb, though I could tell from the throbbing sensation that I was going to have a bruise.

"Daphne!" I called. "Somebody help!"

I continued to shout until my voice cracked. I knew it was no use. Someone might have been able to hear me if they were inside the restaurant, but there was no *way* my voice would carry through the thick freezer walls and out onto the street.

*Think, Caroline. Think!*

A heavy sense of doom settled over me like a blanket,

and I began to hyperventilate. I wasn't getting out of there. I was trapped, and it was freezing. I was going to die in this electric tomb.

Suddenly it felt as though the darkness was boxing me in — pressing down on my chest. The tightness further restricted my lungs, making my breathing all the more labored.

*Get it together*, I growled to myself. Panicking wasn't going to solve anything.

Fighting against the drum beat of my racing heart, I forced my breathing to slow. I counted to three as I breathed in and counted to three as I breathed out.

*In . . . out. In . . . out.*

After a moment, I felt my heartbeat slow, and the tight ache in my chest seemed to dissipate. I could breathe again, sending much-needed oxygen surging to my brain.

Once I was no longer hyperventilating, I became aware of other noises around me. I heard what sounded like a fan directly overhead. I couldn't see it, but as I took a step closer, I could feel the cool air of the evaporator fans.

Reaching up, my fingers skimmed what appeared to be a cold metal cage surrounding each fan, and I was hit by a flash of inspiration.

If I could find a way to stop the fans, it would probably stop the cooling. Stopping the cooling would buy me time — maybe enough time to live.

Groping underneath, I searched for some kind of switch or cord, but there wasn't one. Maybe I could wedge something between the fan blades? Surely *that* would stop them.

Fingers numb, I dug around in my pocket until I located Gran's house key. I took a deep breath and slid it between the thin bars of the cage, drawing my fingers back quickly.

I heard a loud *ching!* of metal on metal as it hit the fan blades, but the key just bounced off harmlessly, landing in the bottom of the cage.

Easing it out, I tried again, but it just pinged off the blades.

I needed to hold it in there in order to stop the fan.

Fishing the key out one more time, I brought the thick part up through the bars of the cage to halt the rotating blades.

*Ching!*

The key shot out of my fingers as if it were coated in butter, skittering onto the floor. I heard the dull scrape of metal on metal, and when I reached down to retrieve the key, I felt a thin gap between the wall and the floor. That's where my key had gone.

No! Hot tears welled up in the corners of my eyes as the magnitude of my failure crushed me.

I'd lost the one tool I had that might get me out of there. *Now* what was I going to do?

I began to pace, tears streaming down my cheeks as I silently berated myself for being so stupid.

Why hadn't I turned around and run the *second* I saw it was Selma? I knew she was the killer. I'd just been hoping to get confirmation before running to Will with what I knew.

Will. *Oh, Will.* If I froze to death in here, I'd never get to see his stunned expression of admiration when I revealed that Selma was the killer.

I'd never get his somber apology for fake-arresting me, followed by what was sure to be a scorching-hot kiss.

I'd never be Will's girlfriend — just that girl who froze to death stuck in a walk-in freezer. Not cute.

Then I had an idea.

Back when I'd been cornered by Jay Mathers's killer, I'd somehow channeled all my rage into a miniature earthquake. I'd brought down a solid brick wall, much as I'd tried to deny it — just as I'd caused Doris's photo album to reveal itself to me.

Maybe if I concentrated, I could generate another one of those handy earthquakes or blow the door off the walk-in.

Taking a deep breath, I tried to concentrate the anger and desperation swirling inside me. I thought about how humiliated I'd felt to find out my fiancé was playing me. I remembered what it had felt like to be fired and eviscerated by Doris during my pitch.

I let those emotions well up inside of me, trying to distill them into raw energy. As I did, I felt a slight tingle race across my palms, but that could have been the cold.

I waited for the ground to tremble or for the freezer door to fly off. But there was no big boom. No earthquake. Nothing.

Sinking down onto one of the cardboard boxes, I let out a groan that was half a sob and wrapped my arms around myself. I was never getting out of there.

It had taken getting locked in a freezer for me even to accept that I had powers. But just because I was gifted with the Blackthornes' ability to manipulate the world around me, it didn't mean I could summon that power on command without ever trying to wield it.

Of all the things I'd tried to escape the freezer, saving myself by magic had to be the silliest.

As despair threatened to overwhelm me, I tried to look on the bright side. If I died in there, there was a possibility I'd get stuck between this realm and the spirit realm and get to party with Aunt Lucille twenty-four/seven.

But if her spirit was forever tied to The Grand, did that mean I'd be stuck haunting the café? The *last* thing I wanted was to be a ghost in a café full of delicious food and not be able to eat it. That would be my luck.

Just then, a soft scoff from the other side of the freezer door interrupted my dark train of thought.

"Oaff!" I heard some scuffling on the other side, followed by a muffled thud. "This dang door — is stuck — again!"

My heart leapt at the sound of that voice. Daphne was *there* on the other side of the door! She was trying to open the freezer!

I scrambled to my feet as fast as I could, but it took me a moment to unstick my throat. "Daphne?"

Silence.

"Help!" I cried and then coughed loudly as I shouted in the cold, dry air.

"What the —"

There was another loud *thunk* followed by a laborious huff, and the freezer door swung open.

Relief as I'd never known poured through me, and I shoved the plastic curtains aside and stumbled out of the walk-in. I nearly groaned as the warm outside air hit me, and a giant shiver worked its way through my body.

Daphne staggered back a few paces. The plump little redhead was wearing a white apron over her volunteer outfit, and she was staring at me as though she'd seen a ghost.

"Caroline?" Daphne made a choking sound. "Oh my gosh! What were you *doing* in there?"

"I-I was t-t-t-trapped," I managed, my teeth still chattering.

"You poor thing! I kept getting alerts on my phone about the temperature regulation thingy, but I just thought it was going haywire again." She reached out to rub my arms and gave a little jump. "Sweetie! You're *freezing*."

She turned and darted around the corner, returning a few seconds later with a fuzzy gray cardigan. "Put this on. Your lips are blue!"

I gratefully accepted the sweater from Daphne, wrapping the whole thing around myself like a blanket.

"What were you doing in my freezer?" Daphne demanded, clucking like a mother hen as she looked me over, rubbing my arms through the sweater.

"Long story," I heaved, unable to stop my teeth from chattering. "S-Selma . . ." I trailed off. I needed to warm up before I tried to explain. I could hardly string two words together.

"Selma?" Daphne frowned. "What's Selma got to do with this?"

"S-s-stay away from her," I managed. "W-we need — to f-find — the p-police."

CHAPTER TWENTY-TWO

It took two cups of Daphne's delectable hot cocoa and fifteen minutes in the sweltering July heat to recover from my time in the freezer. Once I'd stopped shivering and inspected my fingers for frostbite, I made my way to the town square — determined to find Will and share what I knew.

When I reached the square, a huge crowd had already gathered. The competition for best in show was underway, and the finalists were in the ring.

Shoving my way through the mob of people, I earned several dirty looks from both humans and canines. Will was nowhere in sight, but I now had a clear view of the ring.

Inside stood Detective Pierce in full uniform, standing beside the vicious-looking German shepherd that had mauled me by the kiddie pools. I saw Jeffrey and Mr. Bittles standing next to a woman with a Yorkie, and —

I had to do a double take to be sure my eyes weren't playing tricks on me. Gran was leading Snowball around the ring toward the very last podium. She moved slower than I'd seen other handlers move with their dogs, but she was managing a peppy power-walk in her purple tracksuit.

Snowball pranced around the ring with his head held high, his tail sticking straight up in the air and his tiny dog legs working fast. He hopped deftly onto the last pedestal and stood absolutely still as the judge approached.

"He's *very* athletic," Gran told the judge. "And stunningly handsome, don't you think?"

The judge didn't answer Gran, though his sidelong look seemed to communicate that he couldn't talk to her about Snowball's merits while he was judging the competition.

Gran continued to chatter as the judge inspected Snowball's teeth. I half expected Snowball to nip at him, but he was the picture of professionalism as the judge gave him the once-over.

As the judge eyed the rest of the contestants one last time, the crowd grew very still. Everyone seemed to be holding their breath, and for a moment, I forgot the whole reason I'd returned to the dog show in the first place.

"Third," the judge said, pointing with his whole arm toward Detective Pierce and the German shepherd.

"Third place," echoed the M.C., "goes to the Colonel. The Colonel is led by owner/handler Detective Wesley Pierce."

Detective Pierce grinned broadly and accepted the yellow ribbon.

"Second," barked the judge while pointing at the Yorkie, led by the woman in the pantsuit, who immediately burst into proud tears.

"Second place," boomed the M.C., "goes to Rocky, led by our very own Mayor Barbara Sutherland."

The judge made two more hand signals I didn't understand.

"And the award for Mountain Shadow's favorite goes to Snowball — owner/handler Virginia McCrithers."

I whooped loudly and clapped my hands as the crowd burst into applause. Gran's eyes widened in surprise as someone presented her with a huge white-and-gold ribbon.

"And first place goes to Mr. Bittles, led by owner/handler Jeffrey Hanover."

The applause for Gran morphed into another round for the little whippet, but it wasn't nearly as enthusiastic as the cheers Snowball had received.

The rest of what the M.C. said was lost on me. I was already shoving my way toward the other side of the ring, where I'd spotted Will pumping his partner's hand and congratulating him on his win.

I opened my mouth to catch Will's attention, but before his name had left my mouth, a clawlike hand gripped my arm.

A paralyzing chill shot down my spine, and I turned my head to see Selma Lewis.

"I'd think *very* hard about what you're about to say," she hissed, digging her fingernails into my skin. "How do you think it's going to look? One of the committee members hearing your grant proposal winds up dead — then you accuse another of murder?"

"I don't care how it looks," I growled, narrowing my eyes. "You killed Doris, and then you tried to kill me!"

"You can't prove anything."

"Watch me," I snarled, yanking my arm out of her grip and losing some skin in the process.

"Caroline?" Will's concerned voice carried over the crowd. "Is there a problem?"

"Officer!" Selma cried. "Thank *goodness* you're here! This woman just confessed to me how she *murdered* poor Doris. She was just —"

"You confirmed that Doris had bruises along her right side," I broke in, locking eyes with Will and ignoring Selma completely. "Isn't that right?"

"Yeah," said Will, his eyebrows knitting together as his gaze darted from Selma to me.

Her declaration had caught the attention of Detective Wesley, whose hand rested on his sidearm as he looked from me to Will.

A few people standing nearby were listening in as well, and I knew word of Selma's accusation would quickly spread all over town.

"Doris was bruised from where the lip of the steel tub cut into her side," I explained. "But because it was on her right side, she could only have been strangled by a left-handed person."

Will's eyebrows lifted in surprise.

I shot a glare at Selma. "Selma is left-handed."

"So is ten percent of the population," she said in exasperation, giving Detective Wesley a look that demanded he put an end to this nonsense.

"You dog sit for Katy, owner of The Pampered Pooch. You had her key, which is how you broke into the dog wash after the murder to plant false evidence."

Selma scowled and crossed her arms over her chest.

"Is this true?" Will asked Selma. "Do you have a second set of keys?"

"Well, yes — keys to her *home*. But I didn't break into her shop, and I *certainly* didn't plant any evidence." She scoffed. "Honestly, officers, are you just going to let this woman slander me like this?"

"It's a compelling theory," said Will, not taking his eyes off her. "But without any proof —"

"Mrs. Lewis, would you mind showing Officer Hamby your left wrist?" I asked.

"Whatever for?" Selma huffed.

"Well, for one thing, you're wearing long sleeves when it's ninety-two degrees outside. When I discovered Doris's body, I noticed there were scratches along the inside wall of the tub. I'm guessing it's from that bracelet you always wear." I pointed at the braided silver bracelet at her wrist, which she'd been wearing the day of my pitch. "It's titanium, right? A silver or white-gold bracelet wouldn't scratch a stainless-steel sink. But you have sensitive skin like I do, so you wear titanium." I gestured at my own neck. Selma's was still an angry pink. "I noticed your heat rash when you treated Mr. Bittles for that seizure this morning."

"Those scratches could have been from *anything*," Selma protested.

I raised my eyebrows. "Maybe. But Doris was quite the ray of sunshine. She must have put up a fight. I'm guessing the inside of your wrist is bruised from where the bracelet dug into your skin."

Selma's eyes went wide, and the flush from her neck seemed to creep up her cheeks all the way to her hairline.

"Mrs. Lewis," said Will in an even tone. "If Caroline's

theory is way off base, then one look at your wrist should clear things up."

"This is ridiculous," Selma replied, pushing her sleeve down farther and puffing up with indignation. "Doris was a dear friend of mine."

"Oh, yes," I said. "A *dear friend* who exposed your secret when you were in college and got you kicked out of Druxton."

"I'll thank you *not* to drag my name through the mud any more than you already have," she hissed.

Somehow, Selma's furious whisper chilled me more than if she'd shouted.

"We can discuss it in private, if you like," said Will. "Down at the station."

Selma's eyes bulged with indignant fury.

Will shrugged. "Or you can show me your wrist."

In truth, I hadn't laid eyes on Selma's wrist, so I didn't know for sure that it was bruised. But judging by her deepening flush and the fact that she didn't make a move to roll up her sleeve told me I was right.

A long moment passed in strained silence. Will shot a glance at me, and I could have sworn I caught the briefest wink. When his gaze settled once more on Selma, she seemed to crack under the scrutiny.

"She had it coming, you know," Selma announced to no one in particular, her voice shaking with violent rage. "Always so self-righteous. Doris pretended to be my friend, but she was a snake in the grass." Selma sniffed, her eyes shining with unshed tears. "One afternoon she caught me crying in the ladies room and wheedled the story out of me. I told her about the pregnancy in confidence, and what did she do? She turned around and told our den mother, who had to report it to the dean."

Will's eyes darted over to me, clearly wishing someone would fill in the blanks.

"I thought I'd put it behind me when I married Rhett and moved to Mountain Shadow. But Doris's husband got a job here, and . . ." She sniffled and shook her head. "Doris has lauded it over me all these years. I never told Rhett about . . . b-before. And when I saw Jeffrey —" Selma broke off. "Something inside me just snapped."

"You saw Jeffrey and Doris at the dog wash," I said. "She was there bathing Crumpet, because he'd been puking all morning."

I glanced into the crowd, and my gaze landed on Jeffrey. He was standing off to the side of the ring, stroking Mr. Bittles as he watched the dramatic scene unfold.

"At first I thought Jeffrey was the killer, since he lied about seeing Doris at The Pampered Pooch."

Jeffrey's mouth fell open in a scandalized expression.

"But when I heard about Crumpet getting sick, I realized that Jeffrey probably slipped something into his food to teach Doris a lesson."

"I did *no* such thing!" Jeffrey cried, clutching Mr. Bittles to his chest.

I ignored him and turned back to Will. "Jeffrey thought she poisoned one of Crumpet's competitors at a previous show. Based on Mr. Bittles's seizure, I'm guessing Doris poisoned him, too, but it took days for the stuff to hit him."

A sharp gasp went through the crowd, and I narrowed my eyes at Selma. "You had the idea to place the call from the pay phone to get Doris alone. You knew Katy didn't have a security system. You saw the opportunity to put your past behind you, and you took it."

"Yes." Selma stared down at her hand, twisting her wedding band on her finger. "Well, she's gone now. Good riddance."

A deflated energy seemed to leech from Selma, and a somber silence settled over the crowd.

Will was the first to recover. He produced a shiny set of handcuffs, and Selma calmly placed her hands behind her back.

"Selma Lewis, you're under arrest for the murder of Doris Ashcroft." Will slapped a cuff on her wrist. "You have the right to remain silent . . . Anything you say can be used against you . . ."

But I barely heard anything Will said after that. I was staring through the crowd at Jeffrey, who was still seething from my revelation.

I wondered if he'd pieced together the fact that Selma Lewis was his biological mother — or whether he was too busy worrying about Mr. Bittles losing his title.

"Aren't you going to *congratulate* us?" came a familiar voice from behind me.

I turned to find Gran watching the proceedings, Snowball standing off-leash beside her.

I broke into a wide grin. "Congratulations, Gran. And congrats, Snow. You were terrific. Mountain Shadow's favorite, huh?"

"Eh." Gran waved away my compliment and pulled an expression that said it was no big deal. "I knew he was a shoo-in. I was sort of hoping for the blue ribbon, but what difference does it make? Dogs are color-blind! I suppose they felt sorry for the skinny little whippet."

"I'm sure you're right."

She stared at Jeffrey and shook her head with a tsk. "I always knew he was a slippery one. Never thought he'd go to such lengths to win, though." She sighed and shuffled off in the direction of her house. "Come on. I promised Snow we'd have surf and turf for dinner if he brought home a ribbon. I need you to drive us down to the fancy seafood place in the Springs."

"Uh . . . okay," I said, hurrying to catch up. "But I don't think the fancy seafood place in the Springs allows dogs."

Gran turned to look at me with a mischievous twinkle in her eye. "Snowball is not *just* a prize-winning dog, Caroline. He's my emotional support animal."

CHAPTER TWENTY-THREE

I was standing by the coffeemaker the next morning, waiting for my first delicious cup of joe, when Gran's doorbell chimed. Snowball sprang from his bed and took off across the floor, barking like a maniac. He crossed paths with Desmond, who'd been cleaning himself by his water dish, and sent Des hissing into the next room.

"I'll get it," I called to Gran, who was still in the middle of her dance workout.

I was wearing my cat-print pajama bottoms and hadn't combed my hair, but I figured it was probably the delivery guy with the wrong address this time.

Desmond and Snowball were still going at it as I pulled the front door open. Bellamy Broussard was standing on Gran's porch, dressed in a smart pair of camel slacks and a cayenne-colored shirt that perfectly complemented his Mediterranean complexion. A judgmental line creased his brow as he took in my cat pajamas and unkempt hair.

"M-Mr. Broussard," I stammered, tucking a curl behind my ear. "What a nice surprise."

Bellamy pulled a tight smile. "I'm sorry. Did I wake you?"

"Oh, no!" I said, shaking my head as a flush worked its way up my neck. "I was just making some coffee. Would you . . . like to come in?"

So what if it was ten o'clock on a Monday and I was still in my pajamas? After being fake-arrested for murder, nearly frozen, and catching Doris's *actual* killer, I thought I deserved a morning off.

"No, thank you. I'll be quick. I'm here to discuss your application for the Main Street revitalization grant."

"Oh." My stomach gave a horrified jolt. I hadn't realized this was a business call. I would have made Gran stall while I washed my face and put on some actual pants.

"You recently made some additions to your application . . ."

I opened and closed my mouth like a fish as I tried to work out what he meant. Despite everything that had happened yesterday, I'd been too tired to sleep after Snowball's victory dinner. I'd drafted a late-night email to the committee explaining that Gideon had come on board as an investor. I'd forgotten about the email the moment I'd sent it, which was why it took me so long to respond.

"Y-yes," I said after too long a pause.

Bellamy's lip curled. "Well, bringing on Gideon Brewer as a partner was a wise decision. The committee feels that your project has potential and that reopening The Mountain Shadow Grand as a premier hotel would bring much-needed jobs and economic growth to the town." He raised one impeccably groomed eyebrow. "All of us would prefer to see The Grand restored rather than continue to endure the eyesore it has become."

My heart was beating so hard and fast that I could hardly contain my excitement. Could Bellamy be saying what I *thought* he was saying?

"After much deliberation, the committee has voted to approve your proposal, pending a signed contract between you and Mr. Brewer. A copy of your agreement should have been included with your original app—"

"Th-they approved it?" I stammered, cutting him off. "Meaning I got the grant?"

Bellamy's expression was cool as he said, "You will need to open an account specifically for the management of grant funds. Once you've filled out the appropriate forms, the funds should be available within seven to ten business days."

I blinked back at Bellamy in amazement. Seven to ten business days? Meaning I could start renovations on the hotel in less than two weeks? I could hardly believe what I was hearing.

"Th-thank you," I stammered, holding out a hand for Bellamy to shake.

He took it stiffly and pumped it twice, pulling a constipated-looking smile. "Congratulations," he said, looking as though the sentiment cost him great effort. "I look forward to seeing what you do with the place."

The double meaning of his words wasn't lost on me, but I was so ecstatic that I couldn't bring myself to care that Bellamy Broussard thought I was a hack. I was grinning like an idiot as I closed the door and floated into the kitchen, my mind completely numb.

"Who was that?" huffed Gran, making her way in from the living room at a slow shuffle-step and wiping her brow with the corner of a towel.

"Bellamy Broussard."

"What did that constipated cockatoo want?"

I snorted. Bellamy's ridiculously stiff gelled hairdo did sort of make him look like a cockatoo.

"He came to tell me that I won the grant," I said, my voice quivering with disbelief.

"Well, yippee skippy! That's good, right?"

"Yeah," I said, forgetting all about my coffee and sinking down at the kitchen table. "It means I might actually have a shot at restoring The Grand and fulfilling Aunt Lucille's last wish."

"Ugh." Gran groaned as she bent into the refrigerator, producing the chocolate syrup and a gallon of milk. "I hope that's not why you're doing this." She straightened up and set the milk on the counter next to the blender. "It's a lot of work to be doing for someone else — particularly when that someone is *dead*."

"It's not just for Aunt Lucille," I assured her. "*I* want this. I want it more than anything."

Gran raised one bushy gray eyebrow. "Scary, isn't it?"

"What?"

"Getting exactly what you want."

I sucked in a deep breath. As odd as that sounded, it actually was.

"Well, why don't you go make yourself pretty, and I'll find Snowball's vest." Gran winked. "I think this calls for a celebratory breakfast."

---

A PARAKEET CHIRPED from a cage to my right, turning her

head on a swivel. I shifted uneasily on the antique couch, making the silk cushions creak.

I'd never been a fan of birds as pets. They always made me feel as though I was being watched — and judged. The parakeet's cage was positioned beside a clunky old computer desk, where a worn tarot deck rested next to the keyboard. Spiral notebooks spilled over the other side of the desk, some of them lying open to reveal complicated-looking diagrams with notes scrawled in the margins.

Jinx's home was a mishmash of American antiques and vintage Asian decor. Oil paintings of cranes mingled with silk geisha tapestries and a corner cabinet stuffed with mismatched crockery. Oriental rugs covered nearly every inch of the scuffed hardwood floors, and a bevy of houseplants crowded the foot of the stairs.

The warmth of the eclectic furnishings somewhat offset the gloom of the old house, with its dark wood-paneled walls and the anemic sunlight filtering in through floor-length curtains.

A grandfather clock ticked loudly from the foyer, and I folded my hands in my lap. I was beginning to regret my decision to go there, but it would be rude to leave now.

I wasn't even sure why I'd dug out Jinx's business card again. She hadn't been much help with the Roy situation, but I needed answers. Someone who billed herself as a medium seemed the best place to start digging into my newfound abilities, but now that I was sitting in her house, I felt a little foolish.

After my experiences with Aunt Lucille, Philip, and Roy, I could no longer deny the existence of ghosts. But that didn't mean I believed in psychics. Or magic. Or keeping birds as pets.

The parakeet was chirruping noisily again, climbing the bars of her cage.

Just as I was weighing my options for escape, Jinx fluttered back into the room carrying a heavy silver tea tray. She set it down on the table between us, and an earthy, floral aroma wafted my way.

Rather than her layers of gauzy shawls, Jinx was dressed in a simple pair of orange cropped pants and a colorful billowing tunic. She was fresh-faced with very little makeup and had a fuchsia silk scarf tied around her head.

"Is jasmine tea all right?" she asked.

I cleared my throat. "Sounds lovely."

Jinx smiled as she carefully poured the tea into a pair of dainty handle-less cups. "I thought I might be seeing you soon," she said, setting the teapot back down.

I glanced uneasily at the tarot deck resting casually beside her computer. "Did you . . . have a vision or something?"

"No." Jinx chuckled. "It was just a feeling."

I nodded uncomfortably and took the teacup she offered me, grateful to have something to do with my hands. The steam carried that refreshing floral aroma, and I took a careful sip.

"You can see spirits," said Jinx matter-of-factly. "That's quite an extraordinary gift."

"Is it?" I asked, genuinely curious.

Aunt Lucille's book made me think that Midge must have been able to communicate with ghosts, but I wasn't sure how widespread that ability was among the Jinxes of the world.

"I have only known one other witch who could see spirits as you do."

"*Witch?*" My heart beat a little faster, and cold sweat beaded along the back of my neck. "Is that what you think I am?"

"Not necessarily. Supernatural ability exists on a spectrum. There are mediums who only claim to commune with spirits. Though, the fact that you can actually *see* them makes me think you must have other . . . talents."

I swallowed and rested my tea in my lap. "What sort of talents?"

Jinx shrugged. "Perhaps an ability to manipulate the world around you . . . to cause changes on the physical plane. Or certain extrasensory perception . . . Have you ever sensed that something was about to happen or known things you shouldn't have been able to know?"

I shook my head.

"Some folks are just extra sensitive to other people's energies," said Jinx. "Though, I've never heard of a mortal who could see and speak to spirits."

"I can only see my Aunt Lucille," I confessed. "And the bellhop who used to work at the hotel. They both sort of haunt the place." I gave an inward cringe at my own admission. I hadn't told anyone about Aunt Lucille — or my newfound ability. Part of me was worried that anyone I told would think I was crazy. The other part worried I actually *was* crazy.

"Is that all?" Jinx asked.

"Well, you already know about Roy Wilkerson," I said. "But I only saw him twice. Aunt Lucille talks as though there are other ghosts who haunt the hotel, but I haven't seen any of them."

Jinx leaned forward in her seat, her brown eyes bright with curiosity. "Have you seen any spirits *outside* of your hotel?"

I shook my head. "Aunt Lucille can't leave. At least, that's what she says. I'm not sure if Philip the bellhop can."

"Interesting." A little crease appeared between Jinx's perfectly manicured brows. She appeared to be working something out.

"Is that . . . normal?" I asked.

What was I *saying*? Nothing about this was normal.

"It's common for spirits to become attached to one specific place," said Jinx. "Often a house they lived in or wherever they died."

"My aunt didn't die at the hotel," I said slowly. "But she did spend a lot of time there."

"That can be enough to cause spiritual attachment to a place. Does your aunt's spirit seem . . . in any way disturbed?"

"Not really." Then again, I hadn't really dug into why Aunt Lucille hadn't passed on. I wasn't sure even *she* knew. "I don't know why her spirit's still hanging around. She seems pretty happy, though, as ghosts go."

Jinx chuckled. "And this bellboy?"

"Well, he's new — new to me, I mean. Not the hotel. I don't know him very well yet, but he seems all right."

It hadn't occurred to me that being a ghost whisperer meant psychoanalyzing every spirit I came into contact with. I didn't have time for that.

"So you aren't looking to help them pass on?" Jinx pressed.

I chewed for a moment on the inside of my cheek. Did I

*want* Aunt Lucille to pass on? I'd certainly been enjoying her company these last few weeks, but it seemed selfish to keep her spirit trapped on earth if there was any way I could help her find rest.

"That's not really why I'm here," I said.

"Ah." Jinx gave a knowing nod. "You're here because you'd like to understand why you can see them when others can't."

I nodded. "I've never seen ghosts before Aunt Lucille died. It wasn't until I came to Mountain Shadow that this started happening to me."

I didn't know why I felt the need to clarify that part — it wasn't as though the sudden onset of ghost vision made it any less insane.

"There are those whose abilities don't manifest until later in life," Jinx said slowly. "Or it could just be the free-floating aether that is unique to Mountain Shadow."

I frowned at Jinx. "Come again?"

"Aether is the fifth element — the natural life force in all living things. It exists in us and around us. It is what binds the realms and makes it possible for a witch to manipulate the other four elements that exist on the physical plane."

"When you say manipulate . . . what exactly does that mean?"

Jinx raised her eyebrows. "It can mean different things to different people. Most witches have a dominant element — earth, water, fire, or air. What that witch can do depends on her unique strengths — and how much energy she or *he* is willing to expend. A witch who's gifted with wind and water may be able to shift a storm with relatively little effort. A witch who works with the earth might use their ability to help things grow — or, in extreme cases, shift the earth."

"Like an earthquake?" I asked, my voice coming out very small.

"Yes. Like an earthquake."

I swallowed.

Jinx studied me carefully. "Have you . . . experienced anything like that?"

Hands trembling, I brought the teacup to my mouth and sipped so I wouldn't have to answer right away. For some reason, the idea that I could bend the laws of nature was even more terrifying than seeing ghosts.

Jinx seemed to take my silence for an answer. "It's all right if you have. Most of us come into our abilities at a young age, but for those whose powers manifest later in life, it can be . . . disconcerting."

Now *there* was an understatement.

I shook my head. "But . . . even if I have . . . I mean, even if I *did* do something I shouldn't have been able to do . . . that doesn't necessarily mean it will happen again. Right?"

Jinx raised her eyebrows and drew in a breath. "If your ability to see spirits came about around the same time as this other ability presented itself, it seems likely that these abilities will continue to develop."

My heart thudded against my ribcage. "But . . . It could also just be a one-off thing, right?" I let out an uneasy laugh.

Jinx shook her head. "I'm afraid these things don't tend to go away. And if you don't begin learning to work with your abilities, they could start to get away from you."

Dread seeped into my gut. "What do you mean?"

"You see it frequently in teenagers who have a lot of pent-up emotions. A young witch might intend to light a candle, only to light the whole table on fire. Or she might try to shift a storm closer to get out of gym class and cause a small flash flood."

Yikes. I thought back to the incident with the hose and hoped that hadn't been my so-called powers "getting away from me."

Jinx chuckled at the look on my face. "I speak from experience. These things happen."

I swallowed to wet my throat, which had suddenly gone very dry. "How would I . . . I mean, how does one go about learning to work with their, um, *abilities*?"

"You take things as they come," said Jinx. "You may get the urge to try something you've never been able to do before or perhaps receive a message from a spirit. Let it come. It also helps to get to know others like yourself so you can see that it's not so terrifying."

I clutched my teacup tighter. "You mean, like, join a coven?" That seemed . . . extreme.

Jinx laughed. "We don't bite. I promise. And we don't dance naked under the full moon, either."

I sat back and let out the breath I'd been holding. Although I could tell that Jinx was messing with me, I was secretly relieved that I wouldn't have to take my clothes off.

"I . . . don't think I'm ready," I said, turning my cup in my hands. "I'm not . . ."

I wanted to say that I wasn't a witch, but since I actually didn't *know* what I was, it seemed a little pointless.

"I understand," said Jinx. "And that's perfectly all right. But when you are ready, we'd be glad to have you."

CHAPTER TWENTY-FOUR

It was a balmy August morning when I finally got the call. I hadn't heard a peep from Roy Wilkerson's ghost since the visit with Charles, but I'd sort of been holding my breath ever since.

Per Gideon's advice, I'd signed a contract with Miles Briggs, the first contractor who'd bid the renovations at the hotel. I was terrified that the cantankerous handyman would run the men off the job as soon as they started work, so I was relieved to learn that my little tribute to Roy was finally in place.

It had taken some research to find Roy's final resting spot. The old section of the cemetery was slightly overgrown, with huge spruce trees shading a path that was choked by tall grass. Red thistle peeked through the gaps in the wrought-iron fence along the perimeter, and a few magpies sang in the distance.

Roy's grave was marked by a modest slab of granite — gray with a curved top. It leaned slightly due to the grade of the land and included his name, birth date, and death date. The carving was weathered and difficult to read. Eventually, it would be completely illegible.

According to Philip, Roy hadn't had any family. The Bellwethers had paid for his funeral and the headstone, which seemed the least they could do, since Cecille had pushed him down the elevator shaft.

I'd been in contact with Charles over the last few weeks and, with his permission, ordered a small brass plaque for the headstone. I'd had it mounted beneath the original inscription.

*Roy Wilkerson*
*Devoted Father*
*1893-1938*

I'd also bought a small bouquet of flowers from the florist on Main Street. I hadn't been able to think of anything more masculine for Roy's grave, but the red and white daisies mixed with purple statice flowers looked nice.

The new plaque gleamed in the late-morning sunshine, and I felt a certain lightness of spirit that had eluded me since I'd first come to Mountain Shadow. A light breeze kicked up, causing the spruce trees' needles to rustle and tossing a few stray curls into my eyes.

I had the feeling that Roy was watching — and that he approved of the change to his headstone.

Self-conscious of the other mourners milling about, I knelt down in the cool grass and placed the flowers against Roy's headstone. I felt as though I should say a few words, but I didn't know what.

"Dead but not forgotten," I whispered, resting my

fingers in the grooves of the original inscription. The granite was cold against my skin, but then a ray of sunlight fell across my arm, sending a radiating warmth throughout my entire body.

I stood and started walking back toward the entrance where I'd parked Gran's Pinto, but as I merged onto the main gravel path that wound through the cemetery, I stopped dead in my tracks.

Will was headed straight toward me, dressed in khaki shorts and a soft-looking blue collared shirt that set off his sky-blue eyes. He was clean-shaven as always and smelled amazing — that same delightful fragrance of a pine forest after a storm.

"Will?"

"Caroline?" Will's eyebrows scrunched together as we looked at one another. He seemed just as surprised to see me as I was to see him.

"Fancy seeing you here," I said in an awkwardly jovial voice. Because what's a conversation with Will without the most awkward pickup line ever? I scuffed my shoe into the gravel. "It's, uh . . . pretty dead today, huh?"

Horror lanced through me as I realized my poor choice of words, and something like a spasm passed over Will's face.

Then the corners of his eyes crinkled, and he let out a hearty laugh. "It usually is." A real smile stretched across his face, and Will's whole demeanor softened. "Who are you here to see?"

"Oh . . . just my aunt," I said, glad that I actually knew someone who'd died recently so I wouldn't come across as a total creep.

Will nodded. "Right. Sorry."

I slid my hands into my pockets and shrugged. It was hard to feel sad about Aunt Lucille when I was spending more time with her in death than I had when she'd been alive.

As an awkward silence stretched between us, I chanced a glance at Will's right hand. He carried a beautiful bunch of sunflowers wrapped in brown paper and tied with a striped red string.

"How about you?" I asked.

Will's gaze darted off to the side, and his lips pulled in a sad half smile. "My mom."

"Oh. I'm sorry," I stammered. I'd been expecting him to say he was visiting the grave of a grandmother or even a great-grandmother. This was *much* sadder.

Will shook his head. "Don't be. She's been gone since I was a teenager, but I like to visit now and then."

I nodded in understanding, my heart fit to burst. It was both tragic and unbelievably touching that Will still visited his mother's grave.

"How did she die?" I asked quietly. Then, realizing it was a horribly insensitive thing to ask, I shook my head. "Never mind. I shouldn't —"

"It's all right," said Will. "She had cancer. She was sick for a long time."

I nodded as if I understood, though I couldn't even fathom what that must have been like for him.

"Here," he said, holding out the bouquet. "Mom would rather you have them."

"What? No!" I cried, simultaneously stunned and horrified. No *way* was I taking flowers from Will's dead mom!

"Seriously," he said, one corner of his mouth lifting in a

grin. "She used to love it when my dad bought her flowers, but she was always racked with guilt that he'd spent the money on something that was just going to die. She'd be appalled that I bought a bouquet that was just going to rot at her grave. She'd much rather *you* enjoy them."

Feeling awkward but also touched by his explanation, I carefully took the bouquet. Will couldn't have known this, but sunflowers were my favorite. Nothing brightened a room like sunflowers.

"I'm sorry, by the way," said Will, his smile crumpling into a grimace.

"For what?"

He bugged out his eyes, as though shocked I had to ask. "For treating you like a suspect in Doris's murder." He pressed a hand to his hip and shook his head, looking so much like a cop. "I knew right away you hadn't done it, but — lame as it sounds — I was just doing my job."

"It's all right. I understand." The sunflowers more than made up for it.

Will gave another sheepish grimace, which for some reason I found adorable. "This is the second time you've solved my case for me . . ." He glanced up at me through golden lashes. "Any chance you're trying to take my job?"

"No," I choked, laughing as I said it. "If I never see another dead body, it will still be too soon."

Will grinned. "Trust me. I get it. I honestly never expected there to be so much action in a small town like this. That's part of the reason I applied for the job — a lot less crime than St. Louis. Or so I thought."

"If there isn't enough crime, doesn't that sort of put you out of a job?"

"Yeah, I guess. But that much death wears on you after

a while." He shoved his hands into his pockets and shrugged. "I guess I was hoping for something a little quieter."

"And Mountain Shadow's not delivering?"

"Not so far." Will's eyes twinkled. "But the town does have its . . . charm."

He held my gaze until I squirmed, and, not for the first time, I got the feeling that Will was flirting with me. It was a pretty impressive feat, considering we were standing in a cemetery.

I chewed for a moment on my bottom lip, fighting the grin that was tugging at my lips. Then Will cleared his throat, and I sensed a change in his mood.

"It's probably none of my business, but . . . Are you and Gideon Brewer . . ." He trailed off suggestively, and there was no misinterpreting the question.

"No," I said quickly. "Gideon's just agreed to partner with me on The Grand — as an investor."

"I see," said Will, an unmistakable edge to his voice. For some reason, this didn't seem to put his mind at ease.

"Gideon's the only reason I got the grant to revive the hotel," I added, feeling strangely defensive of my decision to give up partial ownership. "The committee wanted someone with experience. Gideon has a track record of renovating historic buildings and turning them into thriving businesses."

Will nodded slowly, though he didn't seem entirely convinced.

"It's strictly business between us," I added. "Not that I'm in any place for anything other than business."

Will frowned.

What was *wrong* with me? I wondered. Why couldn't I just leave it at "it's just business" and be done with it?

"I was . . . dating someone back in Chicago," I admitted, a little breathless. "Engaged, actually."

Will's eyebrows shot up in surprise, but to his credit, he recovered quickly. "What happened?"

I shook off a full-body cringe. Why couldn't I keep my mouth shut?

Will didn't need to know the gory details of my pathetic love life. He certainly didn't need to know that Todd had targeted me on an online dating app and swindled me out of thousands of dollars.

I pulled a tight smile. "He just . . . wasn't who I thought he was."

"I see."

Shifting my weight from one foot to the other, I gripped the bouquet tighter and tried not to think about how easy it would be for Will, a cop, to dig into my past.

"Well, congratulations on the grant," he said, perhaps picking up on my discomfort. "I suppose this means you're staying in Mountain Shadow?"

I knew I wasn't imagining the hopeful lilt to his voice, and it gave me all kinds of butterflies.

"Yep." I let out a nervous chuckle. "As long as the ghosts don't run me out."

Will broke into a wide grin. "I've heard that place is crazy haunted."

"You have *no* idea."

"Really?" His eyebrows shot up. "Have you actually *seen* a ghost?"

I lifted a shoulder in a coy shrug. "I've seen a few."

"No way." Will's tone was entirely playful, and I let

him think I was joking. The less he knew about my haunted hotel, the better.

"Well, I should get going," I said, hitching a thumb toward Gran's car.

Will nodded, his eyes smoldering. "It was great running into you, Caroline."

CHAPTER TWENTY-FIVE

T*wo months later . . .*
"I just don't know about the green," Aunt Lucille pouted, frowning down at the velvet swatch I'd tossed over the arm of a couch.

She was dressed, as usual, in one of her opulent evening gowns and a pair of elbow-length gloves. That day's ensemble was a gauzy powder-blue number, and between her fingers she held a long cigarette holder. A smoldering cigarette dangled from the end, but the glowing red cherries simply vanished as they tumbled through the air.

"It's so . . . *green*."

"Green is good," I assured her, laying out three more fabric samples beside the first so they caught the dappled afternoon sunlight. I'd narrowed it down to a deep hunter green, a light sage, and a rich forest green.

"Green says luxury. Sophistication. Class." I traced my hand in a slow arch through the air as a cue to help Aunt Lucille think bigger. "Green says money."

"We like money."

"Yes, we do."

She crossed her arms over her chest as she surveyed the samples. "But don't you think red also says money?"

I shook my head. "We're going for a rich, sedate aesthetic. Dark woods. Leather. Gold. Greens." I took a few steps toward the huge wooden counter that still dominated the hotel lobby. "I told Miles I want to keep as much of the original woodwork as possible. His crew will be here the first of next week to start renovating the ground floor. I want lots of natural light coming in through the windows and plenty of greenery in the lounge areas." I gestured toward the dilapidated love seats and wingback chairs, which would need to be replaced.

"What does Gideon think of the green?" asked Lucille, her full lips pursed in a dubious expression.

"Gideon has left the branding to me. He's just helping with cash flow, project management, evaluating bids from subcontractors . . . that kind of thing."

"As he should," said Lucille, raising her hands in a gesture of surrender. "Don't mind my waffling. You're the expert. Though might I suggest fresh flowers? I think they would soften up the place and lend a feminine balance to the heavier, masculine touches."

"I think that's a great idea," I said, standing back to envision huge bouquets of peonies, white lilies, roses, and snapdragons bursting from every table. Showy floral arrangements screamed Victorian, which was exactly what we were going for.

"And what about the bellhop uniforms?" asked Lucille. "I was thinking —"

*Crash! Bang, bang! Crash!*

The cacophony echoed through the huge empty lobby, sending Desmond streaking under an armchair that had nearly lost all its stuffing. I jumped, and every muscle in my body seemed to stiffen as I stared toward the main ballroom in the direction of the noise.

Aunt Lucille looked just as startled.

"What was that?" I hissed.

"I haven't the foggiest!" She took a long drag on her cigarette and inhaled deeply to soothe her nerves.

Feeling uneasy, I called into the void, "Phil-ip!"

Another crash echoed through the gloom, followed by a string of what sounded like swear words.

"Yes, ma'am?" Philip materialized seemingly out of nowhere, clutching his little pillbox hat and looking flustered.

"What's going on in there?" I asked, nodding toward the ballroom. Beyond the ballroom lay the hotel kitchens, which hadn't been used since the late eighties.

"Ah. You see, ma'am, it's Cook. She's a little —"

*Crash! Bang, bang! Crash!*

"Cook?" I looked from Philip to Lucille. "What cook?"

Philip cast a glance at Aunt Lucille. "Not just any cook, ma'am. The *Cook*."

"Who's Cook?" I demanded.

Something like a panicked grimace creased Aunt Lucille's face. Philip opened his mouth wordlessly, and something Charles Bellwether II had said came floating back to me.

*If Cook was angry about something, well, you'd know about it.*

Could this be the same person?

Shoving past the two silent ghosts, I shuffled

cautiously into the main ballroom, which had definitely seen better days. The enormous crystal chandelier was caked in cobwebs, the plaster ceiling was cracked, and every few feet there were pieces of wood missing from the grimy parquet floor.

Another crash like the sound of falling pots and pans echoed from the kitchens, and I continued through the dim ballroom and past the servers' stations.

While the ballroom was a little shabby, the hotel kitchens looked as though they'd been staged for a zombie-apocalypse movie. Every inch of the porcelain backsplash was caked in grease and food splatters. The grimy tile floor glittered with broken glass, and one of the oven doors rested against the cabinets as though it had been ripped clean off its hinges.

Pots and pans covered with cooked-on food were piled in the sink, and the counters were stacked with broken dishes, small appliances, rusty colanders, measuring cups, and old tin cans. Rodent droppings speckled the edge of countertops, and a few cabinet doors hung ajar to reveal piles of dead leaves and refuse.

But before I could start stressing about the cost of cleaning out and renovating the dilapidated space, something whizzed past my head — coming so close to nicking my ear that I felt a cool breeze.

Half a second later, a metal cake pan banged off the wall and hit the floor with a deafening clatter.

"Festering blister! Dog with the runs! Curdled toilet scum!"

A bread board whizzed past my head and crashed into the wall with a *thuck!*

Wheeling around, I staggered back to put some space

between me and the most terrifying woman I'd ever laid eyes on — who seemed to have materialized out of thin air.

Cook couldn't have been taller than five foot two, but her feet were floating a good four inches off the dirty tile floor. Her wrinkled oatmeal-colored skin hung off a bony frame, and she had the pointed chin that instantly conjured the image of a cartoon witch.

Greasy strings of gray hair hung limply around her gaunt see-through face, and her uniform was streaked with some greasy sauce — or possibly blood.

"You think you can come here and tear out *my* kitchen? Ha!" She emitted a high-pitched cackle. "How 'bout I come to *your* house and wipe my greasy arse with your good linens, you infested, weeping scab?"

Cringing away from the crazy woman hurtling insults and physical objects at my head, I turned to find Aunt Lucille and Philip cowering in the doorway.

"Uh . . . guys?" I yelped, ducking just in time to miss the end of a rusty meat grinder Cook lobbed at my head. It hit the porcelain backsplash behind the sink, causing the tile to shatter.

"Oh, dear," said Aunt Lucille, her face twisting in a fretfully apologetic expression. "Did we not tell you about Cook?"

## THERE ARE MORE MYSTERIES TO SOLVE!

Find your next great read at
www.tarahbenner.com.
Watch on YouTube @TarahBennerAuthor.
"Like" the books on Facebook.

Printed in Great Britain
by Amazon